SNIPER!

Stryker went down on one knee, scanning the distant rooflines for the sniper, but the smoke from idling assault tanks made detection difficult. Five more shots rang out and one of the AK-47 bullets slammed into the flat patch of skin between the army chaplain's eyes, splitting his skull.

Stryker couldn't locate the enemy but the sniper obviously had a clear field of fire. In the bat of an eye, several MPs were catapulted off their feet by impacting slugs.

He had to try something—anything—so Stryker jumped a railing just as the unseen enemy began "walking" the projectiles from one side of the courtyard to the other. And then he spotted the source of the death: glowing red tracers from a rooftop directly across from him. It was the time of decision. . . .

ZEBRA BOOKS
KENSINGTON PUBLISHING CORP.

ZEBRA BOOKS

are published by

Kensington Publishing Corp.
475 Park Avenue South
New York, N.Y. 10016

First printing: December 1984

Printed in the United States of America

Dedicated to my cousin and friend, Gary DeCesaro, whose missions into Cambodia first sent me to the world map to see where Southeast Asia was. It was a lackadaisical move, made out of sheer boredom on a rainy Pueblo afternoon, yet it forever altered the destiny of my life.

ACKNOWLEDGMENTS

I would like to thank Harry Berlin of Los Angeles, a virtual walking encyclopedia of tasteless jokes, whose grim sense of humor formed the basis for much of the insulting dialogue in this Vietnam narrative.

And a special note of thanks must go to Tran Thi Tamminh, for critiquing past novels in this series. I know her assistance has made *SAIGON COMMANDOS* more accurate and believable. Tammy provided the inspiration for one of the characters in *DI DI MAU OR DIE*. I'm sure she knows which one.

AUTHOR'S NOTE

DI DI MAU OR DIE is a novel, but it is based on several true stories the author swapped with other MPs at Mimi's Bar, where he was an Assault tank gunner, town patrolman, and graveyard tower rat while assigned to the 716th Military Police Battalion.

The phrase "Saigon Commandos" was a derogatory term, invented by infantrymen in the field to refer to almost any soldier stationed in the rear. But some of the military policemen fighting snipers, sappers, and other hostile hooligans across the sleazy Saigon underworld affectionately adopted the title, proud to be lawmen, and not jungle grunts, battling crime in the toughest beat in the world.

It is interesting to note that, according to the December 14, 1981 *Newsweek* article "What Vietnam Did To Us," a considerable number of Saigon Commandos saw hostile action in Vietnam: of the approximately 2,594,000 military personnel who served within the borders of South Vietnam between 1965 and 1973, some sixty percent either fought in combat, provided close combat support, or were at least fairly regularly exposed to enemy attack, despite only twenty percent of those same soldiers being assigned to first-echelon combat arms units such as the infantry, armor, artillery, etc. where the enemy was pursued and engaged in ground contact on a regular basis.

I'd drop a low-yield atomic bomb on the Chinese supply lines in North Vietnam.

Senator Barry Goldwater,
quoted in *Look*,
April 21, 1964

Vietnam is our greatest adventure, and a wonderful adventure it is!

Vice Pres. Hubert H. Humphrey,
Saigon
November 1, 1967

I do not believe the Americans can win unless they make Vietnam their 51st state.

Gen. Andre Beaufre (senior
French commander
during Indochinese
War). Quoted by
Newsweek, January 1, 1968

Vietnam GI: "We're gonna invade Laos."
Reporter: "Where did you hear that?"
Vietnam GI: "The mama-san who cleans my hooch told me."

Newsweek, February 15, 1971

I would use anything we could dream up, including nuclear weapons . . . We seem to have a phobia about nuclear weapons . . . I think there are many times when it would be more efficient to use nuclear weapons. However, the public opinion in this country and throughout the world would throw up their hands in horror when you mention nuclear weapons, just because of the propaganda that's been fed to them. I don't believe the world would end if we exploded a nuclear weapon . . . At Bikini . . . the fish are back in the lagoons; the coconut trees are growing coconuts; the guava bushes have fruit on them; the birds are back. As a matter of fact, everything is just about the same except the land crabs . . . the land crabs are a little bit "hot," and there's some question whether you should eat a land crab or not. . . .

Gen. Curtis E. LeMay, Former commander,
Strategic Air Force, and Chief of Staff,
U.S.A.F., at a news conference
announcing candidacy for vice
president October 3, 1968.

1. Blowout on Thunder Road

Monsoon storms afforded soldiers in the Orient little warning. With the ominous clouds above swirling about like vast silver grins, they simply arrived, dumping sudden sheets of intimidating liquid thunder over land and man. Then they moved on, often on all sides at once, until it almost appeared you were viewing the downpour from the eye of a hurricane.

Private Simon Cox peeled his flak jacket away from the olive drab T-shirt as he shifted about on the uncomfortable metal seat. Beneath him, the huge V-100 Assault tank with its balloon tires and swivel-mounted heavy machineguns rumbled along Highway 1-Alpha at fifty klicks an hour. Galloping. Like some beautiful, wild stallion, soaked with strength. The powerful vehicle rocked up and down slightly, front to back, in a sleepy, soothing sort of rhythm. *Yea, though I walk through the valley of death, I shall fear no evil, for I am the meanest sonofabitch in the valley. . . .*

Cox watched the black, funnellike storm floating along the horizon on his right, seemingly pacing the tank, gobbling up palm trees and stilt-supported bungalows in its wake. A warm, steady drizzle coated his cheeks and shoulders, but there was none of the uncomfortable pelting that had accompanied the brunt of the downpour as the driver raced directly through the middle of it.

Naw, couldn't let it pass by up ahead. He spat out over the M-60 on its support bar between his legs, jutting up like some nightmarish erection, come to scare all the village maidens. *Little Fuck had to charge right thru it!* He frowned, recalling how the spec5 behind the controls had giggled when the four MPs riding topside were nearly blown off by the strong wind gusts. *Well, payback is a bitch, Little Fuck . . . payback is one hell of a bitch!*

Bored, buck-private with no-time-in-grade Simon C. Cox shifted about on the hot surface of the tank, careful not to lose his handholds as it rumbled along, until he was away from the rear gunner's position, facing forward. He slowly pulled his face mask and helmet off, slung the straps over the lip of the canteen on his web belt, and gazed out at the sprawling hamlet rapidly approaching on the right. The dilapidated cluster of structures would have been entirely obscured by the dust of the two speeding tanks ahead, but because of the rain and the mud and the recent coating of blacktop by the combat engineers, visibility was as unlimited as the mist cloaking the horizon permitted.

Behind them, four more V-100s. Chugging along at a hair above cruising speed. Hanging in there. Bouncing along like hot metal humping slick asphalt using the most cumbersome set of screaming tubeless rubbers you ever saw.

A genuine, down-in-the-Nam, payroll convoy. Hog-60s on the turrets and all. Impressive as a wet dream with a woman beside you. Hollywood material.

Motivated by money.

A payroll convoy. Thirteen million apple pie greenbacks minimum. Prosperity packed to the Far East.

The unforecasted (weren't they all?) storm had grounded the choppers normally used in transferring the monthly payroll to points north of Saigon.

Their current destination: Bien Hoa by the boonies. Lovely home to some 38,000 nationals, and half that many wing-nuts (as the flyboys were called by their army counterparts). A teeming town called just another suburb of Saigon. Regardless, a strategic hamlet of the grandest proportions. Vast and ever-growing. Hub of the American air effort in Southeast Asia, outside Utapao. Paradise to all the papa-sans, who, for so many years—grim rumor had it—killed off their newborn daughters rather than lose the farm feeding them. Sons were powerful medicine and security in one's old age.

Now Daddy's little girl supported silicone implants as well as the old man. Tricking by night in Fifty-P Alley, and sleeping by day.

How quickly thousands of years of culture, pride, self-esteem, and sovereignty could fly out the window on dragon's wings, when the mighty Bald Eagle was chasing it.

"Fuck it."

Private Cox glanced down at the military policeman manning the 50-cal in front of him. "Say again," the military jargon, after so many months with the 716th now, was no longer military jargon, but off-the-cuff slang. *Correction . . . that's a rog . . . Lima-Charlie. . . .*

"I said, 'fuck it!' " the specialist 4th class spat a thick glob of *crahl*—steamed bamboo slivers mixed with a tobaccolike paste of liquored sweet rice and mashed sugarcane cubes—out over the barrel of his weapon and wiped his chin with a thickly muscled, deeply tanned forearm, eyes narrowed and glazed at a group of village girls, frolicking in the paddy at the edge of the government housing project.

"Fuck what?" Cox found himself on the verge of laughing at the man's overly dramatic expression, but you just didn't giggle at a short-timer with heavy metal between his thighs, and a trembling-from-burnout trigger finger.

The MP's monster mask faded as he turned to look back at Cox, but their eyes didn't quite seem to meet. The spec4 had that shell-shocked and combat weary look about him, like he was acknowledging Cox's presence and passing from a football field away instead of face to face. "Fuck the pension, brother."

"Huh?"

"Only eighteen years and a wake-up, and I can collect my pension," he said sarcastically. "But no, I don't think I wanna spend nine thousand odd days bustin' my balls on this metal monstrosity!" He slapped the hull of the tank as it rumbled uncaring beneath them both.

"I dare say you've gone dinky-dau on us, ol' chap." Cox produced his best British accent as the V-100 slapped through a pot hole and they tensed to keep aboard.

The spec4's lips flashed a set of brilliant white teeth against the backdrop of sooty cheeks and wild whiskers. "Fuck the bloused boots." A Death's Head grin curled his lips back now, as he lifted his green and black canvas jungle boots for Cox's inspection. "And fuck the whitewalls." He ran his fingers against naked temples where meticulously cultivated sideburns had once grown. "Screw policing my hog!" He rose to a catlike crouch, the wind in his face, and ran his thumb along the gun grease coating the breech of his huge weapon. Eyes wide with excitement now, he sucked the oily fingers clean, as if he had only run them through melting ice cream. "And motherfuck getting up." He tore his wide-banded wristwatch off and heaved it at a group of orphans standing along the side of the road. "At four o'clock in the goddamned morning! Just to play soldier!"

"I hate getting up before the most reverend sun!" Cox responded, aware it was most closely what the man would want to hear. *Humor the crazy sonofabitch till you can transfer to another rhino at the next laager.*

The spec4 reached over and slapped Cox on the shoulder roughly. "Fuckin' stract, Cox! You're all right after all. I don't care *what* the other Saigon Commandos say about you." He fell away into a self-amused chuckle but abruptly returned to the matter at hand.

And he waved that hand out in a slow arc that encompassed the entire village spreading out before them and the shimmering turquoise paddies beyond it and the haze in the distance. "Just doesn't make sense to bust my ass the rest of my life for a lousy hundred bucks a month take-home, fighting some corporate giant's war so his punk kid can hide out in a Harvard fraternity house. Ya get my drift?"

"Yah, yah." Cox avoided the man's eyes and stared at the combat patch on his right shoulder instead. *Swc-ds and battleaxes*. "Chuck these jive duds," he said and began to unbutton his fatigue shirt, lost in the intensity of the moment. "And boogy over the hill."

"No, no, no!" The spec4 made to pull at the hairs of his bushy crewcut in resignation. "You *don't* get my drift!" He stood up on the roaring tank now, miraculously keeping his balance, and pointed at a group of teenage girls standing in the middle of the nearest approaching rice paddy. Murky water up to their thighs, the girls were all topless—some bathing shamelessly, others washing laundry with their bare hands. "I'm talking premature ETS, brother . . . early *Out*, man . . . disability retirement, at the least." With his other hand he gestured at an American airman in beachcomber shorts, lounging in a fishnet hammock between the stilts that supported his bungalow above the edges of the probing canal water. Two young maidens with long ebony hair and jutting breasts were making a show of fanning the guy with palm fronds while he sipped Coca-Cola through a straw.

Cox didn't doubt the dude had heard their convoy approaching from miles off, and had paid the women to put on the loyalty display on the spur of the moment, just to impress the doggies. "You mean . . . go native?"

"*Go native?*" he responded incredulously. "*Go native*,

you ask?"

"Do I stutter, lizard lips?" Cox folded his arms across his chest, nearly falling off the Assault tank backwards.

"Son, we went native the day we all passed the pop VD quiz back at Camp Alpha's in-processing center." He flipped the off-duty airman an admiring thumbs-up, and the nineteen-year-old responded by slowly stroking an invisible shaft in his lap, totally contented.

"Please elaborate." Cox gave his best Mr. Spock-to-Captain Kirk impression, but, tainted with irritation, it did not come across convincing. That would be illogical.

Looking a bit spooked, the E5 piloting their shuttle glanced up and back at the two MPs, rolled his eyeballs skyward, then forced them quickly back to the roadway, lest he spot the starship *Enterprise* hanging motionless above the castlelike clouds blanketing the northern horizon.

"Where you from, Simon?" The spec4's eyes remained glued to one of the village girls. Long silky hair shining with the raindrops and upturned nipples glistening from the monsoon's arousing kiss, they had paused in what they were doing to watch the MPs pass. Recognizing the V-100s at a distance—it was hard to miss the colorful *Captain America* and *Thor* murals painted across the front hulls—the girls knew the more disclipined round-eyed *canh-sats* would not chase after them like the infantry grunts always did.

Cox stared at the young women too, but his eyes narrowed with suspicion nevertheless. "Why do you ask?"

They were almost abreast of the firm, healthy maidens now, and he felt the harsh fabric across his crotch grow taut and uncomfortable.

"I asked where the FUCK *you from*?" The hog hustler bared his teeth impatiently without actually looking back to confront the private. "Simon says: Answer the fucking question, douche-bag!"

"Cheyenne!" Cox yelled the answer back at him, surprised at how automatically the word shot from his lips when pressured.

"Cheyenne?" The spec4's grin returned and he gave a whooping war cry, slapping his fingers against his lips as he wailed loudly. Some of the girls, only fifty feet away now, imitated him, smiling shyly from behind their own Indian calls. One woman, startled, draped her hands across her breasts and sunk down slowly to her waist, bending her knees so sensuously Cox feared he might ejaculate all over the inside of his pants right then and there. "Cheyenne?" The spec4 repeated the city's name. "You mean like in Apache—or *squaw*?" He slurred the last word out, making it sound dirty as a two dollar flip-flop in a Hong Kong whorehouse.

Cox frowned. "Wyoming," he said dryly.

The spec4 didn't miss the change in facial expression. "See?" he said. "That's just what I'm getting at. *Wyoming*." He dragged the three syllables out until he matched Cox's apathy. "Cold and grey, boring and—"

"Not always." The Wyoming Kid came to an unexplainable defense of his hometown.

"Boring and insipid." The spec4 left no room for compromise. "Gonna go back there after your *Tour*

365 and log trees in some mountain forest the rest of your life, boy? Gonna watch your life leak out between the cracks of your log cabin just so you can be close to nature? Gonna *die* an old papa-san, telling fairy tales about the river dwarfs and hillbilly gremlins to the little country kids who just return after midnight to steal the carrots from your garden?"

"Wyoming is *beautiful*!" He meant it, thinking about how the mountains turned purple and the canyon mists rose at sunset.

"Or maybe you'll just stay in the Green Machine like all the other lifers!" The spec4 sounded like he was in a fighting mood. *What the hell have I done to deserve this?* Cox wondered, almost aloud. *I didn't even breathe out of sinc.* "Drift from duty station to frigid duty station, GI town to GI town. And for what? *Why?*"

"Why?"

"Yes, why? When you can have all this!" The man cradling the brackets of the big MG in his arms again threw his palms out to reveal Vietnam in all its splendor.

And sure enough, a collage of sights and sounds he had never noticed before seemed to unfold in front of Cox, though he couldn't tell you why, couldn't embrace them as this other man did; couldn't rationalize why the emotions, the electricity in the air was clinging even then to the descriptive praises the spec4 had yet to speak. "All *this* could be yours!" He pointed back to the falang with the amber maidens fanning him. Cox's eyes locked onto the bungalow dwellers frolicking in the rice paddy. The spec4 was pointing at him now. "And only *you* can make it happen, sport!"

"Me?" Cox's eyes didn't stray from the scene spread out in front of him—the edges of his peripheral vision were actually lighting up with brilliant colors now. Like some artist was adding the final touches to an island masterpiece that was already more paradise than the fortune it would someday be worth.

"Stay with me in the 'Nam, brother." Cox could feel the bond of friendship in the words now, but he refused to look down at the specialist. "I need a partner. Are you interested? I can see it now: *Fox and Cox Investigations, Saigon office*. Hell, even with only one or two clients a month, we'd rate enough to live like kings here the rest of our lives. And, hey hey, you know the custom here, lad: Vietnamese men are allowed as many wives as their whanger can handle!"

"Says who?"

"Says me, and all the QCs I've ever talked to—and who should know better than our illustrious Arvin counterparts, right? Besides, even on an off month, you'd have your disability check to fall back on."

"My disability check?"

"Sure." Spec4 Parlin Fox III sounded confident as a smooth talking car salesman. "Even if we *don't* bag a couple cheating wife investigations per month to tide us over, so long as you got some insurance to back you up when the grocery bill's due, no sweat."

"Insurance? But—"

"Surely you don't picture yourself puttin' in twenty years into an organization—and I use that word lightly—where the incompetent lead the unwilling to do the impossible for the ungrateful."

Where had he heard—no, seen that phrase before? Probably on the concrete walls of the shower room beneath the MACV olympic sized swimming pool back in Saigon.

"But—*insurance?*"

"On the job injury, bonzo! Medical discharge, monthly disability check . . ." Fox curved his fingers into the shape of a pistol and popped an imaginary round into his thigh—the fleshy part. "Even with a monthly income that small, you can live like a king in this country. You know that. And it's guaranteed to arrive in your little ol' postal box in downtown Saigon the thirtieth of every month, just like clockwork—while you sun yourself for the rest of your life on the terrace of some boonies bungalow in tropical paradise."

Paradise? Fox read his thoughts from the incredulous expression.

"Aw, what the heck. So a little mortar spirals in every third week or so to keep things lively, and of course the random rocket into downtown Saigon every once in a while is what the Pearl of the Orient is all about, right?" His toothy grin was ear to ear, as he caressed his machine gun like a woman's thigh.

Cox just stared back at him uneasily.

"Don't tell me you forgot about San Francisco Sal already?"

Cox let his memory roll back to that first week with the 716th. He couldn't picture the MP's face, but he remembered the incident. And the name. Salvatore Dominguez. A mountain of a young man who had worked the docks at Fisherman's Wharf through the twilight of his youth until Uncle Sam called. Cox watched the fuzzy flashback as his mind's eye recreated the high speed race through the streets of Saigon alongside a half dozen other MP jeeps after Sal radioed for assistance: He was pinned down by a sniper, and had sustained a leg wound.

"You don't really think some crafty old Charlie Cong zapped him, do you?"

Cox could see it all clearly now. They had rolled up to the intersection of Pham Ngo Lao and Pham Thanh Gian, a mile east of the airport, amid a swirl of twirling red beacon lights lancing through the midnight mist, and brave ol' Sal was lying in the street beside his patrol unit, blood spurting like a weak fountain from the wound in his leg. The grimace of pain etched across his features as he returned fire up at the rooftop overhead was genuine as a heart attack, and damned if Cox hadn't seen the sparks erupting across the blacktop around Dominguez with his own eyes!

"What are you trying to tell me?" Cox wasn't buying it.

There *had* been somebody up on that rooftop firing down at them when they rolled up on scene. He had experienced that much himself—had seen the muzzle flashes just before rolling for cover beside the groaning Salvatore.

"It was Sal's old lady up on that building, *nuoc-mam*-for-brains!"

"Horseshit." The driver of the Assault tank glanced back at both of them, frowning as he shook his head from side to side.

"Whatta *you* know about it?" Fox lashed out at the man whose eyes were shielded by the dark CVC mask.

"Well, *I* was there, you know!" Cox cut in, his tone telling the spec4 the talk was unwarranted.

"So was I," the driver added, without looking back at them again. "You know everyone rolls on a shots fired call—it's S.O.P."

"I'm tellin' ya." Fox was adamant. "They planned it well in advance. Sure it was painful. But it *was* a flesh wound, right? And how come that alleged 'sniper' up on the rooftop was such a fucking dead-eye with a rifle that he or she managed to slamdunk a round in a non-lethal section of ol' Sal's anatomy, yet failed to damage a single part of any of the ten jeeps coasting up all around him before he or she disappeared into the night?

"Huh? You explain that one for me! Go ahead, explain it if you can. I'm tellin' you, boys—ol' Sal was smarter than we gave him credit for—definitely occifer material—a First Louie at the least. You know he's lounging surfside down in Malacca right this very moment, don't you? Takes a train down to Singapore every week so his cunt can cool off in one of those air-conditioned cinemas where they show the Chinese Kung Fu flicks dubbed in English with British accents? And don't kid yourself, pals—ol' Sal trots on down to his P.O. box every month, scarfs up the disability check from Uncle Sammy like clockwork, then laughs his ass off all the way to the Bank of Hong Kong. A flesh wound in the thigh, I grant you, but the crafty motherfucker hurt his back falling to the ground, hey hey—on-the-job injury, amigos—workman's comp and a one-way ticket to Kuala Lumpur, courtesy of the Green Machine.

Now, don't ya just love it? My hero, ol' Sal, didn't even dishonor his fellow cops, during the perpetration of said crime, either. Cuz, as you know, they don't give MPs Purple Hearts."

Pvt. Simon C. Cox knew he could have nailed his counterpart to the wall if he brought up the fact a self-inflicted gunshot wound would have left powder burns around the point of entry, but he didn't feel like arguing anymore.

Instead, his eye remained glued to the lovely maidens that painted the scenery his Assault tank was rudely passing through. *We should stop and introduce ourselves*, he mused. *Take five. Time for some of that good old mandatory PT: Exercise our tongues!*

Cox breathed in the warm, moist air smothering the road. He let his eyes narrow slightly as his chest expanded with the pleasure of sucking in the life of the tropics. A sheet of elusive rain rushed across them, pelting his cheeks with heavy, angry drops. Cox smiled at finally being a part of the 'Nam. He let his eyes open up again—it wouldn't do to miss *any* of it. He wanted all his senses to devour this land. Somehow, he knew there had never been anything like it before. The chance would not be repeated.

He found himself wishing he had brought along the camera with the zoom lens that goofy canh-sat Jon Toi had sold him. He'd bring those virginal bosoms right up to his nose, focusing in tight. The thought brought another smile to him, and he leaned back on the side of the rumbling tank as it slowed to negotiate a burned-out QC jeep, still smoldering in the middle of the road.

Spec4 Fox, belts of 7.62 ammo wrapped across his

chest, was whistling "The Good, The Bad, and The Ugly." Cox was amazed at how the tune seemed to fit in on that payroll convoy just then.

Off in the distance, there came a dull report and a splitting crack as a metal projectile scratched through the humid air, but the danger did not immediately register in the young private's mind. He was debating on whether to yank down his zipper, jerk out his whanger, and wave at the ladies with it as Thor thundered through their town.

His attention diverted, the last thing Private-with-no-time-in-grade Cox would see before the LAW, shoulder-launched rocket tore his smile through the back of his skull were the upturned nipples of the beckoning young amber-colored cherry girl.

2. Dirty Copper

Two huge black and white magpies screeched down at the slender Vietnamese man rummaging through the torn and twisted steel carcasses of the seven Assault tanks strewn about the roadway, but he ignored them completely, which further enraged the birds perched on a leaning tamarind tree. The wide branches of the tamarind had shaded this stretch of Highway 1-Alpha since a French plantation owner had planted it decades ago. Now, peppered with pieces of shrapnel, it bled sap. High overhead, the magpies shifted about on the branches, actually intending to defecate on the shifty-eyed human, but the man was nobody's fool—he stayed out of the shade.

A sudden explosion beneath the smoldering chassis of one of the disabled V-100s fifty yards away sent the birds to screeching again, and when the three Vietnamese in civilian clothing pried open the hatch and poured in two banana magazines of 5.56 tracer, leaning hard into the sound of screams bursting out at them, the magpies finally flew away.

Saigon policeman Trinh Tri paused to watch the birds disappear beyond the treeline, then he resumed inspecting the wreckage. He, too, wore civilian clothes: a light brown safari shirt over old khaki pants that made him look more like one of the Japanese foreign correspondents than a canh-sat—and his mirrored sunglasses hid his eyes, but there was no smile on Tri's lips, and it was obvious he found no pleasure in murdering Americans. Especially military policeman. They had extracted his ass from many a bar brawl, and he had also gone out of his way in the past to lend them a hand.

This afternoon was purely business.

He had never set up such an intricate ambush, using so much firepower and explosives, but it had gone off without the slightest setback or unforeseen obstacle. The QC he had transferred to the 716's Canh Luc Hon Hop program had done well. Provided invaluable inside information regarding the MPs' contingency plans, strong points, weaknesses, and back-up routes. Too bad the man was so loyal he was sacrificed for the good of the ambush. Tri would see to it one of his lieutenants hand delivered a couple thousand piasters to the corpse's widow.

Tri gently stuck his finger in an ear and rubbed it around. His head still ached, and, from past experience, he knew it would be days before his hearing was back to normal. It would screech—not ring—painfully the rest of the day. His men had set off two dozen land mines simultaneously. Nine of them had caught the underbellies of the monstrous tanks with the balloon tires, flipping six of them onto their tops.

Anti-tank weapons were then employed to crack the tough dinosaur egg-of-a-shell enveloping each cell of four men. Those who weren't killed outright were finished off by thermite packs or gas.

The incident seconds ago with the M-16s had been unfortunate, but Tri realized no witnesses could be left behind. He had almost been destroyed by someone's testimony years ago, but the threat had been eliminated in the nick of time, and a lesson had been learned. Tri seldom forgot life's little lessons, and he never forgot anyone who would contemplate driving a dagger into his back. No man worth his salt would.

But the display of brutality with the automatic rifles had been uncalled for—yes, it was truly regrettable, the more he thought about it. You don't pluck the wings from a grasshopper, enjoying the creature's agony. You simply eat its legs for food. The incident could have been controlled had the men on this "mission" been his platoon from back at the police barracks. But he was dealing with mercenaries—outlaw cutthroats Manh Tung had rounded up somewhere down in the Delta.

Granted, the fiends knew how to ambush a heavily armed military police convoy, but their idea of winding down after work left a sour taste in his mouth.

Thirty-five MPs lay dead before him now. He wondered if he had worked with any of them in the past, or knew them by name. He found himself hoping that crazy Mike Broox was not among the casualties—the kid was always buying him ice coffee at the foodstall in front of MACV gate four. Tri shook the thoughts from his head and resumed searching the debris for the lockbox. It was not where the dead canh-sat said they kept it on earlier convoys to Bien Hoa.

Tri kicked over the hatch lid from one of the demolished V-100s, and a terrified rat scampered off through the ashes, disappearing in the piles of debris further down the road. The rodent had not been harboring the lockbox either.

Tri rested his hands on his hips as he surveyed the men searching the rubble all around him. He glanced over at the villagers gathering behind a cluster of bamboo and reeds at the edge of the rice paddy fifty yards away, to watch. The half dozen bare breasts swaying like agile palm trees in the breeze as the girls carefully maneuvered through the shrubs along the canal bank did not interest the police captain in the least. He had more chippies back in Saigon than he could handle. Sex had become boring to him. A mandatory daily task to reinforce his own picture of himself. The women who had once been the highlights of his evenings were now a royal pain in the ass. Power had become his mistress. Money and weapons would bring more power his way than he could handle. Tri did not waste time pondering what goals awaited him, what pleasures were the reward of such power. He was a firm believer in karma. And a grim mixture of fate. The ambush had been successful. He had shed no blood over it. The task at hand involved gathering up as much loot as possible before the MPs failed to check in by radio, and MACV sent a couple patrols racing down Thunder Road to check on them. Afterwards, what would be would be.

Tri took his time searching for the lockbox with the documents in it. He was not worried about an unexpected patrol sauntering down into the midst of his little gathering. He had LP sentries set up two miles down both stretches of the road. The listening post on the Saigon side had earlier radioed the warning that the convoy was approaching.

Tri produced one of his polished snarls as he watched the topless maidens sneaking about behind the wall of reeds—so foolish if they actually thought they were invisible to the mysterious raiders who had themselves been lying in the elephant grass all morning. He whistled at one of the mercenaries with an RPG slung over his shoulder. A whistle was one of the lowest forms of insult in Vietnamese culture, reserved only for summoning dogs and beggars, but the bush soldier grinned when Tri caught his attention and pointed over toward the clump of bamboo stalks.

Moments later, a rocket-propelled grenade erupted from the tube atop the man's shoulder. Tri's eyes followed the silver plume of smoke as the projectile rushed along the waves of shimmering elephant grass in a mild arc and exploded in the paddy directly between the two closest girls. Murky water spewed skyward as the female spectators were catapulted heads over heels through the air in a crimson shower.

Screaming hysterically, the few remaining survivors bolted for the village, as eyes disappeared from behind cracks in window shutters. Tri's men watched calmly as the girls scattered, and none of them raised their rifles to punctuate their message: Go about your business—there is nothing to see here amidst the smoking tanks and dead bodies. *It's Vietnam at its most routine. You've seen it all before. . . .*

Tri watched with slight amusement as one of the girls—he wondered if she was wounded, or just too scared to run from the paddy—crawled slowly deeper into the reeds and eventually disappeared beneath the surface of the polluted water. Though he envisioned himself emptying a clip of smoking tracers into the area where the air bubbles where floating up to the top, he turned his back to the rice paddy and continued inspecting the Volkswagen-sized chunks of metal strewn about.

No doubt the girls' old bent-over papa-san would come running down the hill, yelling his rage and protest; demanding more—much more money than the few hundred piasters Tri had paid him earlier to order his daughters to frolick about half naked in the rice paddy, creating a distraction to the convoy drivers. But Tri *had* instructed the old man to get the bitches out of there immediately following the ambush. It just would not do to have witnesses loitering around when CID dispatched its investigators later. And if the fool *did* make his appearance, demanding more money for sacrificing half his family, Tri would just blast him out of his sandals too—*to hell with them all!*

But a hush fell over the village on the outskirts of Bien Hoa, and nobody appeared to create a disturbance.

As Tri gathered more and more bundles of tattered MPC scrip, his disposition mellowed somewhat. Perhaps later, next month maybe, he'd send a messenger to deliver a water buffalo or two to the old bastard. That would brighten up his disposition and dilute the hate somewhat. A water buffalo was worth a score of useless daughters anyday!

After all, he had to give the old man credit: The feminine ploy had worked to a tee. *A Saigon tea.* He smiled to himself. The ambush had gone beautifully: The MPs had dropped their guard just long enough.

Tri's men now went from American to American, placing muffled hollow point slugs quickly, methodically behind the ears. Tri winced each time a shot discharged. His mind was really not so neutral or without conscience as it forced images of the lead crashing through skullbone, burrowing deep down into the brain, tearing through memories and lost knowledge, wasted experience, exploding out the front of the cranium, deflating eyes through which man lived, logged, and lusted through life—through which his soul now oozed forth like a warm, invisible mist. But the police captain endured the eerie visions without any display of emotion on his face. You did not let these men—the mercs—witness any sign of weakness. Like tigers in the jungle, they could smell fear. After that, they stalked you, and you were at their mercy, for even if you took out one or two of them, they always kept coming, just like the VC, until your ammo was depleted, and it became hand to hand. Tri was a fine physical specimen for his age, but he knew his limitations. He was no match for some of these young bucks. They would tear him to pieces. Right now, only the scent of money kept them at bay.

Tri's boot smacked against something solid in the piles of ash, and he stooped to retrieve a small fireproof file box the size of a shoebox. Too small to be what he searched for, but nothing was ignored in this type of raid, and he drew his revolver and carefully blasted a round into the hasp on the side. The brown, metal case popped open and several of the men gathered around as he went down on one knee to examine the contents.

Five manila envelopes were crammed into the case, and Tri snickered as he discovered the dollar bills stuffed into containers stamped Classified Documents. The greenbacks were officially prohibited in the 'Nam. GIs had to use MPC, or Military Payment Certificates, which were a form of colorful play money the Americans called scrip. Tri held up a handful of the bills—fifties and hundreds—then forced his shirt pockets full as the men laughed along. The payroll officer from Finance obviously had something going on the side, too.

A young man with a hint of military bearing about him rushed up through the ring of mercs encircling Tri and came to the position of attention, reporting with a sharp salute that cracked more than a couple grins.

Tri did not return the nineteen-year-old's salute. Instead, he appeared suddenly irritated. "Yes?" he snapped.

"No sign of the lockbox, uncle," the youth whispered respectfully, his forehead dipping forward ever so slightly as he spoke. He did not look at the older man's eyes but stared at his throat as he bowed. "And no sign of the silver ingots." Staring at Tri's sinking Adam's apple made him even more nervous, and his eyes fell to the ground. *I beg you not to shoot the messenger*, he prayed as he waited for a response.

Trinh Tri glanced up at two men searching through

the tank that sat on melted rims where the rubber tires had long ago burned away. He cleared his throat noisily and spat at the ground. A small puff of smoke rose from the layer of ash covering the ground at his feet.

Without saying another word, Tri started over toward the two Vietnamese thirty yards away. The messenger followed behind at a respectable distance. One of the mercenaries gathered around the broken documents box and casually folded his arms across his chest as he watched the police captain walk away. None of the group followed the two strangers.

The short, stocky thirty-year-old closest to Tri spotted the canh-sat's approach out of the corner of his eye. He felt those corners widen, startled, and he concentrated on searching through the debris even faster, though he now paid no attention to what his hands touched.

His partner had not noticed the officer's approach yet. He continued humming a popular Vietnamese war hymn as he tossed twisted chunks of scrap metal back over his shoulder. When the short man beside him quit digging, he looked up for the first time. And felt his heart skip a beat at the sight of an incensed Captain Tri approaching.

Tri had been watching the skinny weasel from day one, maintaining an eyeball on the crafty character's every move. Things of little value seemed to disappear wherever the man went: a map case here, a coffee mug or pencil box there. He could hardly be trusted with booty from a payroll convoy, strewn about a cluttered ambush site amidst bloodied bodies. Tri had considered dismissing the man early on in the caper, but had given him the benefit of the doubt more than once and dismissed his antics as just a bothersome nuisance. The ringleader had far too much on his mind as it was. But he knew now he should have cancelled the man's ticket long ago.

The words *and no sign of the silver ingots* bounced about in Tri's mind as he brushed the shorter man aside and stepped forward to confront the weasel nose to nose. "You betray this hunting party," the off-duty Saigon policeman hissed at the man as he drew his revolver again. "And there is no honor—or forgiveness among thieves, despite the old saying."

The weasel stared back, wild eyed, at Captain Tri. Being ethnic Chinese, his Vietnamese was poor. He conversed in pidgin slang at best, and even then only when absolutely necessary. So it was doubtful he even understood any of the words that were thrust at him in a rapid torrent, mixed with a spray of spittle.

The weasel would never have to wipe the drops of mucous from his cheek, for an instant after Tri finished his epitaph, the revolver was rushing up between the two men.

Tri calmly pressed the barrel of the American-made .357 Magnum against the man's yellow teeth—Vietnamese have a bad habit of smiling when they become frightened, embarrassed, or bewildered—muttered, *"Xin loi, manoi,"* and pulled the trigger as if the pistol were an expensive pen and he was just writing off a company expense.

After the blood splashed back at him, sprinkling the front of his shirt, and the man crumpled at his feet, Captain Tri reached down and pulled several of the silver ingots from inside the man's rain poncho.

He held out the ten ounce ingots in front of him, allowing the rain to wash away the blood coating them, then held them up high over his head for all to see. "This scumbucket attempted to steal from us!" he announced, kicking the dead man in the testicles. The body did not ignore the assault but continued jerking about spasmodically in the mud with renewed vigor. "I am going to order my subordinates to behead his worthless ass and separate the parts of his body by several kilometers. . . ." The Vietnamese believe a dead man without his head is cursed to wander about the scene of his murder forever, unable to find his way to either heaven or hell. "Think about what you have seen here today before you contemplate imitating what this fool just tried."

Grinning inwardly with satisfaction, Tri turned to the man who had addressed him as uncle and directed him to deposit the body in the rice paddy.

Ten minutes later, the youth appeared in front of Tri again, dragging a charred and blackened lockbox the size of a footlocker. This time Tri displayed no sign of irritation. An ear-to-ear smile on his face, he helped carry the box over to a motorscooter hidden behind a nearby stretch of tamarind trees. As he supervised, three of the mercenaries kept the box balanced across the edge of the seat as another tied it securely down with twine.

Tri checked his wristwatch, then pulled a paper sack from under the Honda's seat and stripped down to his shorts. He slipped the neatly folded police uniform out of the sack and quickly donned it, then mounted the motorscooter as two men kept it upright.

With the U.S. Army vehicles completely stripped of

all their equipment and cargo now, Tri told his assistant to round up the men and insure they dispersed into the jungle as had been previously rehearsed. Then two of the mercenaries ran along on either side, pushing his Honda until it was traveling fast enough for him to keep his balance unaided.

Capt. Trinh Tri then quickly disappeared down the highway to Saigon in a puff of scooter exhaust. He'd have just enough time to get back to Sin City for the graveyard shift tour of duty.

3. A Cursory Inspection of the Goods

"So what do you call a Vietnamese man with thirty-five dogs?" Sgt. "Cob" Carmosino asked his partner for the third time as they approached the International Hotel in the heart of downtown Saigon.

Mark Stryker, ex-Green Beret turned military policeman, folded his arms across his chest and focused his attention on the four people arguing just inside gate four on the Tran Hung Dao side of the complex. He wasn't really ignoring Carmosino. Stryker's concentration the entire day had been centered around the ambush that had claimed thirty-five MPs only two days earlier. He had known every man except two: newbies fresh off the boat, now stiffs stuffed in a body bag—KIAs with less than a week in-country.

The disturbance taking place at the edge of the 716th headquarters compound would present a diversion to take his mind off the tragedy that had so obsessed him these last forty-eight hours.

Cob Carmosino, in his early thirties now, and, also like Stryker, a giant of a man, nudged the buck sergeant beside him with his elbow.

"Huh?" Stryker scratched at the old bullet hole scar across his left earlobe. It was itching to beat hell again, and that usually meant another monsoon cloudburst. He scanned the skies, frowned at the blanket of dark clouds rolling in over the city of three million, then brought his attention back down to the three MP privates arguing with a Vietnamese female down the block.

"I said . . ." Carmosino was growing impatient as he repeated his question. It wasn't that he did not feel loss and anger over the ambush. But Cob, who had eluded death countless times already as a rocket dodger in Danang, did not dwell long on the past. His friends would tell you the man's grim sense of humor had brought many of them back from the edge of insanity. It had a habit of cropping up loudly at the most somber of occasions. "What do you call a Vietnamese man with thirty-five dogs?" His Brooklyn accent cracked a smile across Stryker's melancholy expression—as it always did—but Mark did not take his eyes off the well-endowed lady-of-questionable-virtue their jeep was rapidly approaching.

"I don't know, Cob." He feigned a cop's combination of fatigue and boredom. "But I get the feeling you're gonna tell me whether I want to or not."

"A *rancher*, stupid!" Carmosino erupted into laughter as he slapped Stryker on the back and brought the jeep smoothly up beside the three enlisted men sporting day-shift khakis and black helmets.

Stryker forced a chuckle and rolled his eyes skyward again, but after the joke sunk in—some Vietnamese hoarded back alley mutts, considering them delicacies—he suppressed the urge to laugh out loud also.

Carmosino, always an expert at detecting attempted discipline, nudged Stryker with an elbow again. He did not appear at all interested in the argument taking place a couple scant feet to his left. "Hey hey, pretty good, eh ol' Marco Polo? Wanna hear another one?"

Stryker shook his head from side to side in resignation, but directed his words to the senior MP standing in front of the ebony-haired woman with fire in her eyes. "What's the problem, Uke?"

"What's numba one on the Saigon bestsellers' list these days?" Carmosino cut in, ignoring the raised voices of the woman and three privates trying to calm her down.

Stryker raised his hands palms up and shrugged his shoulders—you didn't ignore a man with two Silver Stars to his credit and a pocket full of Arcoms. You did your best to humor him.

"Fourteen ways to wok a dog!" Carmosino bellowed nearly out of control as he dismounted the patrol unit, but his ear-to-ear grin instantly faded as he stepped beside the three privates. The tallest one's helmet liner barely came to his chin. "What the fuck's the problem on this post, troopers?" He directed his question to the private with the inscription *Peace Hell, Nuke Hanoi* stenciled across the back of his helmet in small white letters, just above the hometown graffiti.

"Caught this cunt trying to sneak off post with a ring hidden on her person, sarge."

"A what?" Carmosino shifted into a defensive stance by placing his side to the woman, but the safety measure was negated when he playfully imitated the woman by resting his hands on his hips.

Incensed at his display of body language—the stance

told her he was not impressed by her command of English profanity—she stomped one black highheel down on the sizzling blacktop. The woman pointed her dainty finger up at Carmosino, but stammered and finally said nothing.

"A high school class ring," the private held the silver ring with the black stone up for his sergeant's inspection.

"It was *hidden*?" Carmosino rolled the heavy jewelry about in the palm of his hand until he found the year of graduation: 1967. "Where?"

"When we were checking her purse." The MP with mosquito wings on his khakis stepped forward to supplement the Uke's explanation. "A roll of stolen toilet paper fell out—"

"Rolled across the ground," the third MP added.

"She screwed up by bending down to pick it up," the Uke said, "and the ring rolled right out the top of her blouse and clattered between our boots. She musta had it down her bra or something."

Carmosino tossed Stryker the graduation ring. "Hhmmm," the buck sergeant mused. "Class of 1967 . . . couldn't have grabbed his diploma more than six months ago, tops. That'd make him a seventeen . . . maybe eighteen-year old. We got any cherry-boys that young in the 716th, Cob?"

Carmosino stared at the three teenagers standing beside him, confronting the whore, and frowned—this time with a bit more gusto in his expression as he shifted his boots around.

"We can trace the owner later," Carmosino finally said. "I'm sure there's initials inscribed inside it."

"Without a victim, we've got no crime," Stryker

jested, tossing the ring up a couple feet and catching it in the palm of his hand, over and over again.

"The important thing," Cob said, sounding stern—probably for the benefit of the enlisted men present, "is that she's got no other private property belonging to Americans hidden on her person."

"And how do you propose verifying your suspicions?" the Uke asked, the sparkle in his eyes challenging the veteran cop.

Carmosino stared down at the woman wearing the miniskirt and tight blue blouse. "Where'd ya get this, honey?" he asked simply.

It almost seemed the fire in her eyes cooled to a dim glow as her snarl melted into a slight smile, but her tone was still laced with hate as she remained defiant. "One, two, three . . . mother*fuck* MP. . . ."

Carmosino felt none of the anger that would have coursed through his veins had a man uttered the phrase so common to the streets of Saigon. He simply shrugged his shoulders for the fifth time that afternoon and walked over to the fieldphone clamped to the static post's kiosk.

After shoving a light current of electricity through the wire with a brisk whirl of the phone's lever, he spoke to the MP at gate one, requesting a Vietnamese policewoman at their location.

Hanging the phone back up with a satisfied grin on his face, Carmosino was basking in the sudden fear that radiated from the girl's eyes when she heard the word *canh-sat*.

Stryker locked eyes with one of the privates. "Was she originally signed onto the compound through *this* gate?" he asked with little hint of humor in his eyes.

"And if so, by whom?"

The MP privates exchanged worried glances, and the Uke consulted his clipboard. He quickly scanned the list of Vietnamese names beside the serial numbers of the off-duty MPs who had signed the ladies onto the grounds of the International, but this tart's name was nowhere to be found. With a relieved sigh, he wiped his brow with the edge of his palm and said, "She musta came through one of the other gates, sarge."

The practice was generally frowned upon, but the men of the 716th were allowed to sign a Vietnamese guest onto the compound to take her to the hotel restaurant or gift shop, so long as she remained in the company of her escort. The MPs at the gates were supposed to log the soldier's serial number down, time in and out, as well as the woman's name, national ID card number, and VD card identification number—provided she had one. They weren't supposed to get on post without one, but the MP brotherhood is notorious for bending the rules for fellow cops. And it was no secret the ladies-of-questionable-virtue were eventually smuggled up to the men's rooms a few minutes before the midnight curfew. Stryker was at a loss to explain the rationale behind the little games that went on behind-the-scenes at the International. Why take the risks when you could whore all night at one of the brothels for a couple bucks? Of course, there *were* the men confined to post for the eight hour Alert Teams after their usual twelve hour shifts on the street. And there *was* that flavor about Saigon itself that demanded one live constantly on the edge. But Stryker wondered if the added excitement was worth six weeks punishment at Fort Hustler, where tower rats spent all day butt-stroking dragon lizards.

"Anything else in her purse besides the toilet paper?" Stryker asked. He didn't particularly enjoy belittling the woman in front of so many men. Toilet paper was a rare commodity in Vietnam, so far as the poor were concerned anyway—it was often priced far out of their reach. Even on the bustling blackmarket.

"Any *contraband*?" Carmosino added.

"Just the usual female junk," the buck private in the middle replied. "And some of that weird Viet medicine they all carry so they can keep their lips from getting chapped."

"That's bug juice, jizz-breath," the E2 argued. "Keeps the mosquitoes away."

"You two talking about the same thing?" Stryker rummaged through the woman's purse. She tried to snatch it away from him, and Carmosino grabbed a handful of chest and shoved her back.

"*You* are skating on thin ice, young lady." He rested his right hand on the butt of his .45 for emphasis. "I suggest you behave yourself."

The girl extended her middle finger, engulfed it with her lips roughly, then jerked it back out and spat at the ground.

The privates all grinned and Stryker gave Carmosino a watch-out-or-you'll-really-piss-her-off glance, cocking one eyebrow in mock shock at the vulgarity of her actions.

He withdrew the small pink card from her purse and opened it to the last page. Several of the medical stamps were in red ink, meaning an examination in the recent past had been positive for venereal disease. The latest stamp, however, was black. This whore was declared clean by the United States Army. As of her last examination by medics, anyway.

Stryker heard the jeep approaching behind him from a considerable distance, but the unexpected yelp of a siren announcing its arrival caused him to jump a bit, and he dropped the VD card. It fell close to a puddle of water, and as the woman rushed forward to retrieve it before the precious document got wet, he allowed his eyes the treat of watching her more than ample breasts strain against the tight blouse as she bent over. The topmost buttons were open, and Stryker felt himself becoming suddenly aroused at the sight beckoning him. He turned away, pleased his attention had been diverted by the patrol jeep rolling up to the gate.

Sgt. Ron Brickmann returned his shit-eating grin as he switched off the vehicle's motor and ran his eyes up and down the curves of their prettier-than-usual prisoner. Beside the tall NCO sat Michael Broox, who rode with the Decoy Squad at night, but was The Brick's partner today.

Broox jumped out of the front seat and extended a hand to the slender woman behind the huge M-60 mounted in the center of the jeep. Wearing an unflattering light brown uniform, she wore no sidearm, but sported a glittering insignia over her left breast that identified her as a VNP policewoman.

"Hey Mikey." Cob Carmosino was all smiles again as he ignored both women totally. "Know how to tell if a Vietnamese woman is ticklish?"

Broox responded with a blank stare.

"Give her a test tickle!" Carmosino slapped his knee, highly satisfied with the punch line, but Broox's face remained expressionless as he helped the lady canh-sat down out of the jeep. Carmosino's smile lost some of its shine. "Don't you get it? Test tickle? *Testicle?* Give her a fucking testicle!" The presence of two women didn't seem to inhibit old Cob in the least.

"What does a Japanese guy do when he has an erection?" Broox posed the question icily, still unsmiling—almost like it was retribution for Carmosino's joke. And he rattled the words off quickly, hoping perhaps the conversation would float right past the beautiful woman stepping down between mannerless street brawlers.

Sergeant Cob wrinkled his brow in deep concentration, but Broox allowed the man no time to offer an answer. "He votes!"

Carmosino fell apart laughing. It was not the desired effect Mike had in mind.

Stryker, sitting on the edge of their jeep now, marveled at how the four of them—Brickmann, Broox, Carmosino, and himself—were even able to breathe together, let alone argue loudly on this small plot of pavement, deep in the intense swirl of motion and emotions that was Saigon, South Vietnam. Only a month ago Broox had taken a round in his right arm that had nearly torn the limb off. His buddy, Anthony Thomas, was later responsible for gunning down the Honda Honey who had fired the burst of near-deadly bullets. Brickmann was still recovering from burns received when he got a Molotov cocktail filled with gasoline and soap chips bounced off his back by a phantom in a rain poncho, who had been torching drunk GIs after dark. The Brick had been working the decoy squad during that brush with death. Carmosino had been stabbed in the thigh by a woman on the back of a motorscooter that had cruised up beside his MP unit during routine patrol—probably the same suspect responsible for Broox's wounds. And Stryker? Even he had nearly kissed Mr. Death on the lips last month, when a sliver of shrapnel from a VC mortar had slammed into his lower back. The Cong had launched a surprise attack on a much-publicized execution in Lam Son Square, and Mark had suddenly found himself in the middle of a heavy storm of steel. But they had all survived the worst Saigon had to throw at them. And hadn't they fought back, recovered more than miraculously, and even gone on to make the PM happy by ignoring their "million dollar wounds" (a guaranteed freedom bird back to The World) and staying on in the 'Nam?

"They vote!" Carmosino slapped Broox on the back, knocking the smaller man off balance. "Pretty good: *They vote!*"

"Hey, watch the arm." Broox shied away protectively, shielding his right shoulder. The policewoman beside him threw Carmosino a disapproving glare, then she noticed the prostitute standing in the shade of the kiosk, and her smile returned.

Carmosino rushed forward suddenly, like a wild bush boar on the attack, and slammed an open palm against Broox's shirt pocket. "Carrying your trusty Gideon in there again?" The question sounded more like an accusation. Broox had been saved from stray rounds by the pocket bible twice already: a feat that made him a bonafide lucky charms legend in the eyes of every man in the 716th Military Police Battalion.

Broox slapped the pocket himself confidentially. "Now I carry a fuck book instead!" he said almost defiantly. "If it's all right with you, *sergeant*."

"A fuck book?" His eyes were wide, incredulous, but his tone said Mike's response had its possibilities.

"They're thicker!"

"Hah!" Carmosino made his thumb and forefinger into a pistol and shot Broox with it. "You got me with that one, punk."

"What the hell is everyone in such a good mood for?" Another unit had cruised up to the gate. Stryker turned to see Spec4 Tim Bryant behind the steering wheel. His partner, Ants Thomas—the latest arrival who had posed the question—was hopping out the side of the vehicle. The smiles remained frozen across Carmosino's and Broox's faces. "I asked what the fuck you guys find the time to laugh about, for Christ's sake. . . ." Thomas left no doubt in anybody's mind he was in a rotten mood. "We just lose thirty-five men KIA less than forty-eight hours ago, and *you*, sergeant," he said and stabbed a rigid forefinger against Carmosino's chest, "are fucking smiling about something!"

"Lighten up, Anthony," Stryker cautioned the Pfc.

"But this is a period of mourning, goddamnit!" He kept his finger pressed against Cob's sternum. "I don't care if he *is* a sergeant—he should show some respect!"

"Cob lost some buddies on that convoy also, pal." Stryker was running his mental photo album of pictures past his mind's eye until he viewed every man who had perished on the outskirts of Bien Hoa.

Carmosino's smile lost some of its shine, but he did not appear to take the verbal attack personally. He looked more hurt than offended, and he was not about to respond in terms of military rank. Not in Saigon.

"Thirty-four," he corrected Thomas softly, as the three static post MPs, the policewoman, and the prostitute all looked on quietly.

"The reactionary team never found Treach—the news just leaked out a couple hours ago. PMO is carrying him as Missing In Action—"

"Then we should all be out scouring the bushes for him!" Thomas interrupted. "We should be crisscrossing every damned hamlet between Bien Hoa and Xa Trang, searching . . . he might be wounded! How would *you* like to be abandoned out in the middle—"

"The colonel's already got half the detachment from Bien Hoa conducting a multiple grid search of the scene," Stryker said, cutting him off again. "It's kinda tough to piece something like this together, friend, when you can't locate any witnesses."

"Well . . ." Thomas hesitated. "Shit."

"And who is the little lass none of you apes has found it in your kindness to introduce me to." Tim Bryant was stepping down from his side of the patrol jeep. His eyes were scanning the curves of both the policewoman and prostitute. Thomas, who knew the man inside and out—most of the time—had no idea which woman he was talking about. But every man present knew the only love in his lie was Hue Chean, his wife. A strong-willed woman who had just lost her first child and, herself, was still recovering from a serious bullet wound. Bryant might talk like a flirt, and his eyes were notorious for bulging from their sockets whenever a good pair of cantaloupes walked by, but his heart would never stray from Chean. Broox's favorite story to tell at Mimi's Bar was about the night, months before their wedding, when Chean caught Tim entering a bar without her. She promptly stabbed him over the incident.

Sergeant Brickmann was about to explain what was

taking place at the post, but the policewoman was quickly tiring of all the conversation. She grabbed the prostitute by the arm and roughly led her into the kiosk on the other side of the gate's bulletin board. "Tell her I want to know where she got the ring," Stryker said, loud enough for the pretty canh-sat to hear above the roar of traffic beyond the sagging concertina wire atop the fence line. "And see if she's got anything else on her person—strip her young ass down, if you have to!" He folded his arms across the chest with a satisfied grin and returned the nods of the men.

The policewoman hadn't been alone with the suspect for more than a few seconds when the two began screaming at each other in rapid Vietnamese, and the hooker sent a spray of spittle across the canh-sat's brown tunic blouse. As Stryker and The Brick rushed up to see what all the commotion was about, the tiny law enforcer had cold cocked the whore with a dainty fist, and was sitting on her chest, arms and back pinned to the ground.

"Need any help?" Brickmann cooed unnecessarily.

"She say I swine!" The policewoman slapped the prostitute. "She say I whore with a badge!" And she slapped her again. "She say I suck all your cocks behind Mimi's Bar after work!" This time blood flowed from the prostitute's nose.

"She said all that?" an incredulous Brickmann looked down fondly at the hooker, tears in her eyes.

"She resists my attempts to search her," the policewoman continued, rising to one knee as she twisted her prisoner's arm around behind her back, further subduing her.

"Well, it looks like you've got the situation under

ontrol, honey," Bryant added. All the MPs proceeded o leave the archway at the kiosk's entrance.

"Two of you stay," she directed matter-of-factly.

Stryker and Brickmann halted in the shadows of the uardhouse and reluctantly turned their heads to lance back at her. The policewoman roughly sat the rostitute on the lone chair inside the hot structure and attled off another directive—this one in Vietnamese.

The prisoner began unbuttoning her blouse. Brickmann dutifully shrugged his shoulders and walked ack into the kiosk. Stryker, hands on his hips indicating his reluctance, spent a couple seconds frowning for he benefit of the men watching, then followed The Brick inside.

"Need any assistance?" a hopeful Mike Broox could be heard rushing forward from the jeeps.

"Remain outside." Stryker was quick with his reply. Make sure we're not interrupted by any chefs." Broox kidded to a halt and frowned, then took up a position ust outside the steps to the bright red clearing barrel. Chefs were any soldiers with scrambled eggs on their hats: officers.

Brickmann, on the other hand, felt no such reluctance in participating in the interrogation. It never occurred to him the prisoner could be escorted to the slammer, or some lock-up downtown, where additional police matrons could be located. This was, after all, ust your everyday street corner hooker. Not a real person, with rights and all that hogwash. If the canh-sat wanted them to stand by while she searched the uncooperative prisoner . . . well, this *was* a combat zone, wasn't it?

The woman threw her blouse in Stryker's face, dissolving any compassion he might have been harboring. Her breasts bounced about, barely confined by the thread of a bra, when she bent over to climb out of her miniskirt.

She threw the skirt at a somber-faced Brickmann, who caught it with his teeth.

The prostitute, clad now in only sheer black underwear and her highheels, folded her amber-colored arms across her chest and, in English, asked, "So you are happy? Go ahead and . . ." she hesitated as she grasped for the word, "*frisk* me!"

In Vietnamese, the policewoman ordered the removal of the bra and panties. Stryker and The Brick both understood what had just been said. But what surprised them was the manner in which the bargirl complied.

She merely shrugged, as if she were just preparing to bed down another GI, and slipped the panties down over the curve of her buttocks, then let them ride along her thighs a moment as she glanced up at Brickmann and winked at him. Like it was all just a game. Or perhaps a mental show she put on for herself in order to preserve her sanity.

The panties fell to her ankles, and she did not step out of them but switched her concentration to the hinge on the back of her bra. "No can do," she presented her best damsel-in-distress voice. *Naw, that couldn't be jammed.* Stryker smiled to himself.

Brickmann, ever the Boy Scout, rushed forward to assist, and she arched her shoulders back suddenly. The clasp slid smoothly free, and—as if she practiced this bedroom trick every night—shot across the small space between them and struck the MP sergeant on the nose.

Stryker's eyes locked onto the full, jutting breasts that, no longer restrained, sprang forth for his inspection. He felt he could almost judge her age from them, so firm and smooth did they smile up at him, almost beckoning. He knew she was really getting no thrill out of all this—the wide nipples were still flat and unaroused. Stryker saw himself licking them erect, yet in a dual vision, he saw himself standing in formation with several other recruits at the Military Police Academy, taking that all-important oath to serve and protect. His mind was already subconsciously fighting off all the thoughts rushing through him. And he didn't want to know which one would lose out.

But the policewoman was all business. As soon as the prostitute was naked, she hit her with another torrent of angry Vietnamese, motioning for the woman to raise her arms straight up in the air.

"Nope, no bazookas hidden there," Brickmann sighed dramatically as the policewoman inspected the bargirl's underarms. She ran her fingers down through the woman's long silky hair, again searching for hidden contraband, and Stryker flashed back to the night in Korea, during the riots, when he had collared a looter. The blacks weren't the jigabooes all the rednecks at PMO took them for. They held underground classes on how to ice the pigs and blow up your local police station. How to spring back out of the *against the wall, motherfucker* search position to cancel the copper's ticket. Even how to place razor blades under your afro, against your scalp, so when the oinkers ran their fingers through your hair, searching for dope, like they always did, you came away with a piece of the bacon.

Stryker still carried the scar across his finger where the punk's hidden razor blade had got him. But the jive monkey would forever be struttin' his stuff straight into lamp poles from now on. Stryker's nightstick had claimed an eyeball during the twenty minute struggle that followed. That was one dishonorably discharged private who wouldn't be shuckin' anybody back in The World, ever again.

Stryker watched the rivulets of sweat cascade down the woman's deeply tanned curves as the canh-sat told her to keep her arms up above her head. She instructed the woman to turn around, and as Stryker felt the intense heat in the tiny cubicle create a trickle of sweat along the small of his own back, he saw himself in bed with Lai, lifetimes ago, worlds to the north, in their private little bungalow on stilts, outside Pleiku. Tangled in the sheets, slick with sweat after hours of lovemaking, the heat of the tropics oozing in to envelop them. The smell of their juices sweet, not bitter as another storm swept in over the highlands to applaud and bathe them.

The ex-Green Beret was jerked from his memories by another noisy directive rattled off by the policewoman. Again, it was in angry Vietnamese, and though he understood the language, this particular order came across considerably more familiar than the others. It was always the last in a series of search-and-seizure procedures the canh-sats used when searching for drugs: bend over and spread 'em.

The prostitute glanced at the two huge Americans for a moment before complying. She obviously felt she was in for something quite different than what the policewoman intended. Puzzlement danced in her eyes as he waited for the MPs to unbuckle their belts and they lidn't.

As the policewoman probed, both men glanced at ach other uneasily—none of this was affording them he humorous respite or break from monotony they ad been anticipating. In fact, each of them had taken o shifting about nervously as they waited for the poicewoman to complete her body cavity inspection.

"Khien trach!" she announced loudly with obvious pride as she jerked the string of small heroin balloons rom the woman's vagina, and held them up for the Americans' inspection. Like sunshine, relief bathed the NCOs from helmet to jump boots.

The prostitute doubled over from the intense pain of he harsh extraction and fell to the ground, whimpering on her side. "Heroin!" The policewoman's face was also lined with sweat. They all looked like they had just been through a particularly difficult childbirth.

"Yes, heroin," Stryker admitted and he moved forward to examine the moist capsules. As scent of the woman's juices invaded the room, Stryker found himself growing uncontrollably hard. He pressed up against the buttocks of the policewoman from behind, always the flirt.

"Sergeant *Stryker*!" Her voice went up an octave as he pushed in against the crack of her cheeks, and she shuffled her feet to escape, but there was nowhere to go.

Brickmann narrowed his eyes, wondering what they were up to, yet instinctively realizing Stryker was simply returning to his old, take-nothing-serious self.

Stryker grinned as the pretty canh-sat forced her own smile but brushed him away nevertheless. She glided over to the prostitute's side, went down on one knee, and began applying the handcuffs.

After she spent a full minute clamping the "bracelets" in place, she finally managed the courage to glance back up at him, a scolding frown on her lips and mock anger in her eyes. Stryker winked back, and blew her a kiss.

Kip Mather would have been proud.

"Youz guys need any help in there?" Thomas, Bryant, and Broox all chimed in unison, like the trustworthy trio they weren't.

"Radio for a canh-sat patrol to transport," Brickmann replied, his voice a study in nonemotional tone.

"Roger."

Stryker moved forward and helped the policewoman lift the prisoner to her feet. "That's a negative!" he called out to the men in the street. He wondered if they shouldn't start putting her clothes back on, but with the handcuffs in place that would be difficult. "She was arrested on U.S. property, so we'll be the ones to book her."

"Far out." Brickmann made the statement as if in tired resignation. He walked out of the kiosk, leaving the arrest to Stryker.

"You can *book me* Mr. MP sergeant!" The prostitute was regaining lost energy. "But you can't *fuck* me! I won't let you!"

"What?" Stryker cocked an eyebrow at the woman.

"I saw how you looked at me when this VC bitch ordered my clothes off!" She spat the words at him. "I felt your eyes licking me as this dyke violated my snatch!" She kicked out at the policewoman, who lashed back with a vicious slap.

Stryker just set his feet apart and folded his arms

across his chest again, more amazed at her sudden fluency than offended by any accusations.

"Well, no matter what you saw here today, sergeant sir, you only *saw* it!" Despite the handcuffs behind her back, she managed to bring her fists around and grasp the edges of her pubic hair with her long, pineapple-painted fingernails. "*This* piece of heaven will never be yours." She focused weary eyes on his nametag, *"Stryker!"*

The policewoman made her settle down some so she could slide her skirt back on and drape the blouse over her shoulders. She placed the woman's underwear in a plastic bag with the heroin and sealed it. Stryker motioned the prostitute out into the sunlight.

From the back of the group of MPs, a whistle sounded at the sight of the woman's firm thighs as she climbed into one of the jeeps, but Stryker shot them a sergeant's glance, and they all fell silent.

"Take her young ass to the monkey house," he directed Bryant, who was behind the wheel again now. "Thomas and Miss Nhu here," he said, motioning toward the tiny policewoman, "will accompany you to assist with the book-in. But the arrest's yours." He held up the plastic bag so the others could see the baggies inside.

"Thanks, sarge." Bryant was all smiles. "I can use the felony."

"After you mug and print her," Stryker added, "hand her over to Miss Nhu. She can take her downtown to Vo Tanh or wherever and tape a fieldphone to her tits to find out where she got the Horse."

"For sures." Bryant folded the passenger seat forward so the policewoman could climb in, and the prisoner used the opportunity to bid Mark Stryker farewell.

She stood up and raised her skirt from behind so that its edge rode the top of her crotch. "You can never have it, Stryker!" she screamed as the canh-sat struggled to subdue her again. "I know you want me— I could *feel* it in there. But it will never happen, GI! Never! Only in your dreams!"

Stryker stood alone in the dust as the jeep pulled away and the prostitute continued to yell at him as the men listened all around. "When you make love to your whore tonight, Stryker, pretend she's *me*! Do you hear, Stryker? Pretend she's *me*!"

He spent a few moments watching the MP jeep disappear over the hill, then turned and headed directly for his jeep, resisting the urge to see how many of the men standing behind him were trying to hide their hard-ons.

4. The Legendary Jack Flak

"Look, boob-breath, do you wanna snuggle up to her tush tonight, or do you wanna end up volunteerin' for another lonely Fort Hustler static post out of boredom?" Michael Broox braced a scuffed jungle boot atop the western style log fence behind the orderly room bulletin board and resumed chewing on the sliver of bamboo like the old Asian hand Richards was always telling him he was.

The newbie recruit, fresh off a turtle bus from the Camp Alpha in-processing center outside Tan Son Nhut, shuffled his feet about in the dust and buried his hands deeper into the pockets of his embarrassingly new, shiny green jungle fatigues. "Well, I've got the *'Chao ong'* part down, but as for the rest of it, I just can't seem to get the pronunciation right." The private glanced over his shoulder again at the secretary purchasing a baggy of steaming sugarcane cubes from a vendor parked outside gate four of the International Hotel complex. "You don't suppose maybe she speaks English, do you?"

"*That* would be too easy, cunt juice!" Sergeant Richards punched the raw recruit lightly on the bicep and flicked his chin back in the direction of the slender secretary in the blue and silver *ao dai*. "You think she's gonna be impressed by a lousy private, what with all these bookoo-bucks officers running around here? You gotta come up with an approach none of the goofy butter bars would ever waste their time trying. You gotta speak the lingo, boy, speak the lingo. Now listen to the syllables again carefully as I repeat each one. And get it right. Pronunciation *is* important when you use this language. One three-letter word can mean half a dozen different things if you change the tone every time you say it, okay? Now listen." He repeated the phrase again.

"I just don't know." The eighteen-year-old was nervously wringing his hands as he bent his head closer toward Richards, eyes glued to the buck sergeant's lips as he repeated the seven-word phrase.

"What are you—some kind of wimp?" Broox coaxed the kid on. "Here we are wastin' our time trying to bed you down with an honest-to-God professional girl—"

"Not some fifty-P-whore from Tu Do," Richards cut in.

"And you're tryin' to back out on us. What the hell kind of brothers they turning out back at the academy? You a gutless wonder or something? A ball-less babysan? How the hell we gonna be able to count on your sorry ass when the mortars and rockets start comin' in, or a sniper zeroes in on us downtown?"

"Okay, okay!"

"And ya ain't got all fuckin' day, sport." Richards glanced back at the secretary again. In her early twenties, she was probably the most beautiful woman employed by the 716th. A goddess. No one in the battalion—no one on record, that is— had ever gotten into her pants. No one had even *claimed* to have achieved the impossible feat. "Sure, she comes out every afternoon like this—hell, you could set your watch by the lady. But them bastards inside headquarters work her buns off all day, and only allow her a fifteen minute break."

"And all these Vietnamese are raised expecting their mandatory two hour afternoon siesta," Broox said.

"Just goes to show you what a good wife she'd make," Richards added. "She's half Americanized already."

"Just one more time," the recruit whispered.

Richards repeated the phrase in slow Vietnamese.

"Now break a leg." Broox wrapped an arm around the kid and headed him in the direction of the mysterious woman sucking on sugarcane cubes under a brightly colored vendor's wagon umbrella on Tran Hung Dao Street.

"Good luck." Richards winked the kid a confident expression.

"Thanks, sarge."

And break a leg he almost did.

After he bowed politely in front of the startled secretary, he whispered the phrase he had memorized to the syllable, and was promptly knocked off his feet by a swift round-house punch to the chops from out of nowhere!

Richards and Broox, holding each other up, were doubled over with muffled laughter. This was the tenth rookie in two weeks they had coaxed into their little bait-the-FNG (fucking new guy) trap. The secretary, hardly amused (yet always on-target with her dainty, lightning-fast fist) cast an icy glare at Richards and his partner, then dumped what remained of her sugarcane cubes on the private lying on his back in the dust, and stormed off to her office.

"What the hell happened?" Stryker had appeared on the steps of the orderly room. His right gunhand rested on the butt of his holstered .45 automatic. He didn't like seeing his MPs lying on their back in the street—even the rooks. It brought back too many bad memories.

"Aw, Gary here taught him how to greet Miss Diem, from the PM's office, sarge." Broox shifted the blame expertly.

"Aw, roasted VC rectums, you little sawed-off runt!" Richards threw a lazy punch at him, mildly offended.

"I'm sorry I asked," Stryker said frowning as he kept his eyes on the private fifty yards away. He had still not gotten up off his back. "I should have known you two were behind this."

"The rook there," Richards said pointing at the cold-cocked newbie, "wanted to meet Miss Diem—"

"*Every*one wants to meet Miss Diem," Broox cut in. "Under the sheets, after curfew, in a sixty-nine position."

"So Mikey here told him some of his back-alley sleaze lingo—"

"It always works for me." Broox produced one of his most innocent smiles.

"And Miss Diem was apparently not impressed."

Stryker cleared his throat. "What did you tell the poor bastard to say to her, Broox?"

"Aw, nothin' sarge."

"Mike!" The big sergeant was not one to be easily conned by a member of the notorious Decoy Squad.

But Broox remained silent. He knew how far he could go with Stryker. And the point of no return had not been reached yet.

"He said, 'Gorgeous, would you do me the honor of clamping your luscious vaginal lips across the length of my rosy red tongue?' " Richards translated, and Broox's smile faded.

"There's no words in Vietnamese for gutter talk like that." Stryker's eyes went narrow as they burrowed into Broox's mental shield. The private was refusing to return his stare.

"Sure there is." Broox continued to stare at the dirt between his boots. He swallowed hard—this was no time to have scuffed boots. Stryker sounded like he was in the mood for a uniform inspection.

"Horseshit," the ex-Green Beret countered, confident Mike was full of it. And he'd damned well prove it, if the hotdog wanted to get down to semantics—*he* had all the graveyard shift to make his point, and that was all the time in the world.

"Yah, where do you take your language lessons, anyway?" Richards sided with Stryker, and Broox cast him a betrayed glare.

"Jon Toi told me how to say it, and he sure as hell knows his pussy talk." Broox was sounding more and more defensive.

"Jon Toi the canh-sat?"

"Yah."

"He's a family man." Stryker flashed back to the little room in Toi's small flat back at the police barracks. The walls were papered with glossy photos of murder victims, suspects gunned down by the police, and missing persons who had eventually been found floating face down in the *Song Saigon.* A chill went down his spine, and he shifted his feet about and walked out from under the roof overhang, seeking the warmth of the tropical sun, but it was laughing down at him from behind the blanket of storm clouds smothering the city. "Toi don't use that kind of language."

"Well, *somebody* told me how to say vaginal in Vietnamese," Broox said and stood his ground. A Phantom jet rolled along the edge of the storm front just then, waving its wings as the sonic boom rattled glass in those few buildings daring enough to be equipped with it. Broox nodded his chin confidently, as if the monstrous machine in the sky had punctuated his point. Richards cocked an eyebrow skyward, impressed with the omen.

Stryker bit his lip. He was not one to fuck with fate, buck karma, or ignore messages from heaven. "Get your lousy asses inside." He forced a smile and grabbed both men by a bicep before propelling them in through the swinging doors of the briefing room. "Everyone's late for my guardmount!"

"Hey, don't be tarnishing the merchandise!" Broox brushed off the spot where Stryker had grabbed Richards. "This here is a genuine NCO too, you know. Show some respect, Stryk!"

Richards got his partner in a playful headlock and dragged him deeper into the cavernous building. "Shut the fuck up, Mikey."

Pvt. Don Mallory watched the clouds swirling about directly overhead. The stars cleared from in front of his eyes. It was actually daylight. Heads and faces of curious bystanders were poking into his field of vision from all sides. The sound around him was a collage of nervous laughter and muffled chatterings in a foreign language—*Asian*. The back of his head was throbbing with pain. He stared up at the clouds, trying to focus on the dark blurs that raced past beneath them—*gunships!* With rotors beating at the hot, sticky air. The smell of the garbage in the gutters made him think of his high school locker room and the time he had had the wind knocked out of him on the football field. He had woken up on his back, staring at the sky, just like now. But there was no faceguard blocking his field of vision, and spittle was not collecting at the edges of his mouth from the plastic against his teeth. And the faces staring down at him had narrow, alien eyes. They were definitely not the cheerleaders from Highland High School!

His mind began to race backwards, until he saw the slender woman in the gossamer-thin gown (sensuously slit up the sides from ankle to waist, closed at the throat, draped over black silky pantaloons) deck him with a sudden right. The fist had not hurt. It was not even thrown with much power behind it. But somehow those girlish knuckles had caught his jaw just right and knocked him off balance. The pain ringing between his ears was from slamming the back of his head against the asphalt.

How the hell did he get into these situations? And who were those two clowns that had given him the free language lesson? He doubted he'd be able to identify them out of the thousand-odd MPs in the battalion. What even made him think they might be connected in some way with his current misfortune?

He shook his head like they did in the westerns after

the big bar fights, but his vision remained blurred, and he decided to remain where he was—on his back.

Clouds of dust were rolling in between the faces staring down at him, and soon a dull rumbling noise was invading his private little world of hurt. Private Mallory had no way of knowing just then that a patrol jeep had coasted up to within inches of the right side of his face.

"You okay, brother?" Someone with powerful hands was lifting him up out of the dust. He wished the guy would just let him be. The motion was making his head vibrate, like a plugged tea kettle ready to burst. "Don't tell me Miss Diem is assaulting newbies again."

"Yes . . . Miss Diem . . . beautiful Miss Diem with ripe mangoes for tits." Did he really say that out loud? Did all these people hear him say that?

"Looks like Broox and Richards have been up to no good again."

Broox and Richards. Yeah, the names banged a gong now. "Beautiful Miss Diem."

"Lady with a twenty-two-karat chastity belt locked beneath them tantalizing tits, soldier. Dream on!" The guy was helping him over to the jeep, bracing him upright in the passenger seat. "Think you can keep your chin up till I get you over to the dispensary?" he was asking.

"Oh, I'm okay, I'm okay." Mallory finally glanced over at the husky MP climbing in behind the wheel. "No need to see no doctor. I'm not even bleeding."

"Then un-cross your eyeballs, boy," the guy said with a laugh. "But a concussion can mean pretty serious business, you know. Especially in this heat—in the tropics."

"I'm okay, sport." *Sport?* Did he actually call one of the short-timers sport?

"Suit yourself."

"It's almost worth it, ya know?" Mallory rubbed the knot rising along the back of his head. "I could get off just dreamin' about that woman's thighs."

"Ain't no secretary worth physical injury, pal. Not on *this* installation. Ching ching!"

"She could sit on my face any day."

"I'd say she did better than that." The vet chuckled. He slammed the gears into reverse and maneuvered out of the throng of pedestrians that had gathered around them. The motion made Mallory nauseous.

He glanced over at the twenty-five-year-old with the spec4 patch just below the Eighteenth Brigade combat patch. Solid build, clean shaven, short blond hair—*and he thought all cops grew mustaches!* Why did he look so familiar? "Don't I know you?" He couldn't believe he actually asked that. He hoped the guy didn't frown at the question or move farther away. Had his tone really come across with fairy-light quality? Mallory wasn't sure—he couldn't really hear his own voice beyond the throbbing of his head.

The specialist glanced over at him with a tight smile. "I don't think so, *sport*, but who knows—what town you from?"

"Colorado. I mean Thornton. Thornton, Colorado."

"Where the fuck is that?"

"North of Denver a couple klicks. Suburb. Nothin' much to look at, except fifty-nine bars. They got fifty-nine ass-kickin' bars in Thornton."

"Can't say as I've been there."

"Oh."

"Spent a year at Carson, though. You know Carson?"
"Yah. No comparison. Fort Carson's cold. Too many mountains. Thornton's hot fun in the city, so far as sticktime's concerned. You should ride with the cops there—they call it the Big T. They'll show you a ride along you'll not soon forget."
"Yah, okay, pal. Next time I breeze through Denver on my way to Bangkok, I'll be sure and stop in Thornton." The spec4 rolled his eyeballs skyward.
"A most notorious police force in Thornton."
"For sures."
"Road with 'em half a dozen times before I joined the MP Corps and signed up for the 'Nam. It was good experience."
"I can imagine."
"No you can't. They bust balls in Thornton. They kick ass and take names. Heroes after my own heart."
"Well, I never been to Thornton."
"The gang punks call 'em Thornton Thumpers."
"Oh."
"With awe and respect, mind you."
"For sures."
"Best city cops I seen in a long time, and I been around."
"Uh-huh."
"The boys in blue play it by the book there, but there's enough scumbucket potential floatin' through town on a daily basis that they wear their sap gloves thin, too."
"I'll make a point of visitin' Thornton on my next R and R, sport."
"You won't regret it."
"For sures."

"You play football?" Mallory scratched his chin.

"Nope."

"Then where the fuck have I seen you before?" He stared hard into the spec4's eyes, and the man braked to a gentle stop halfway through the entrance to gate four and returned the blank look. "I'm sorry. I meant—"

Then Private Mallory saw it. Over the guy's shoulder, taking up four racks of the sidewalk vendor's stand located beside the military police kiosk. The latest issue of *Time* magazine. And plastered across the cover was the face of the MP sitting next to him. "You're—you're—"

"Jack Flak." He held out his hand.

"You're Jack Flak."

"For sures."

"Pleased to meet you, Mr. Flak!" Mallory grabbed the hand and pumped it heartily. "Damned proud to fucking meet you!"

"Call me Jack." The MP with the Paul Newman grin displayed a modest and slightly embarrassed twinkle in his eye.

"Outfuckinstanding!" Mallory lost all his rookie insecurity as he announced his discovery to the MPs manning the gate. "I'm sitting next to Jack Flak!"

"Give the young man a Twinkie dipped in cunt juice," said one of the khaki-clad sentries and laughed.

"*Chao ong*, honorable infamous one." The other MP whipped a semi-formal salute on the driver as he grinned from ear to ear.

"Aw, knock it off, guys." The humble cover boy shook his head, blushing now. He gunned the accelerator through the gate, leaving the privates in a cloud of dust.

The magazine cover showed Jack Flak with three other MPs atop a roaring V-100 Assault tank that had been caught on film racing to the scene of a burning tenement the VC had rocketed downtown the month before, but only Jack's face was clearly visible—the others were obscured by gunsmoke and rainfall.

Private Mallory had seen the magazine during his last week at the school, in Fort Gordon, Georgia. Reading material had a way of arriving weeks late in a combat zone, and as he processed through Camp Alpha, the magazine was on the racks there also. It was all the guys could talk about. *Imagine that . . . a Saigon Commando on the cover of* Time*!*

But Jack Flak brushed it all aside with his usual display of no-nonsense modesty. What was a fancy back-in-the-world rag, when he'd already had his puss plastered across the front pages of every Saigon newspapers on Tu Do Street. Jack Flak had a knack of shining in front of the cameras at just the right moment. The photographers had been there when he rescued the woman from the apartment house fire, and they had been there when he saved the choking child at the open-air restaurant. And hadn't they magically appeared when he stopped off at a vendor stand for a mug of coconut juice and ended up dusting the liquor store robber who had foolishly backed out of the establishment right into Jack's lap? The PM had even jokingly accused him of setting them all up once—just for the publicity. But how could you fake a robbery-in-progress and a baby-san choking on a wishbone?

"So how's your head feeling, hero?" Jack Flak asked Pvt. Donald Mallory as their jeep slowly cruised in and out of the zig-zag maze of sand-filled barrels that reduced the speed of vehicles approaching the MP Headquarters building. "Looks like you've lost the slight daze in your eyes."

"Oh, I'll be all right." Mallory rubbed his bump and the pain stung back at him like an angry, determined honey bee. "No sweat, Jack, no sweat."

"So you'll be assigned to the Seven-Sixteenth here, eh? Know which company yet?"

"Well, my orders said Bravo, but I've since been told that's been amended to read Charlie because of the ambush up in—" He hesitated more from the taboo of mentioning the deaths of so many MPs rather than his inability to pronounce Bien Hoa.

"Yah, yah, total wipe-out, brother. Real numba ten bummer. Bien Hoa's always been bad news. Well, what was I getting at: I see by your . . ." He searched for the proper word. "Misfortune here today. You've taken an interest in the local girls—"

"I've already seen all the VD films at Camp Alpha." Mallory interrupted him. He wasn't in the mood for a lecture.

"I'm sure you have." Flak worked on maintaining his smile. "That's not what I was getting at." He began to wonder why he was even wasting his time on the FNG. But he went on. "If you're really interested in meeting some of the local gals, enroll in a language class, or taxi out to some of the social clubs far from the GI district. You're bound to meet some nice young lady who's not after a plane ticket stateside, or your ration card. Most of the bargirls crowding the neon boulevards that spoke out from the International are nothing but trouble. Take my word for it: some of them have even *killed* just so they could impress the neighbor cunt next door by hanging this helmet liner." He tapped his forefinger against his helmet. "On one of their bedposts. Now tell me *that* don't take a twisted mentality."

"Miss Conceited there at the sugarcane stand didn't quite strike me as your run-of-the-mill hooker," Mallory said.

"Hell, I wasn't even talking about *her*. Nobody's gotten into *her* pants since . . . well . . ."

"Since who?" Mallory's ears seemed to perk forward like an annoyed race horse's.

"Look." Jack Flak worked at changing the subject's direction of travel. He brushed the base of his model's nose with a smooth knuckle and grinned. "All I'm saying is let me know when you're in the mood for some enlightening conversation and not just a sweaty crotch to plunge into. I'll set you up with a real cherry girl who don't give a shit how much you make a month, how long your pecker is, or what's your home address so she can blackmail you by threatening to send photos home to wife numba one."

"You sound more like a pimp than a street cop." Mallory was not sure why his lips were rambling on into territory rooks seldom ventured. His mouth was taking him toward the shitter again. Here was this rare vet taking an interest in him, and he was becoming difficult. Maybe it was the knot on the back of his head. Innocent by reason of involuntary irrationality. "On what do you base your experience in this field?" He found himself imitating the specialist who had jeeped him down to the International from Alpha that first day last week—what was his name? Schaeffer or something?

Jack Flak raised the fingers on his left hand so that

the intricately carved twenty-two karat gold wedding band became visible. "Been in the 'Nam three glorious years now, pal. Been married to the most *dep gai* two of those Tour Three sixty-fives. Haven't regretted a single sunrise with her, either." His smile brightened as he gazed off at the clouds and saw his own private little silver lining.

"Good for you, Jack Flak."

"Just trying to save you some grief, newbie."

"Gracias, amigo," the kid said sarcastically.

"Known a lot of guys in old Saigontown lost their hearts in the 'Nam and went back to The World forever changed. Ruined their whole outlook on life. And *those* sorry cases involved street girls of questionable virtue, *sport*. Just trying to save you a world of grief."

"I didn't come over here with the intention of letting love of pussy fuck up my marbles. I got my priorities, ya know. I've yet to let a woman come before my career and the street."

A light chuckle escaped Jack Flak. *There goes another rook talkin' 'bout the street like he knows the difference between his asshole and his airhole.* "We'll see, my friend, we'll see."

"I'm serious." Mallory clenched his fists by his sides, out of view. "All I wanna do in this lousy town is waste a bad guy or two then book a flight back to the States and get on with some real police work. Ain't no bitch gonna break my heart over a midnight romp in the rack."

Jack Flak just giggled again, and with his left hand he imitated a Soviet-made rocket twirling through the night sky down onto a random tenement in the heart of his favorite city. His lips made the same fluttering noise the DIs back at the school made when describing a barrage of 122s descending from the clouds in some past, almost forgotten surprise attack. Mallory had no idea where the connection was. "Remember what you just told me." Jack Flak chuckled for the third time as he parked the jeep outside the briefing room doors and started to lock the steering wheel chain to the brake pedal. "A month or two from now when some shady lady downtown is lying across your chest and your little mind is racing a thousand miles in every direction trying to figure out how you can remain in that rack forever without me or Sergeant Stryker coming around to look for your AWOL ass, *chump*! Just remember what you told me today when your shackup starts looking better to you than your beloved nightshifts with your scuzzy old buck sergeant partner. Remember your little ain't-no-bitch-gonna-break-my-heart speech when Miss Right has cried in your arms 'cause she don't wanna surrender you to the Green Machine every night, and you've fallen under her spell—Vietnamese women have that power, you know. Don't let 'em cry all over you, boy." He waved his finger in front of Mallory's nose. "Or they'll have you under their spell until you both meet in the next life!" Jack Flak shook his head in resignation and slowly climbed out of the jeep, muttering, "Fuckin' rookie. What the fuck do I care."

Pvt. Donald Mallory watched Jack Flak saunter in through the briefing room doors, hand resting on the butt of his holstered .45 as if he just might be walking into a sudden, unscheduled gunfight. The kid from Thornton, Colorado watched the veteran street cop disappear into the clouds of cigarette smoke drifting out from the gathering guardmount, then he let out a hearty sigh and checked the rain flap on his own holster. Some day he'd taper it down with a razor the way Jack Flak did, so the hammer and rear slide assembly would be visible. The unauthorized alteration of government equipment made the black holster look more professional, tough, and *sharp*, so none of the sergeants said anything other than to give it a second glance of envy. Few sergeants were afforded the luxury of bending the rules, except perhaps Stryker, Richards, and The Brick. Then there was Raunchy Raul, too, but *that* was another story altogether.

Mallory glanced over his shoulder, back toward the fruit vendor's stand, but the old papa-san was gone, and so was the beautiful secretary in the form-hugging *ao dai.* Mallory took in a deep breath, straightened his web belt so the brass buckle was straight with his gig line, then he reluctantly followed the legendary Jack Flak into the briefing room.

Sergeant Stryker slammed his nightstick against the top of the podium twice and cleared his throat. "Awright, awright. Lemme have your attention, gentlemen." None of the three actions were necessary. The room, despite being crowded with fifty normally rowdy MPs, was deathly still. It was a mandatory type of silence, in view of the events two days earlier. It would be up to one of the sergeants to break the ice. The patrolmen would sit there stone-faced and glassy-eyed, with their arms folded tightly across their nametags, the whole guardmount, unless someone in a position of authority showed them it was permissible to abandon their guard and let the walls down. "We got a lot to cover this afternoon, and not much time to get it all down in your little pocket notebooks."

Stryker scanned the cavernous room from left to right. Men from the day shift, who just happened to be in the building and took it upon themselves to sit in on the Stryk's briefing, wore bright tan khakis. Stryker checked his watch: five-thirty P.M. These boys in brown had six hours to go till their eleven-to-eleven day shift was over. The MPs directly in front of him, and to the right, however, were clad in green jungle fatigues, and made up the six P.M. to six A.M. relief shift. They kept the streets under control, until the graveyard shift hit the bricks one hour before midnight curfew. All fifty of the soldiers seated in front of him wore the black helmet liners with the white letters up front, a green and gold Eighteenth Brigade combat patch decal on the right, and the numbers seven-one-six on the left. The backs were covered with all form of graffiti from hometowns to profanity. "And speaking of pocket notebooks . . ." None of Stryker's usual *fuck-it* attitude had shown through yet, and the men before him were unsure how to react. "Just how many of you clowns are carrying them this week?"

A few hands shot up in the air—teenagers who hadn't kicked bad high school classroom habits yet—and some of the men patted empty pockets then shrugged, but most just returned their watch commander's blank expression. "Put your hands down, put your hands down." Stryker had both his in the air now, waving them all down. "But consider this fair warning: we don't stand up here and spout off thirty minutes of crap just so it can go in one ear and out the other. If it's not on your hotsheet or BOLO bulletins, you'd best be makin' notes—especially if what's leavin' my lips pertains to your beat. Any questions? We're going to be having more than the usual number of inspections beginning next week, and from now on, that includes skimming over your notebooks."

"That's an invasion of my constitutional privacy." Thomas stood up before Bryant and Broox could keep him seated.

"Shut the fuck up, Anthony." Stryker consulted his clipboard before going on with the briefing. He didn't check the room for any who might have questions. Stryker considered the directive self-explanatory.

"But sarge!" Thomas was, it seemed, charged-up to bait Stryker in front of the men. It was a scene that was expected to be made, and it always involved the same two men.

"Sit down, Ants!" Even Richards had grabbed onto the private this time, and he was finally forced back into his chair.

"Last week Charlie shot his wad into Cholon again," Stryker continued, unsmiling, "and the rockets not only took out forty-three civilians but a Cuan Loc Hon Hop patrol. Before he died from loss of blood . . ." Stryker looked up briefly and nodded to himself at all the helmets that dipped down in mourning, the way it should be. "Private Vincent had the presence of mind to radio in the approximate launch points of the incoming projectiles, and an Alert Team of seven V-One hundreds was fortunate enough to race out in time to catch the VC with their pants down: in other words, we got a half dozen rockets intact."

"We already know all about that, illustrious leader," Sergeant Brickmann called out from the back of the room. "Half of the men in this room were aboard those

Assault tanks. Tell us something we don't know, so we can conclude this extravagance of valuable time and abscond to our appropriate baliwick." The Brick was notorious for his meticulously lengthy dissertations.

"Yah," Thomas added from the safety of his folding metal seat. "Let us expedite this little rendezvous so we can hit the bricks with no further adieu. I got some ladies of questionable virtue I got to be filling FI cards out on down along Tu Do way." And he pulled out a silky scarf from his thigh pocket and floated it in front of Broox's face, "Smell *that* scent of womanliness," he bragged to the men around him. "The owner of this little Saigon souvenir assures me she slept *threeee* nights with it between her legs before she gave it to me this morning as we parted company, gentlemen." He allowed the filmy length of silk to flutter in front of the men's noses again before leaning back in his chair and letting the scarf settle across his face. "Definitely a tiny slice of heaven!"

"The *reason* I bring all this back from the grave," Stryker said, giving Brickmann and the others an annoyed glance, "is because the experts in MI have completed their analysis of the armaments we captured. And Specialist Linda Covert from Psy Ops is back again to narrate a slide program her team put together recently."

The lights dimmed, and Spec5 Covert entered somewhat hesitantly. This time she wore unflattering coveralls, as opposed to the tight-fitting uniform she had donned last time she appeared in front of the Saigon Commandos. She glanced around the room, feigning mock suspicion, but there was no way she could recognize anybody in the growing darkness.

"Bring out the popcorn," Thomas muttered, a smile

from ear to ear now and memories of Sergeant Schultz's involvement in the last Linda Covert briefing fresh in his mind—Lydic and Schaeffer had commandeered the porno flicks Raunchy Raul recently brought back from R&R and substituted them for the survival films the Psy Ops lady was *supposed* to be showing.

"Just like the days of my youth," Bryant chimed sarcastically, as the slide projector was turned on and the screen became a bright glowing square on the bamboo wall. "The only thing worthwhile about high school: when they showed films once a week."

"Get your balsa airplane wound up," Richards whispered over to Broox.

"We congratulate you men on making an exceptional cache seizure," Miss Covert began after brushing off her buttocks in the darkness. The first slide was flashed across the screen: a Soviet 122mm rocket still on its bamboo launch stand, pointed at the heart of the city. The MI photographer had a sense of drama about him: He took the color photo inches from the rear fins of the projectile, so that the charred and blackened tenements downtown rose in the distance, miles in front of the nose cone. "Not only were some basement bomber type missiles recovered, but both Soviet and Chicom weapons were located in perfect operating condition. The president of South Vietnam and his advisors have all already seen these slides, and I am proud to announce here today that the Seven-sixteenth MP Battalion has been put in for still another presidential unit citation. And I'm sure you'll all get it." She smacked her lips with obvious pride. "You certainly deserve it." There came a sudden, slight fluttering noise above the hum of the projector, as a rubberband-propelled balsa wood airplane took to the muggy, smoke-laced air and began buzzing the room.

"This, I'm sure nobody needs to tell you," continued the shapely blonde with the fake eyelashes, "is a Soviet One Twenty-two millimeter GTG rocket. It has a maximum range of eleven thousand meters, so it has to be launched within five or six miles of the intended target—lucky for us. That's why you men were able to swoop in on the bad, bad VC before they could beat feet for their tunnels under Tu Do. . . ."

"Hey, I like the way she talks." Thomas nudged Bryant with his elbow. "Just like a regular fuckin' GI type."

"This particular model is the niner-Mike-toowah-toowah-Mike," Miss Covert continued as her bottom expertly swayed out of the flight path of the balsawood airplane. It crashed into Stryker's podium with a dull thud as she tapped the bamboo screen with her pointer stick. "Payload is high explosive fragmentation. . . ."

Stryker was not watching Spec5 Covert just then. He had already seen the slides at a special screening for NCOs earlier in the day. Thomas was still snoozing beneath his perfumed scarf, and now the fragrance had drifted up to the big MP sergeant behind the teakwood podium.

"The rocket's length is just over seventy-five inches, and it weighs a mere hundred and one pounds. For you technical experts out there, the whiskey-hotel filler in the nose cone is fourteen and a half pounds of RDX and aluminum combined . . . the fuse is DKZ dash B-Bravo with a good old PD on the end," she was saying, but Stryker was no longer listening—or hearing the words anyway. Instead, his eyes were glued to the silk scarf, and his mind was seeing his hotel room down at the Miramar as he found it only a week before the ambush outside Bien Hoa.

He had come home from an eighteen-hour shift keeping the rooks in Precinct One in line, to find Kim had moved in a plush, princess bed, complete with lacy white canopy and silver, satin sheets. It was so big and soft you could sink two feet even before taking both feet off the floor, completely losing yourself in it.

Stryker had always been used to what he thought of as "plain" sex before: sparse hotel beds, a rack in the barracks, a mat on a primitive hut floor—even the bamboo or teakwood floor itself! The closest he had come to anything so daring was a fishnet hammock strung beneath his bungalow-on-stilts up in Pleiku—making love under the floating moon of the highlands had been more eerie than satisfying, but he would never forget it.

And now, after Kim had entered the bedroom wearing a see-through gown from some mail order catalog off Hollywood Boulevard Broox had given her, lovemaking in Saigon would never be the same.

He breathed in the perfume rising from the scarf across Thomas's nose, and visions of Kim's flawless face drifted in front of the glowing screen as a slide of a Chinese 102mm rocket replaced the Russian 122. Thunder from the advancing storm in the distance echoed across the compound, penetrating even to this, the womb of headquarters building, and the vision was replaced with the sad, somber face of a Lai he hadn't seen in months. He wondered where she was, what she was doing. If she was all right. Who she was with. The thought she might be two feet beneath the muck of some Pleiku rice paddy shot through him like a tracer round, and he shook the vision of worms crawling through the eyesockets of her skull from his head and tried to concentrate on the American woman's briefing.

"You guys went and captured yourself a crateload of one-zero-toowah-Alpha-thurees, also." Spec5 Covert swatted a probing hand from the darkness off her thigh but managed to ramble on without losing a heartbeat. "Those babies are only just under a yardstick long, but they pack a real punch with their two and three-quarters pounds of TNT. Weighing in at a total-tube of thirty-seven pounds, its maximum range in good weather is five thousand meters.

"This is another Chinese Communist import into the squirmish between Vietnamese," she said bitterly as a third slide flashed through Stryker's memories. "You gentlemen captured a couple bicycle loads of these hummers. Thirty-three inches of Type Sixty-three, one-oh-seven millimeter with an HE-Frag payload of about three pounds of, once again, TNT. She weighs in at forty-two pounds and has a range of eighty-three hundred meters, which in American lingo is somewhere around five miles or so . . . Ohhhhhhh!" She suddenly screamed as she whirled around and latched onto another probing hand. She twisted Broox's hand until the wrist popped a couple of times and he flipped out of his seat onto his knees, groaning. Spec5 Covert climbed his face like an out-of-control truck roaring up a runaway semi ramp at a hundred klicks an hour.

"Hey, help, you guys!" Broox called out as she slapped him silly. "She's got the wrong man—I'm innocent!"

The lights flicked on, and Covert gathered up her slides, threw the men in the front row a disgusted look, then glided out of the room, glaring. "How did it feel?" Richards laughed, nodding.

"I'm telling you, it wasn't me!" Broox rubbed his wrist.

"Aw, come on, Mikey!" Brickmann and Schultz cast unbelieving grins at the private.

"Seriously!"

"It was totally divine," a guilty Thomas said, sighing in not-so-mock ecstasy. "Utterly absorbing. Well worth the risk to life and limb. . . ."

Broox promptly slugged him in the shoulder, and both men were deluged with guffaws and a barrage of paper airplanes from all over the room.

"Awright, awright, knock off the crap!" Stryker was checking his watch again. "We've got too little time, and too much to cover." He glanced at his clipboard.

"Item number one: Private Fox has been Absent With Out Leave over forty-eight hours now. Any of you clowns know where he's at, or what he's up to?"

"Fox?" Bryant shot to his feet, mouth open and eyes wide.

"What is it, Tim?" Stryker felt a shudder slide down into the pit of his gut. "You look like you've seen a—"

"Fox was on that payroll convoy that got ambushed outside of Bien Hoa, sarge!"

"He wasn't on the Alert Team roster." Stryker raced through the pages tacked to a bulletin board beside the podium. When he found the list of men he himself had compiled just eighteen hours before the Assault tanks had rumbled north through the rain with their cargo of payroll money, he scanned the thirty-five names again so quickly letters ran together in a blur of black and white.

"That don't mean nothing, Mark." Sgt. Gary Richards remained calm in his seat, though his eyes seemed to be dancing with the hint of excitement now. "You know how the off-duty clowns and some of the eager-for-action newbies always hitch a ride out of town in hopes of seeing some blood and guts in the boonies. Fox might have done the same thing."

"I swear I saw him ridin' tailgunner on Simon's V-One hundred!" Bryant was adamant.

"Okay, okay." Stryker held his hands out for calm. The room was coming alive with an uneasy hum of emotions and boots shifting around.

"Anybody know if he was off duty or whatever?" Richards glanced around the room.

"He was on his fucking vacation time," Bryant said.

"I thought he was gonna trek down to Malacca Malaysia or something," said Broox. "To see . . ." His voice trailed off suddenly, as if he was just about to accidentally reveal a long-kept secret.

"Yah, he *was* on vacation." Sergeant Brickmann stood up, frowning as the weight of the situation began to balance itself out on the collective shoulders of all the NCOs in the room. "I remember shuffling the numbers so I could give him some extra comp days."

"Crazy fuck shoulda gone to Honolulu," mumbled a disgruntled corporal in the last row. " 'Stead of some goofy payroll convoy out to the sticks."

"Some guys'll do anything to score a hard-on," the man beside him muttered.

"Stupid hotdogs."

"A laugh a minute, ain't they?"

"Ching ching, GI, ching ching." The words came out slow and tired.

"Tim." Stryker's eyes zeroed in on Bryant as he leaned down across the podium. "Bust ass over to the PM's office and tell them everything you know about this. If Fox was aboard that payroll convoy, he's an MIA, because he sure as hell wasn't found among the dead." Spec4 Bryant swallowed hard, a look of intense seriousness coating his features, then he nodded and bolted from the room.

Several of the men were moving toward the doors after Bryant like a school of fish darting in a sudden direction without warning. "Let's go—let's go—" came the murmur as the crush swelled against the exits.

"Hold it! Hold it!" Stryker raised his voice and even used the podium loudspeaker for the first time since any of the Decoy Squad could remember. The MPs crowding to get out of the briefing room froze in place, many in mid-stride. "I already told you: The bossman's got all kinds of help up north searching the ambush sight with fine-toothed combs. Bryant'll tell the CO what he told us, and the CO'll pass the word to the NCOIC up north. If he wants additional troopers up there, he'll radio for 'em, okay? Besides, it'd take you a half hour to get up there and make a nuisance of yourselves, even if you ran Code Hot, downhill, on a *good* day." Another drumroll of angry thunder rumbled down across the city, as if to accent his point. "And today *ain't* exactly what I'd call your classic good day.

"So take your seats, and we'll breeze through this briefing and inspection in no time so youz clowns can boogie on out to your beats." Stryker switched off the microphone as several groans filled the room at the mention of a uniform inspection. "Just kidding, just kidding." He raised his hands in resignation. "Don't get your peckers in an uproar."

Sgt. Raul Schultz had spent the last ten minutes browsing through a week-old *Saipan Post* newspaper. Cob Carmosino was leaning over one of Raunchy Raul's shoulders, reading along. Carmosino did it more to aggravate Schultz than anything. "Damn freelance reporters from Sydney givin' a bad slant to our participation in this police action," Schultz grumbled to the man beside him.

The private on his right glanced down at the picture depicting some grunts torching a VC rice cache. The three men staring at the photo knew it was just a rice cache, anyway. But the caption made no such mention and left the naive reader to think the marines were murdering innocent villagers by fire. "Fuckin' Aussie oughta be hung by the balls over an anthill," the private muttered before going back to blowing huge pink bubbles with his chewing gum.

"Hey Schultzy." Carmosino saw an opportunity opening for one of his jokes. "Did you hear about the photographer the MPs arrested yesterday?"

Raunchy Raul's eyes lit up with anticipation of good news. "Really? Fuck no! Tell me about it." He shifted about in his seat to meet the other NCO face-to-face.

"Yah, they charged the guy with shooting people and blowing them up!" Carmosino tried to keep a serious expression on his face, but only a couple seconds passed before he cracked up.

Schultz's own grin belly-flopped into a frown, and he directed an icy glare at Carmosino before turning back around. "That was bad, Carma, real lousy, in fact."

"Fucking corny-Cob," the private muttered under his breath, ignoring the sergeant's stripes.

Carmosino reached over and grabbed the nineteen-year-old in a playful headlock. As Schultz sat there ignoring the horseplay, Carmosino slowly increased pressure on the chokehold until the kid passed out in his chair and ceased resisting. "Goofy rooks gotta watch what they say around us seasoned vets a little more, right Schultzy?"

"That's a rog, Carma, a fucking righteous roggg."

"Okay, okay, let's get back down to business." Stryker finished making some notes on his clipboard before resuming the briefing and trying to restore order in the room. "Reilly! Take off that goddamned Aussie bush hat!"

Scattered laughter and applause filled the guardmount.

"Gentlemen." Stryker's face took on a serious expression every man in the place automatically saw clean through. "We've got a kiss-ass congressman trottin' through town next week—if the shrapnel will just cease flyin' for awhile—and the PM has asked me to *ask* you fellows to clean up your act. I'm talking about all the crap on the back of your helmets. This clown—no, I don't know which state he's from yet—anyway, he'll possibly be participating in one of the guardmounts, following on the heels of one of the butter bars, acting like he knows what kind of gigs he's looking for—you know the act. So let's at least paint over some of the profanity and racial slurs, okay? Especially those derogatory to the proud Vietnamese people, okay? We *are* guests in this country, okay?"

"I'll be on the first Boeing back, if it's all right with you!" an anonymous voice called out from the back of the room. It was followed by the mandatory scattering of dry laughter and light clapping. Somebody whistled his endorsement of the suggestion.

Stryker expertly ignored it all and concentrated on a quiet private in the front of the assemblage instead. "That goes for you too, *Uke.* I doubt the PM wants to see graffitti about nukin' Hanoi right about now. Ever since good old Goldwater made the remark about shittin' atom bombs on North Vietnam, they've been real touchy over the situation back on Capitol Hill, from what I hear."

Without looking up, the private flashed Stryker the thumbs-up, then resumed polishing his tiger claw necklace like the whole guardmount was a bore and *let's get the fuck out on the street and cut the chatter!*

"Davis." Stryker's chin pointed toward the middle of the room, and Craig's eye's widened in hesitant response. "The CO requests you cease wearing the teakwood crucifix while you're in uniform. The request, which everyone present knew was really a command from higher up, did little to phase the black MP. He merely nodded respectively in reply. "If you wanna wear it under your T-shirt, no sweat, but the damned—uh, darned thing is as big as your automatic, and more eye-catching." Stryker consulted his clipboard again, but immediately glanced back out at Davis. "And the motorpool NCOIC is fermenting a case of the ass over the Kill A Commie For Christ bumperstickers you keep slapping on the bumpers of your patrol unit. He's tired of scraping them off every week, so knock it off for awhile, okay?"

Davis nodded obediently again and turned to the soldier seated beside him. Shrugging his shoulders, he said, "No sweat. Don't mean nothin'."

"There it is."

Stryker, his eyes still on Davis, seemed to pause in reflection for a moment before saying, "And by the way, can ya tell me where I can get a couple of those?"

More mild laughter.

"Okay, got another bitch from Schell in the Commo bunker here." He checked off a line on his clipboard. "Everytime he runs a radio check in the wee hours of the twilight, somebody comes over the air with a toilet flush instead of a Code-Four. Now come on, gentlemen, is that very professional?"

"I'm tellin' ya, sarge." Broox stood up in front of the men again. "It's them faggots in Alpha Company!"

"Fuck *you,* ya little fart!" came the reply from the right half of the room as Broox was again bombarded with paper airplanes. An empty Coke can bounced off his shoulder and clattered across the floor in front of Stryker's podium.

"Okay, awright!" Stryker's hands were up in the air again. "Regardless of who the culprit is, I at this time call for a truce and cooperation by all you out on your beat. There's a lotta people listening to our net, believe it or not. From the foreign copulators—I mean *correspondents* at the Continental—to the secret police in the underground whorehouse beneath the Presidential Palace. I'm not even going to include all the PRs you clowns got rigged up downtown so your manois can listen to you while you're beatin' the bricks instead of *them.*"

More laughter should have followed Stryker's little speech, but a private in the back of the room was bouncing to his feet instead. "At*ten*tion!" came the call at the top of his voice.

A few MPs near the doorway rose to their feet, but the vast majority in the room just gave a bored glance over their shoulders at the officer bounding in from the blinding dusk outside.

"At ease, at ease. Remain seated." A smiling Lieutenent Slipka sauntered down the center aisle, his hands out to his sides, palms down, motioning the enlisted men not to get up just for him.

Stryker whipped an informal, half salute on the tall, blond-haired lieutenant with the blue-tinted sunglasses, and Slipka shot back his Hollywood grin in reply. "Just a few things, just a few things, gentlemen." He waved out at the MPs staring back like a celebrity fresh in from tinsel town, then glanced back at Stryker. "If I may, Mark?"

"Have at it, Lou." The ex-Green Beret bowed his head slightly and presented the guardmount with a slight wave of his hand.

After casting a suspicious scowl at Raunchy Raul, Slipka produced a pocket notebook and said, "I know you men will be on your feet or coasting through curfew checkpoints for the next twelve hours, but the chaplain has informed me a mass for the military policemen killed in action outside Bien Hoa will be given at zero-seven hundred hours tomorrow morning in the compound courtyard. The PM has already arranged for full military honors prior to the bodies being airlifted back to The World. The news media will be there. And the PM, the CO, and—I—would like as many of you as possible to be there, in uniform, at oh-six-forty-five sharp. Unless you're tied up with night-shift paperwork, of course."

"Every last man will be there, Lou." Stryker left no

doubt or discussion about the matter, and Slipka nodded thankfully. Not one groan of protest filled the silent room. Even without Stryker's guidance, the men of the 716th would have been at the memorial without the need for coaching. It was the least they could do for their fallen brothers

"All right." Slipka's somber expression returned to its former clown's mask. "Back to more pleasant tasks. As you all know, we have a sort of celebrity among us these days—"

"Hack up a Big Mac for Jack Flak!" came another anonymous cheer from the dimly lit back of the room.

Slipka ignored the interruption and remained smiling as he pulled a copy of *Time* magazine from his thigh pocket. He unraveled it and displayed the cover for all to see. The act was followed by a crescendo of somewhat sincere applause.

"Everyone in the commander's office agrees this is what we'd like to see more of on the newsracks, gentlemen. Definitely a class act! A real piece of pro-police journalism! One of the best—"

"Looks to me like he needed a haircut, Lou!" Another private in the back of the assemblage interrupted the patrol lieutenant and his remark was punctuated with cheers of agreement.

"Okay, okay." Slipka was still smiling as he raised his hands to quell the friendly disturbance. "We'll overlook the hair over his ears *this* time." He shot Jack Flak a fatherly wink. "Now for the official bureaucratic presentation." He pulled a wadded-up piece of paper from the other thigh pocket. "Will Specialist fourth class John Strollinski report front and center!"

"*Strollinski?*" A bewildered Broox and Thomas exchanged incredulous looks.

Several heads turned to stare back at Jack Flak. They had never known him as *anything* other than Jack Flak. Even his nametags said Jack Flak! The only darn nametags in the whole battalion that bore both first and last names!

"Well stroll on up here, Strollinski!" Stryker motioned for the blushing MP to back in more limelight. "The lieutenant's got something for ya."

The man everyone would always know as Jack Flak reluctantly rose to his feet and started toward the podium. Slipka began reading from the piece of paper even before the spec4 made it halfway through the cluster of seated soldiers. "In recognition for his unplanned and unforeseen but nevertheless beneficial public relations escapade," the lieutenant read aloud from an obviously *un*official document, "the Saigon provost marshal hereby presents Specialist fourth class John 'Jack Flak' Strollinski with a seven day pass to Saigon's sister sin city, Cockbang, Thailand!"

"Well all right!" Several of the other men gathered around the surprised MP to congratulate him and read the gag certificate.

"And let it be known the PM is not one to stay out of his troopers' personal lives, gentlemen! He is well aware Jack Flak here is married to a very beautiful and cultured maiden of the Pearl of the Orient. Unfortunately, regulations prohibit utilizing battalion funds to finance Mrs. Flak's airfare so she can accompany her husband to the Kingdom of Siam. However . . ." Slipka enjoyed providing a solution to everyone's dilemma, "the PM is also confident you men would not hesitate in coming up with the necessary funds I've just been talking about." He clipped the edge of his helmet so that the black liner rolled off his head in the blink of an eye and into the palm of his hand, upside down. "Now cough up the contributions."

Wallets sprang forth without protest, and in five minutes, a tearful Jack Flak was over a thousand dollars richer. Grateful beyond words, his head sunk between drooping shoulders, a usually statuesque Strollinski returned to his seat, greenbacks, P-notes, and MPC scrip overflowing from all his pockets.

"That's all I have, Mark." A jubilant Anthony Slipka clapped Stryker on the back as they moved away from the noisy enlisted men congregating around Jack Flak's seat.

"Then that culminates the briefing," Stryker announced into the podium's loudspeaker. "Hit the streets, heroes!"

After the men filed out to their jeeps, Stryker and Slipka left the briefing room last, walking up behind Broox and Thomas as the two privates were just finishing a one-sided conversation with a Vietnamese girl who worked inside the popcorn stand at the outdoor theater on a side street behind the International.

"Yes, I do declare," Broox was proclaiming in pidgin Vietnamese. "Honey, I'd definitely love to mop out your hole with my tongue!"

The girl, confused by the tones and pronunciation the husky MP was directing at her, cast him a nose-in-the-air glare and sauntered back toward the theater, supplies from the PX under one arm.

"She'll figure it out in a couple of hours," Thomas said confidently, arms folded across his chest and helmet tilted strategically along the bridge of his nose.

"And she'll be back here ricky-tik, with her pantaloons down and her vaginal lips puckered. . . ."

"What the devil are you gentlemen discussing?" Slipka asked loudly. Thomas's helmet practically flipped back off his brows, and Broox's heart skipped a beat.

"You shouldn't oughta be sneakin' up on street vets like us that way, lieutenant," Broox said seriously. The remark caused Thomas to crack a you-gotta-be-kidding grin.

"Looks like the movie's already starting." Stryker motioned toward the tall screen, saving the day. "Either of you know what's playing?"

Theme music drifted out from the theater, answering his question. With an oriental flavor to the notes, Nancy Sinatra was singing "You Only Live Twice." Between the charred walls of some Tran Hung Dao tenements, part of the tall outdoor screen was visible, and the men watched as a blur of naked women performed their underwater dance across the opening credits.

"Ah—James Bond." The legendary Jack Flak had joined them on the orderly room porch overlooking the streets and the formation of sparkling patrol jeeps.

"Makes you wanna fly right off to some faraway exotic land, full of intrigue, mystery, and adventure," Stryker sighed with a smile as his weary eyes took in the misty temples rising beyond the skyline of blackened tenements. The intensity that was Saigon seemed to breathe back at him as the traffic blared by, and the emotions and senses sucked in the sights all around: sleek, agile women in their tissue-thin gowns floating past on the warm breeze, their dark, almond eyes pausing to inspect the American inspecting *them*, only to dart away, returning moments later; the bonzes in gold and orange robes going from door to door with their rice pots, collecting daily rations of free food, never failing to direct a sneering frown at the concrete and aluminum towers of foreign influence rising up on street corners throughout downtown. "Makes you wanna take a sampan right down the forbidden lagoon to never-never land."

"For sures," replied Jack Flak as he hopped into his patrol unit. "Fucking sincerely for sures."

Stryker glanced to his right as the humid evening air was suddenly torn by metallic cries of wounded iron leopards. Three MP jeeps, with men scrambling aboard on both sides and struggling to hold onto their gear, were racing toward the main gate, sirens screaming and lights flashing.

Stryker, never taking his eyes from the serious looks of concentration and anxiety on the faces of the drivers, (they usually looked bored, or worse, eager, when beginning their "hot runs" crisscross downtown), played with the squelch control on his web belt pak-set, but the portable radio replied with only garbled static and irritating feedback.

Jack Flak had his own ear cocked to the more powerful radio clamped to his unit's rear seat, and Stryker watched a bolt of surprise lance down through his normally calm expression.

"What is it?" he called out, expecting word of a sniper attack downtown somewhere, or possibly an MP requesting backup at a bar fight on Tu Do—early in the evening for that, but possible. Saigon did not conform to back-in-The-World routines.

"What's all the commotion?" Lt. Slipka added.

"They've found Fox!" Jack Flak was standing on the floorboards of the jeep, one hand braced against the windshield as he steered with the other, pulling out of the tight parking lot in reverse.

"Is he alive?" Stryker was already airborne, flying over the balcony railing, then sprinting to his own jeep.

"We don't know yet!" Flak took his seat as he set the dual red lights on the roof of his unit to twirling lazily against the last hint of dusk. In the distance, lightning spider-webbed down through the ominous black clouds that had smothered the edge of the city, sucking up the last of the sunset's orange and gold glow.

Slipka jumped into Stryker's jeep, just as the big sergeant turned the souped-up engine over, and it rumbled to life. As thunder rolled down from the dark, menacing skies, Stryker seemed to duck a bit, lest the spirits of the storm slamdunk bad luck off the top of his helmet. A death's breath later, thick sheets of rain, like warm gauze, fell across Saigon, soaking the sound of countless sirens heading north, into the jungle.

5. Temple Magic, Temple Curse

"Tell us, man—tell us what happened. We're all your friends here." The MP lieutenant with the blue-tint glasses and ice blond hair stared deep into Parlin Fox's blank eyes, then glanced back up at Sergeant Stryker and gave a hopeless nod in the negative.

Mark Stryker and the dozen military policemen gathered around the army ambulance, stood in the heavy rain, drops falling from the edges of helmets onto noses and over the poncho-covered shoulders to spit-shined combat boots below. Forming a perimeter around the swamp where the missing MP had been found stood a laager of Assault tanks, their powerful engines rumbling idle, mist rising from their hot, green steel skin. Surrounding the V-100s, hostile jungle. The village that once stood fifty yards away had been burned to the ground in a house-to-house sweep by the canh-sats that had located the dazed spec4 with the tattered uniform and multiple shrapnel wounds.

"Try, brother." Sgt. Ron Brickmann was down on one knee beside Fox now. "Try and remember what you saw over there at the ambush—who you saw."

"I will never forget his face. . . ." Parlin Fox the Third stared light years beyond The Brick as his words trailed off.

"Good, son, good." Slipka had joined the huge NCO in the mud. Legs dangling over the edge of the ambulance's rear doors, Fox turned to lock eyes with the lieutenant, and a chill ran down Slipka's spine at the images he thought he saw dancing like death, deep in the man's eyes. "Tell us about it."

"I will never forget."

Slipka turned to face Stryker and the others. Some of the men had built a small fire beside one of the tanks to heat C-rations. He realized now, for the first time, it was only the reflection of that fire he saw dancing in Fox's jungle-green eyes.

The lone survivor of the ambush two days earlier was not seeing all his brother MPs huddled around him protectively. He was not hearing the monstrous Assault tanks parked in a tight circle all around them, lancelike fifty caliber machineguns pointed out at the high treeline. He was not feeling the plank floorboards of the four-wheel-drive jeep ambulance beneath his buttocks, or the raindrops bouncing off the helmets all around, forming water streaks on his face and chest.

Instead, Fox was in another world altogether. His ears were still ringing from the detonation of two dozen landmines simultaneously all around. His eyes were still seeing the Assault tanks in front and to the right of his own disappearing in a puff of smoke, only to flip up out of the silver cloud, end over end through the dusty air, landing with a sickening crunch on their tops, crushing his friends beneath them. And then his own V-100 was being thrown toward the clouds, though it was only really a dozen feet or so off the asphalt. A secondary explosion caught the Assault tank in midair, catapulting it into the trees, and Fox himself farther beyond even that.

No, Fox was not feeling the rain on his skin or the floorboards beneath his torn and shredded fatigue trousers. Fox was feeling the rigid branches as he sailed through the air, crashing across them. He was feeling the gnarled fingers of the tamarind trees slicing through his uniform and ripping at his skin, trying to tear out his limbs by the roots.

And then he was rolling across the paddy dike, hidden in drifting clouds of claymore and gunsmoke, and slamming face first into the murky water. Pushing himself up off the body of the dead American beneath him, he would never forget the surprised look in Treach's lifeless eyes before his fellow MP dropped back beneath the surface of the muddy water.

Fox crawled through the stagnant rice paddy faster then he had ever low-crawled through any punji-laced, concertina-lined confidence course back at the school. And when he came to the opposite dike, fifty yards away, he dug to the pit of his gut and found the energy to flip over it, landing on his back in the connecting paddy. But this one was dry—the mud not mud at all but dust littered with rice stalks no doubt abandoned by some farmer the VC had kidnapped and marched away in the middle of the night long, long ago.

Fox's chin was an inch into the dirt as he hugged the earth, watching the Vietnamese advance through the swirls of smoke. Going from body to body, murdering the wounded. He felt his hand instinctively moving down toward his pistol. The next thing he felt was sudden terror when he realized his entire web belt had been torn away from his body by the impact of the blast.

Then Fox felt rage. Anger at his helplessness, his inability to come to the aid of his friends. He listened to his brothers screaming as they burned to death, trapped inside the disabled tank cells the enemy—whoever they were—were now burrowing into with thermite packs.

Those men who had been riding atop the tanks, like himself, and who now littered the roadway like mangled mannequins, stared defiantly up at their assailants before they were viciously gunned down.

Fox closely watched the Vietnamese man who appeared to be in charge of the operation, though the MP specialist got the feeling he was not dealing with Viet Cong or NVA here today. He memorized the man's features. And he logged in his mind forever the selfless acts of bravery had seen displayed by thirty-five of the finest men he had ever known who were cooked to death or shot between the eyes.

He swore to his gods, he swore to the Asians' Buddha, he swore to the spirits of the jungle—anyone who would listen, that he would not rest until he tracked this bastard down and devoured his heart!

Then Spec4 Fox's lust for vengeance melted to trembling horror as he saw two dozen armed men combing the surrounding jungle for survivors.

And a defenseless, seriously wounded Parlin Fox dug. He dug with all his might. Deep into the dust.

Until it turned damp, and then underlying paddy water sucked and gurgled at his fingers.

Fox dug until he had dug himself into a grave, and then Fox buried himself. He rolled onto his back into the shallow grave, biting his lips to stifle the scream of pain rising from the bloody wounds to his arms and legs, and covered even his face with dirt.

Fox ignored the ants biting every inch of his body. He told himself the stings were his imagination—that ants did not live in rice paddies, though he had seen them enough times while walking patrol along the raised dikes between paddies. The soldier ants marched their own little patrols along the tops of the dikes, and the soldier humans trampled them with their jungle boots.

Fox tried to steady his breathing. If he kept sucking in the hot, humid air like this, he'd inhale the leaves covering his nostrils, and then he'd really be in a world of hurt. He thought of lying on the beach—that was why he was so hot, basking beneath the dirt. He concentrated on sand. How it felt beneath his feet after a swim in the cool northern Pacific. Where his girlfriend had taken him to that nudist colony in Oregon. He concentrated on all the swaying breasts, full and sagging, and he kept telling himself the ants still biting his testicles were just his imagination. And finally the pain went away. Almost like a mirage evaporating.

He could hear them.

They were all around. Laughing. Joking in Vietnamese. *Fucking bastards!* He wanted to rise from his grave and kill them all with heart attacks. Superstitious as Asians were, it might work.

He knew they could hear him breathing, though they couldn't. He was positive every heartbeat was bringing them closer to him like a signal gong.

His blood! They would track his blood trail and pepper his grave with banana clips of AK tracer. The depression in the earth would be noticeable from fifty yards.

He should get up and run. Bolt for it.

But Fox lay there frozen, unmoving. Not yet ready to die like a hero. Not ready to die anything, for anybody. He had never seen that warrior's never-never land, or the hint of it, in the jungle mist, like so many others had professed to have seen.

And the vermin who had pulled off the successful ambush of seven V-100 Assault tanks on Highway 1-Alpha south of Bien Hoa failed to find him.

Oh they beat the bushes, and they cursed the bubbles rising from surrounding rice paddies, and they shot up a few palm fronds. But they never found Parlin Fox the Third.

The specialist fourth class from Gary, Indiana lay in his grave for two days, too weak to move, too comfortable and suddenly carefree to care, his loss of blood stemmed by nature's earthen bandages pressing in all over his body. And the meanest little white boy from Pitts High School, who vowed never to return to that town again, even in death, floated in his cloudy dreams of limbo until Sergeant Farthing's tracker dogs dragged the worried NCO through two rice paddies full of muck until they pawed open the top of his shallow, makeshift grave, saving Parlin Fox from worms and maggots, the pixies of the rain forest, and apathy at being buried alive.

* * *

Stryker hesitated before dismounting from the back of the Honda scooter. He kept his massive palms gently against the slender waist of the woman in front of him and felt his senses shift instinctively into phase yellow: caution; trouble was brewing somewhere near, possibly within striking range—expect the worst—don't get caught off guard—circle around—stalk the hunter—strike the attacker from behind.

He kept his face hidden in the strands of long silky hair floating in the warm night breeze before him. They shielded him now from the dim rays of the yellow street light suspended above a nearby corner. The woman driving the Honda—a girl really, in her late teens, whom Kim paid on a weekly basis to ferry her man home to her from work at "the office," lest she know his whereabouts at all times—the woman shuddered when Stryker hesitated to dismount. Was he really inhaling the scent of her modest perfume? Kim would have her breasts on a platter if she thought the girl was trying to hustle her man! Or was he tensing for something the night offered? It had happened before. The evenings after his shift with the MPs when she'd drive him home, only to see him intervene in a neighbor's family disturbance or a gang fight down the alley.

The Honda's springs lifted the body of the scooter up an inch, and her feet raised off her heels and onto her toes again. He was finally getting off—without making a move toward her ear with his tongue, the way he did in those dream fantasies she sometimes had about him, or a caress of her breast with his rough-looking hands, the way she so often secretly desired. The girl sighed. Stryker patted her on the tight rump, whispered *cha co* like a big brother, and disappeared in the swirling dark.

But Stryker did not mount the rear entrance stairs to the Miramar Hotel like he usually did. Instead, he followed his feelings, down the side street on his left, knowing the irritation in his gut would lead him to the source of his discomfort. He hated retiring for the night when *something* told him all was not right down below, on his beloved block in Saigontown.

Hardly a minute had passed before he spotted the jeep bumper protruding from the black cubbyhole. A scratched and crackling green, it bore the numbers seven-one-six-B-seven-four.

A grin creased the MP sergeant's wary expression. Abandoning a bit of his concrete-jungle caution, Stryker moved flat against the tenement wall to his right until he came to a darkened doorway. His smile still growing with every pantherlike step, he glided past the doorway and continued moving silently along the wall, slowly moving nearer to the military policemen's patrol jeep.

"Gotcha!" A cold barrel was jammed up against the base of Stryker's neck from behind.

"Damn." Stryker's smile faded instantly, but relief also flooded his system, drowning the moment of instant terror, when he recognized the private's voice. "You were waiting in that dark doorway back there."

"You're getting old, sarge." The kid laughed softly. "You breezed right past me!"

"Very good, damned good, in fact. You'd make Kip Mather proud, you cocky sonofabitch."

"And *you* said you could spot me a block away from the *nouc mam* on my breath, *sarge.*"

"You can take the forty-five out from the back of my head now, Uhernik." His tone was both patient and pleading.

"Bet you thought I was catchin' a few Zs back here, didn't you bossman."

"No, I didn't, Nick." Stryker winced as the pistol was pressed tighter against his skin. The cold steel made the hairs along the back of his neck rise slightly, like a burst of static electricity had just rolled across him and then swirled away. "Now holster your fucking weapon, trooper."

"Bet maybe you even thought I was poundin' some manoi's pelvis back here, didn't ya sarge—right in the back seat of my patrol unit over there." The kid blew a gum bubble and smacked his lips with satisfaction.

The pistol barrel did not waver. "No, no, 'course not, 'course not."

Uhernik popped another bubble and holstered his weapon as minute pieces of gum slapped the back of Stryker's neck, where the barrel had been. "Just so long as you didn't suspect me of snoozin' on the job, sarge."

"Fuck me if I thought that, Nick. Fuck me for sures." He imitated Jack Flak, and both MPs smiled below the settling starlight.

"Because, like my trusty buddy Nilmes would say: You snooze, you lose."

"Gotta keep you two separated." Stryker chuckled softly. "Maybe I'll schedule Nilmes a couple of months out at Hustler."

"Naw, now back off, bossman. Carl's cool. Carl's realllll cool."

"So I've heard." Stryker thought back to the first weeks Nilmes had been in-country. Stryker had been the one to break the rook in.

"Eight and skate."

"Knock that off. You know it drives Slipka batty. And he's out on the prowl somewhere tonight. By the way, just what exactly *were* you doing parked back there blacked out, anyway?" Stryker cocked an eyebrow suspiciously.

The private hesitated, then shrugged his shoulders. If you couldn't trust Mark Stryker, who could you trust? "I was staked out for Fuzznuts."

"*Lieutenant* Fuzznuts?" Nobody ever used the officer's real name.

"Yah. Sorry wimp of a jerk."

"That dude that's been hasslin' Angi?" Stryker rubbed his chin.

"Same-same. Cornered her at the central market again yesterday, trying to get her to go out with him."

"Maybe you shouldn't be messin' with an officer, though."

"Fuck him and his bar."

"He could bring smoke on your ass." Stryker paused to reflect on some past experience with an officer in another combat zone. "You might wake up in Khe Sanh."

"Don't mean nothin'."

"Mortars kissin' you goodnight every night of the week could mean a *big* difference."

"Fuck it." The private spat his bubblegum out onto the blacktop before glancing around to make sure nobody was moving into their territory. "Don' mean nothin'."

"Quit talking like a fuckin' grunt."

"Okay, sarge."

"Maybe you should let me or Slipka handle Fuzznuts."

"I can take care of my own problems."

"Where have I heard that one before?"

"Fuzznuts lost his military driving privileges last month. And it's three hours past curfew. He always roars down this back alley right about now, squealing the tires of his damn Renault, laughing with his half dozen whores, nose in the air, scarf in the wind. Fucking rich brat West Pointer. I'm gonna plaster his ass to the monkey house wall on traffic charges, sarge."

"That's an abuse of your authority." Stryker was beginning to sound like a sergeant, but he felt for the kid and his dilemma.

"This is Saigon, sarge." The private glanced up at the flares floating along the edge of the city. "This whole town is an abuse *to* my authority."

Stryker thought he detected a note of bitterness in the younger MP's words. At least he's not wearing mirrored sunglasses. Stryker smiled to himself. But that usually comes during the dangerous period in a cop's career: after three, and before five years on the street. When he gets overconfident, gung-ho and cocky. This kid's only been on the beat less than a year, he thought to himself. He should be invisible, unsure of himself, low-profile, feeling his way along the law enforcement bureaucracy, yet here he is going after an engineer battalion lieutenant's commission. "Think about what you're saying, son," Stryker cautioned him, unsure how far he should venture into the combat zone of counseling—dangerous territory. They were both tired.

"When I'm done with Fuzznuts, he's gonna wish he never—" But the private's words trailed off in midsentence, and he glanced beyond Stryker's shoulder, then slowly pulled the sergeant deeper into the shadows of a doorway.

"What is it?" he whispered, knowing better than to turn around just then. A flash of web gear or shifting of shadows could alert whoever it was out there to their presence.

"Someone moving toward us, down the block." Uhernik tapped Stryker on the bicep—the signal he could look now.

The MP sergeant watched the slender man approach for a few seconds, then said, "Probably a canh-sat walking his beat?"

"At three fucking o'clock in the A.M.? They're all cooping down on Le Loi somewhere." Uhernik unsnapped the tailored flap on his laminated holster and rested the palm of his hand on *Suzie Wong's* butt. Thumb resting against the fourth safety, his forefinger curled itself around the trigger, basking in the touch of cold steel despite the muggy heat in the air.

As he darted beneath a streetlight, the man's face took on Caucasian features.

"Hold it!" Stryker remained in the shadows except for his gun arm, which was extended straight out now. "Military police!"

"Kruger!" Uhernik yelled at the same time. "It's Kruger!" The rook's fingers went limp as recognition drained caution from his tense frame.

The American army deserter, once an MP himself, whirled around to face them. A .45 automatic, the same service weapon he had taken with him the night he went AWOL rather than face murder charges, was in his right hand, moving toward them out of reflex.

"Paul! Don't!" The MP private locked eyes with the deserter, but they were lifeless orbs Uhernik stared into from twenty feet away. Sunken, with dark rings below them. The man's facial skin had shrunk around his cheek bones, was pulled in tight at the edge of the lips, and appeared a sickly yellow beneath the uncaring moon. "Put down the gun!"

A deafening explosion went off beside the private's right ear as Stryker squeezed off a round without hesitating. The MP sergeant had seen the signs in the man approaching them like Walking Death. Kruger, the condition he was in, wouldn't even recognize his mother tonight.

The bullet slammed into his forehead, catapulting him off his feet backwards. The top of his skull and half his brains splattered against the brick wall behind him even before his back folded across the pavement, almost soundlessly, without grace, like two garbage bags accidentally knocked from the back of a trash truck. Uhernik knew worse than squashed tomatoes would be oozing from the tattered container that had once been a man. "Well fuck me," Stryker muttered.

"Huh?" The clap of the stinging discharge off the tenement walls rising up all around them was still ringing in Uhernik's ears.

"I was aiming for his chest."

Both MPs, their shadowy forms against the backdrop of distant Tu Do Street neon, cautiously walked up to the corpse with the mangled face. Somewhere behind them, in the distance, a helicopter gunship rushed past, low above the rooftops, rotors beating rhythmically in the thick midnight air, but it was gone just as quickly, except for the dull flapping of aluminum and steel, lingering like some curious phantoms in the dark.

Uhernik went down on one knee and pressed the palm of his hand against Kruger's chest. Stryker imagined the body sitting up suddenly, arms rigid, reaching for the private's throat.

"His heart's still beating." The kid's voice cracked slightly with the words, but they came out emotionless.

"He's dead," Stryker replied matter-of-factly.

"I know he's dead, but his fucking heart's still beating," Uhernik countered with a total lack of urgency. The observation came across more as simple surprise than excitement.

"Then make the sign of the cross over his ass or something and beat feet over to your jeep to call this abortion in." Stryker slid his .45 back into his shoulder holster. He had changed into civilian clothes before leaving the International and was now wearing loose-fitting silk pants, tongs, and a dragon shirt over the holster.

"Sure sarge. Okay."

Stryker felt a sudden chill in the air as he resisted the temptation to check Kruger's pulse. A wisp of steam rose from the gaping wound in the top of the man's head, and Stryker nodded his head from side to side, unaware he was even making the movement. Steam! Not in the 'Nam—not here! The steam, rising like incense from a joss stick, flashed him back to that evening in Korea, years ago, when his partner was gunned down during a liquor store robbery. Killed instantly by a carbine shot to the chest, he had lain in the street while Stryker engaged the suspects in a gun battle that eventually, even after the cavalry arrived, lasted another four hours. And the whole time, Stryker's partner had lain in the street, on his back, helpless, seemingly abandoned, steam rising from the hole in his chest. *You never forsake your partner.*

"Dispatch has got CID and an MPI Shoot Team en route, sarge." The private was beside him again. "Shit, you're gonna be up the rest of the night with paperwork." Uhernik's eyes were darting along Stryker's frame, from shoulder to angle, feeling sorry for the overworked NCO who was obviously on his way home in his skivvies, yet perhaps in awe of an off-duty MP who could still shoot so straight.

Up all night. Stryker gritted his teeth. If it's not the after-action paperwork, it's the hours-long adrenaline surge.

"Yah—well, fuck it, Nick."

"A man after my own heart." Uhernik slowly walked back to his jeep, smiling as he shook his head in both respect and admiration. He hopped in behind the seat, ignoring the Vietnamese that were emerging onto their balconies overhead, awakened by the discharge, and, as first MP on the scene, began his Form Thirty-two report.

Down the street, on an adjoining back alley, a honking jeep barreled past, carrying Lieutenant

Fuzznuts and his whores from the engineer headquarters where they doubled as daytime secretaries. Uhernik gritted his teeth and pressed the pen harder against the three carbons, but he did not look up.

Stryker squatted, oriental fashion, beside Paul Kruger's mangled head. Blood that had been running along the blacktop in the other direction seemed to slowly alter course toward him, until the edges of his tongs became saturated, but he did not move back.

"I'm sorry, Kruger," he whispered, so that the kid in the jeep wouldn't hear him. His lips barely moved—he did not want the assholes in the balconies to think he was *dinky-dau,* talking to a corpse like that. "I'm sorry, man, but you shouldn't have pulled your piece on us. I had no choice. I had to look out for the rook over there. I had to cancel your ticket, bud. I had to bring smoke on your ass. I know you understand."

Stryker's words came out troubled, sincere. He was beginning to think about the shooting, about the pros and cons of taking life. About the after effects. But he caught himself.

Stryker slapped the dead man lightly on the side of the face, the same way he horseplayed with some of the privates after guardmount, then he rose to his feet and moved away. "I know you understand."

A woman up in one of the balconies of the tenement across the street from the Miramar had groaned noticeably when Stryker patted Kruger goodbye. The MP sergeant glanced up at her and smiled. "It's okay," he said, aware she could see his shoulder holster beneath the thin shirt flapping in the breeze. "We knew each other. He one time MP, same-same me." Stryker decided to fuck with her mind.

"One, two, three—motherfuck MP," she screwed back. After spitting the familiar and over-used rhyme down at him, she threw her ample bottom around, disappeared back into her apartment, and slammed the sliding bamboo door shut. Across the street, and again high overhead, someone laughed at them both. Perhaps at all three of them.

In the distance, a lone siren was approaching, then others. A landing airliner, miles to the north, at Tan Son Nhut International Airport, raced its engines briefly, drowning them out. Then the jet's roar died away, and the sirens were louder than ever. Somewhere on the other side of town sporadic small arms fire was exchanged for a few seconds between two unknown and unidentified groups. Stryker listened to the Waco dispatcher droning off calls across the net: a sniper atop a roof overlooking Lam Son Square, some foreign correspondents causing a disturbance at the Continental, Reilly requesting to go to Channel Two with a hot pursuit.

He hesitated, then walked back over to the body and patted down the dead man's pockets. Just a tattered wallet. Black imitation leather, with a metallic green map of Vietnam molded onto the inside. No currency. Inside the flap, a cracked and faded snapshot of a Vietnamese woman.

Stryker ran his fingers along Kruger's ankle until he located the dog tag on the bead chain. He glanced at the name, unsure why he suffered a pang of self-doubt, but the serial number and the blood type and the religion were all there. Beneath the name Paul Kruger.

He almost jerked the dog tag free, then he remembered this was no firefight. He wasn't even on duty, though everyone knew he was a twenty-four hour cop. They all were. But CID would have a case of the ass as it was. They'd say he shouldn't have removed the wallet before they arrived. *So screw CID anyway.* Visions of agent Harry Sickles hanging by the throat from a ceiling rafter flashed before his mind's eye, and he swallowed hard, burying the groan of age-old pain.

Stryker glanced down at the black and white photograph again. He remembered her. Vo Dehb. She had been a waitress at the Queen Bee, until Kruger flipped out after arresting the robbery suspect and sticked the handcuffed man to death. She had taken him in then, and they had both disappeared underground.

He had seen her a couple times while on routine patrol. Venturing from their safe house somewhere to purchase scraps of food for her man-in-hiding. He had approached her a couple of times, more out of friendship than anything, never really wanting to pursue her or catch Paul, but she had always darted away, through the crowds, like a runaway dog who, once beaten nearly to death, would never trust its master again.

He wondered where she was now. Who she was with. If, perhaps, she was watching him even now, from one of those balconies up there, or a dark doorway down the block. Stryker made a mental note to tell the men at briefing to watch for her. Now that

Kruger was gone, he felt an obligation to protect her, to shelter her. Though in the pit of his gut he knew Kruger had been the weak one. Vo Dehb had always protected and sheltered *him*. She did not need help from the MPs.

She was a survivor. Even though Stryker knew no one ever left Saigon untouched. No one ever survived her.

When he forced his leg muscles to carry him up the three flights of stairs four hours later, Stryker found a suitcase in the hallway outside his hotel room and the door open.

He automatically knew this was no burglary-in-progress, yet his fingers instinctively curled around the butt of his holstered .45, drawing the weapon free.

Kim whirled around from in front of the bedroom dresser, where she was pulling out and folding garments she hadn't looked at in months. Her narrow eyes were pools of restrained fire, and when they locked onto his, Stryker found himself—against all his other instincts—swallowing hard. He did not fear this woman, but he was a cautious man.

"Where have you been?" She rushed forward toward him, then halted abruptly a few feet away, out of reach.

Stryker ignored the inner voice telling him to put her back in her place, and instead feigned intense innocence in his eyes. Holstering his pistol under his arm, he said, "I would have been here hours ago, honey, but I stumbled into another slight delay. You did not hear the shot? Just in the back street down there—"

"Do not tell me your lies!" She reached for the ceramic "Buffy" elephant beside her ankle. It was heavier than she had anticipated, so when she heaved it at him, her range fell short, and the statue shattered into a thousand pieces against the bamboo bureau holding her makeup mirror. Glass sprinkled the teakwood floor between them. "Have you been with her?" She produced the bundle of letters he had secreted into the false panel along the bottom of the dresser. The letters from Lai and from his sister, about Lai. Mark's eyes locked onto the scarlet ribbon binding the striped air mail envelopes, just as she threw the bundle at his feet, and they scattered before him.

"We have already discussed her," he said softly, without emotion in his voice. "I have told you—Lai is gone." He fought the feelings embracing him, but his eyes took on that same distant daze they always displayed when he flashbacked to his woman in Pleiku. "I was delayed by a deserter just in the street below. Surely you heard the shot."

"Shots, my Asian ass!" She shook her shapely bottom at him and slapped it at the same time. "More like a taxi backfiring, no doubt! *Your* taxi, eh? The one that brings you from *her* to *me*!"

"I told you, Kim." He remained calm. "I have not seen her since I left Pleiku—long before I met you. Believe me." He slowly folded his arms across his chest, careful to make the upper biceps bulge forth until they were nearly the size of her thighs, displaying the dormant strength and fury he possessed but never once used against her, or any woman.

Kim, never one to be intimidated, rushed up and slapped him hard, with all *her* hidden fury. Stryker, startled, swayed back on his heels slightly but quickly caught himself, and just as swiftly fended off a fist by grabbing her wrist in midair.

"What about *this*?" She backed away from him, pulling another envelope from inside her blouse. "It came only this morning!"

Stryker recognized the postmark before she snatched it from his sight. Stateside. It would be from his sister. "You are reading my mail again, Kim?"

"Only when it is from your sister!" She was nobody's fool. "I know she searches for your woman for you, too!" And she backed off, smiling.

"Let me have the letter, Kim." He moved forward a few steps, but she fluttered over toward the window.

"*Fuck you,* Mark Stryker!" she snapped back at him. He could imagine the ears of neighbors on all sides pressed against the opposite sides of every wall.

"It could be important." His voice was starting to crack with irritation, and she picked up on it.

"Something from your *moi* bitch up in the highlands jungle!" She taunted him by holding the envelope out over deserted Tu Do Street.

"A family matter, perhaps."

"*You* already told me you have no family any longer—you've told me a million times, all you have left are Saigon." She laughed the words, then sighed before saying, "And me."

"Give me the letter, Kim." He could see from the creases that she had already opened it. She used to steam them open, but who was she to try and deceive a Green Beret? She quickly tired of melodramatics and went back to simply ripping them open when he was away. He wondered how many she had thrown out.

"Do you see my skin?" She pulled her blouse apart, ripping off the bottom two buttons and exposing her breasts to him. She pushed her chest out, taunting him further with erect nipples he knew his lips would not taste tonight. "I have been sitting in that tub in there all night," she said, pointing at the bathroom, "waiting for you to come home. I finally gave up, after five hours."

Stryker smiled, unable to hold it back. "You know I don't like it that way."

"Well, I *like it!*" Her eyes flared out at him again. He rushed her then, but she flung the envelope out into the night and darted out from between exhausted arms.

Stryker, hoping the envelope would flutter down the three flights to the middle of the street, where he could retrieve it, watched with disappointment as the pre-dawn breeze caught it and carried the letter off beyond the rooftops, to be quickly swallowed up by the dark.

"That was not necessary, Kim." Stryker frowned, ignoring the tingling in his loins as she slipped further away from him, her full breasts swaying with the agile maneuver.

"Necessary?" She launched the word at him after she was safely on the other side of the room. "You dare talk 'necessary' to me? After what I have to put up with around here—for you! The boys-who-believe-they're-men I have had to entertain around here while you are off playing watch commander eighteen hours a day—the MP commandos I have had to tell their fortunes over and over, just to make you look good. Do you know how many times I have manipulated my tarot cards, just so your cherry-boy troopers can leave here with a smile on their faces, thinking only fame and fortune awaits them in the Orient?"

"Honey—"

"No. Fuck you, Mark!" She threw a vase from Singapore at him. "No more! I've had it! You will never really be mine—all mine." She cast a hurt look at him. "You will always be dreaming of *her* when you lie in my arms at night. *Her!*" She tossed a whiskey bottle off the shelf next to the aquarium. Vietnamese believe fish in the home to be a good luck charm. Stryker's thoughts told him she wouldn't throw the tank at him next.

"Kim—"

She was gathering up her scarf and purse. "I'm leaving you now." A slight, desperate grin creased her lips. "But if I can not have you, Mark Stryker, I make sure no woman can!"

"Let's talk about this." He started toward the door, but she beat him out into the hallway before he could close it.

"I have put a curse on you, Mark—a temple curse!"

He made himself laugh out loud in response to the threat, but Stryker also felt an uneasy hesitation in the air between them—a shifting of emotion: from love into hate, back into love again, then a collage of both feelings. Though trained to deal in reality, with cold hard facts, Stryker had been in the Orient a long time. He knew there was more to Vietnam than night and day. He had heard disturbing stories about the temple curses. He stared back at Kim silently. Suddenly she seemed all powerful—a sorceress, with his fate, like putty, in her fingers. All his experience, and all that made up his personality, told Stryker to step forward and slap her across the chops, but in the pit of his gut remained that unmoving hesitation, that sudden respect, or fear, for her power. He knew that, even if she possessed no magic whatsoever, the faintest doubts in his mind would give her the strength of a thousand spirits.

She sensed his fear. He could tell, by her change of stance and her widening smile, and he wondered if his voice or his eyes betrayed him. "I offered my prayers to Those in the temple," she announced. "And they have assured me that, so long as you pursue this Lai whore, everything in your life—and hers—will go wrong, Mark. Your job, your future, your destiny—it is all in my hands now, lover." She shaped an invisible figure in the air between them, using the palms of her hands, then she clapped it into oblivion. "And I know you believe in the power of the temples!"

Stryker's eyes were drawn back into the room, and through the open window, he saw the temple spire rising through the mist, several blocks away. Suddenly he reached out and latched onto her arm. She fought like a wildcat, but he held on gently. "Let's go back inside and talk this over, Kim," he said softly, swallowing his apprehension again as static danced along his fingers upon touching her.

Down the hall, a door creaked open and a woman's head peeked out cautiously. Eyes cloudy with sleep, the first thing she focused on was the huge automatic sticking out from under the tall American's arm. "*Choi oi*," she whispered to an unseen partner inside the room, then, after slamming the door shut, she could still be heard complaining about, "that *dinky-dau* GI."

"Come on." He tugged her off balance, toward their room.

"No!" Kim lashed out at him, digging her nails into his cheek. Stryker released her, and blood sprayed against the walls from the four horizontal lacerations.

Mentally exhausted, he gave up, choosing to simply lean against the doorway and await her next move rather than fight on after bittersweet victory in a battle of romance whose war he had already lost long ago.

Kim hoisted her purse strap over a shoulder and yanked her suitcase off the floor, then started off down the hallway, maintaining her balance awkwardly atop ebony-black highheels. "*Cha co*, baby," he said softly, sincerity still in his voice.

She did not look back at him but instead responded with an extended middle finger that elicited not anger, but a deep sigh of resignation.

After she disappeared behind the elevator doors, Stryker glanced down both sides of the deserted hotel corridors and forced a smile. He knew every tenant on the third floor was awake and listening for his next move. He and Kim would be the talk of the breakfast meal down in the hotel restaurant the next morning. "Well, *fuck me*!" he said loud enough for them all to hear, before closing the door behind him, sealing Saigon out. Maybe she'll see all the CID sedans parked outside, blocking the back alley, he secretly hoped. Then she'll be back.

But Stryker knew that, as curious as Kim would be, even after she ventured back behind the hotel to investigate on her own, she'd never swallow her pride and return to him. Not tonight anyway. First, she would punish him.

He walked over to the window and inhaled the warm, moist air as he stared at the distant temple, now bathed in ghostly blues and purples from its perimeter lights the bonzes kept burning all night long, lest the curfew militiamen forget Buddha was more powerful than even the men in the Saigon regime.

Dwarfing the leaning tenements stacked up around it, the temple radiated an ominous, oppressive appearance that beckoned Stryker, challenging him. Challenging all they had taught him back at The School and in the survival camps.

With both hands he slammed the shutters closed. Then he walked over to the dresser and pulled the scrapbook from the top drawer. He opened the cover and sighed, shaking his head from side to side slowly. Kim had torn all the pictures of them together in half, then piled the pieces atop the first page for him to find.

Vietnamese women. He refused to let her behavior rattle him. *They never forget—and they never forgive.*

But Christ: He had just killed a man! Why was he even wasting an ounce of emotion on a woman?

Stryker pulled out his wallet and unbuttoned the photo flap, flipping through the faded plastic pages until he came to the cracked and discolored snapshot of Lai. A drop of blood from the wound across his cheek splashed across the plastic, but he didn't even notice.

Unblinking, he let the eyes in the photograph carry him back into his past, where the woman from Pleiku kept his house, massaged his body and mind, listened to his endless chatter, caught and cooked his meals, waited for her man to come home from work every day, burning her candles in the window if the job sometimes kept him out past the fall of night. Stryker found himself reviewing every gentle, flawless curve of her body by the light of those same candles, and then he was seeing—

The phone beside his pillow rang suddenly, jerking him from the nightdream. The wallet tumbled to the floor as he sat bolt upright, startled, temporarily unsure of his surroundings.

He tensed, his reflexes shifting into phase red, then the phone rang again, and he began breathing as his muscles went lax. *Kim.* Her face flashed in front of him.

After the fourth ring, he picked up the receiver.

It was Stryker's custom never to speak first when he answered the phone. It irritated the caller, but one couldn't be too careful. Yet tonight, he abandoned the routine defenses. "Yes?"

"Mark Stryker." The female voice told him his name like she would allow no argument.

"Yes, this is Stryker." He glanced around the dark room, suddenly feeling like he was not alone.

"I love you, Mark Stryker." The voice was so sensuous, deep and throaty that he felt himself growing instantly hard. Perhaps it was because the voice belonged to a total stranger.

"Who is this?" Stryker checked his watch. It had stopped ticking, and the last time registered on it was four A.M.

"I have been watching you for a long time, Mark Stryker." The woman taunted him on. She spoke slowly. "I love you so much."

"How did you get this number?" Stryker picked up the Zippo lighter from the nightstand and thumbed up a flame. He moved the flickering light about, inspecting the shadows around his bed: He *was* alone, after all. But the window shutters were open, and in the distance: the temple looming above everything else.

"I love you, Sergeant Stryker. Nothing would make me happier than to invite you into my bed." He stared up at the lacy canopy overhead. Kim had slashed through it with a pair of scissors, he noticed for the first time. "To engulf you, to have you explode within my all-consuming lips."

Stryker was not really listening to the woman's descriptive verbs, though he got the gist of her conversation. He was concentrating on the heavy Vietnamese accent despite the confident fluency. The more she spoke, the more he felt perhaps he *did* know her from someplace—sometime in his past. "What exactly is it you want, miss?" Just then, sex, no matter how wild she promised it, was the farthest thing from his mind.

"I want to screw your eyeballs silly." She laughed,

then quickly fell silent. Stryker got a sudden vision of Raunchy Raul and The Brick putting some bargirl up to all this. He could see them listening in on an extension or huddled right next to the woman's ear, mischievous grins from ear to ear. "I want to lick—"

Stryker hung up the phone, drained of energy, and buried his head beneath one of the plush, satin pillows Kim had failed to destroy along with everything else.

Less then a minute later, the phone rang again, penetrating to the depths of his fortress of solitude. He counted ten rings, and after it continued, he picked up the receiver. "I would truly like to oblige you, my dear, but—"

"*Listen to me,* you damned sonofabitch!" She screamed at him this time, her tone the pathological opposite of the loving, submitting voice she had used earlier. Now she sounded dangerous, even demented. "I have watched you rid the streets of this city of its scum for months now. I like the way you operate, Sergeant Stryker, and I would like to reward you with a catch I'm sure you thought far beyond even *your* abilities."

"Just what are we talking about here, Miss—" He made it obvious she was to tell him her name next, but the woman was not so naive or stupid. She ignored the bait.

"How much would you pay to learn the identity of the asshole responsible for the ambush of your people up in Bien Hoa?" She cooed, her tone losing its layers of hate with each word.

Stryker's eyes went wide, but he masked his sudden enthusiasm. "I'm sure we could make it well worth your—"

"Your money means nothing to me," she interrupted him. "I hate the bastard as much as you do."

"I do not hate a person I have not yet met." He was not sure why he had said that.

"But you would string him up in the town square and peel off his skin for what he did to your MPs, if you had the chance." She guessed correctly, sensing his answer through the wire. "Fine. Curfew will be lifted in one hour," she said. Stryker glanced back out the window. Already the dull emerald blue of predawn was splashing the horizon in the east like watercolors spilled from the crescent moon. "At six-thirty, I will meet you in the open-air cafe across from the Caravelle. You will buy me a Vietnamese coffee and a croissant, and I will bat my eyelashes at you and give you the name and address of the man you seek."

For the life of him, Stryker could not match the voice with the sea of countless faces floating in his memory banks. "Six-thirty." He repeated the time, for confirmation.

"And then afterwards," she said, her voice sounding like nylons-against-thigh again, "you will follow me up to my suite, and I will treat you to the finer pleasures of life."

"I have a funeral at seven," he said matter-of-factly.

"Fuck your funeral!" she rasped back at him harshly, her tone monstrous again. "Why waste your time with the dead when you can be with me?"

"I'll meet you at the cafe at six-thirty."

"A wise decision," she whispered tauntingly, and then the line went dead.

Stryker replaced the receiver on the phone and sat in bed for several minutes, watching the temple lose its power over him as the stars began to fade and shafts of sunlight finally pierced the castlelike clouds blanketing the horizon.

He dragged himself off the satin sheets and forced himself to walk over to the windowsill. Below, an MP jeep was still parked down at the shooting scene, the patrolman inside completing his paperwork. The body of Kruger, the deserter, had been removed hours earlier, but a smear of blood marked the spot where his soul had left its corpse, and where Stryker himself had knelt down in the thick pool of crimson.

He thought about tossing a water balloon down on the MP private, and even walked back over to the drawer where they'd been kept, but he was out, and he mentally scolded himself for even being able to contemplate anything so lighthearted after all he had been through in the last twelve hours.

Stryker walked back over to the window and followed the vapor trail of a squadron of Phantoms as they sliced in through the heat waves for a landing at Tan Son Nhut. Down the street, the midnight militiamen were dismantling their curfew roadblock, and in the courtyard below, an old mama-san was setting up her soup stall. The spices she used in the *pho* were already drifting up to Stryker, and he leaned out the window a little to breathe them in, as if that would help.

A few moments later, psychologically invigorated by the sunrise, Sgt. Mark Stryker did an about-face and fell prone across the hard teakwood floor. Totally nude now, except for his shoulder holster, he commenced doing the two hundred push-ups that started every day shift for the ex-Green Beret.

6. Making Noise In Mass

Mimi's Bar on central Nguyen Hue opened early that morning. Rather, it stayed open late from the night before. A half hour before martial law curfew was lifted across the city of sorrows, the drinking establishment was crowded with off-duty military policemen. Some of the more dashing NCOs, bending the rules a bit perhaps, were still in uniform.

Sgt. Cob Carmosino sat braced on a bar stool, six shots to the wind, an aching arm draped over one of the black MPs from Charlie Company, Craig Davis. The big, gentle Davis, a recent winner of the Bronze Star and constant contestant in the race for those elusive acting-Jack stripes, was on duty, fresh from the day shift guardmount, his helmet tilted back on the edge of his head, a bubbling Coke on the counter in front of him. It was the earliest bar check he had ever conducted: One didn't have much choice in the matter when crazy Cob and that Goofy Gary Richards flagged down your patrol unit, feigning a motorist assist, then dragged you off the street into the nearest watering hole to say hi to the boys from nightwatch.

"What about—what about—what about this one?" Crazy Cob was all smiles. "Why are so many of you soul brothers gettin' your ass smoked in the 'Nam?"

Davis grinned at a nodding Gary Richards and rolled his eyes toward the ceiling. "I'm almost afraid to ask," he finally replied.

"Because every time the bullets start flying and the squad sergeant yells 'get down,' the blacks stand up and start jive dancing!" Carmosino exploded into laughter, along with half the men crowding the counter. A gorgeous young waitress in a tight halter top and short miniskirt made her way into the mob, a platter of bottles high over her head.

"Ah yes." Davis rested his already weary eyes on her ample bosom. "The lady of the house. Too bad, gentlemen, I is on duty." He tipped his helmet to the young woman, who kept her nose in the air, ignoring them all. One thing she didn't need was a boss in a perpetual good mood—so long as the money was good, too—who kept the bar open so the MPs could have their after-hours choir practice. Davis ignored *her* cool expression and kept the smile on his face. He liked Mimi's Bar. True, it was just another dive, but he had once known a military policewoman back in The World named Mimi, and the name of the establishment, emblazoned above the front swinging doors in purple neon, served to remind him of her: a woman every guy on the force lusted after, but whom no one ever scored with. Her old man was a cop, too.

"Yes, yes. Lady of the house." Carmosino followed Davis's roving eye as the bargirl bounced her bottom out of sight, around the corner. "That's all you soul brothers ever think about: sex!"

Davis fought off the frown. He detested the title "soul brother," but what could you do when so many people used it—and they even had a back street below Tu Do named soul alley, where the shoeshine boys could dap as good as any of the boys back on the block. "Well, you should know why all us niggers ever have on our mind is sex." Davis turned to Carmosino and gave him a blank stare.

"No." Cob scratched his chin in deep thought. "Why *do* youz guys always have nothing but fucking on your mind?"

With a straight face, Davis answered, "Because of the pubic hair on our heads!"

Carmosino's jaw dropped, and Richards slapped Davis on the back as the men on both sides again erupted into hearty laughter.

"Now that was good," several MPs said. "That was damned good, yes sir."

All eyes at the bar squinted tight as the front doors to the establishment flew open, and bright rays of sunlight flashed into the dark brick cavern. Two Vietnamese policemen walked in cautiously, their short forms silhouetted against the golden dawn outside for a few seconds before the doors again creaked shut. Then they quickly let down their guard after recognizing all the friendly faces at the counter.

"Well if it ain't tricky Trinh Tri, illustrious captain of Canh-sats," Carmosino announced loudly, rising to his feet. "Pull up a chair—pull up a chair! You're just in time. We were just getting ready to string Davis here up to a burning cross."

Tri smiled uneasily—the Vietnamese often smile when they are suddenly terrified or bewildered—and reluctantly hopped up on the bar stool.

"Do you know how they got the nigger out of the tree after the Ku Klux Klan meeting?" Davis leaned forward and flashed his gleaming teeth at the small Vietnamese law enforcement officer.

A silent Tri shook his head in the negative, and the men at the bar fell silent, awaiting Davis's punch line.

"They *cut* his ass down!" he finally revealed, and MPs on all sides exploded loudly. Tri forced a chuckle, his eyes wider than ever at all the noise and commotion. The private beside him remained standing, and Carmosino started to pose a joke to him, then decided against it: He doubted the young man spoke much English.

"Sorry to hear about Nguyen Van Bao," Richards told Tri, putting a sudden damper on the festivities.

"Yes, yes." Tri frowned. "It was an unexpected loss, but at least he died among heroes." The captain nodded somberly. "I am attending the memorial your battalion is putting on this morning." He checked his wristwatch.

"Of course," Richards replied softly.

"I hear your Sergeant Stryker got into the shit again last night." Tri changed the subject, though they were still talking about gunsmoke and death. It seemed they were always talking about those two subjects in Saigon.

Richards's frown deepened. "Yah, poor old Mark dusted another deserter last night. He's always walking into the wasp nests—even off duty. I'm sure he'll be at the memorial. You can talk to him more about it afterwards, perhaps."

"Yes. Perhaps."

"We heard you have located a survivor of the Bien Hoa ambush." The canh-sat Carmosino assumed spoke no English posed the sudden question in fluent English.

"Yes, one man managed to make it out alive," Richards said. "Fox. I don't know if he'll be at the memorial this morning or not. He sustained some serious shrapnel wounds. They've got him in isolation—"

"And under heavy guard," Carmosino added. He liked talk of power, of brute force.

Once again the front doors to Mimi's Bar swung open, and everyone inside shielded their eyes from the harsh sunlight filtering in. More than a few MPs seated near the entrance stumbled over each other in their haste to make room for the latest patron: a snarling pup tiger rushed in gracefully—dragging the legendary Jack Flak at the other end of the leash.

The giggling Flak, wearing only baggy, green GI shorts and a pair of Ho Chi Minh tire-tread sandals, quickly overtook the striped pet, only to crash up against the counter. Men sitting on either side scrambled to abandon their bar stools as the agile animal bounded after its master and leaped up onto one of the stools.

Expertly ignoring the cops scattering on all sides of him, Jack Flak pounded his fist on the counter several times, until the trembling waitress finally appeared. "Service!" The inebriated Jack Flak roared. "Service!"

"Yes—sir?" the bargirl held her platter defensively in front of her shapely torso as she approached man and beast.

His nose held up in the air, Flak scanned the multicolored faces around him without really acknowledging anybody, and asked, "Do you serve blacks in this here bar, *lady*?"

The waitress's eyes darted about the room uneasily, finally coming to rest on Davis, who was slowly nodding back to her in the negative. "Why—why yes sir—yes, we do." She forced the words out, appearing braced for the worst. She recognized Flak as one of the MPs, but she could see no firearm on his person.

"Well then, I'll have a Bloody Mary for myself." He jerked on the leash so that the tiger cub roared slightly in protest. "And a nigger, medium-rare, for my cat here!"

After a short silence, the bar again exploded with laughter, and after the waitress figured out the joke and lost the fear in her eyes, Flak bent forward, nose to nose with her, and whispered loud enough for all around to hear, "How 'bout a little kiss for old Jackie, honey?"

As the men waited with baited breath for her reply, the tiny woman folded her arms across her chest and frowned. "Kissing a cop without a mustache is like eating an egg without salt," she finally said. Obviously taken aback, Flak pulled a crumpled pack of Vietnamese Blue Ruby cigarettes from his baggy shorts, slowly lit one up, then balanced it expertly on the edge of his lower lips. A slight smile now crept across the waitress's features as Flak squinted with one eye, contemplating her reply as he sucked in a lung full of smoke. "And kissing smokers is like licking ashtrays." She repeated the age-old comeback that was just then making the rounds in Saigon. As men on either side of him chuckled aloud, Jack Flak grimaced while the waitress smiled broadly now, proud of her quick wits.

"Aw, come on, baby," he finally said, sensuously rolling his tongue out at her between two fingers extended in the shape of a V. "I'll show you what *licking* is all about." And as the tiger beside him purred loudly in apparent agreement, Flack added, "I'd really like to get into your pants, baby."

Whirling on her heels, nose up in the air again, the waitress said, "No thanks. I've already got one *asshole* in there!" She then vanished behind the pyramids of glasses again amidst a roar of approval from the men all around.

Flak, seemingly undaunted by the rude brush-off, made a point of keeping his own nose up in the air, Harvard style, as he glanced at the men on either side of him and spotted Davis as if for the first time. "Why if it ain't ole Craig, my blood bro from way back!" He flashed a toothy grin, then made the smile vanish with the same breath. "Let me see your hands!" he ordered.

A worried Davis, wide eyes contrasting against his dark skin, hesitated, and Flak again demanded, "Let me see your hands, *boy*!"

Gritting his teeth for the worst, Davis held out his hands, palms up, and Jack Flak gently took them, like a fortune teller preparing for a session.

"You know why the palms of black people's hands and the bottoms of their feet are white?" Flak asked the men closest to him, with a dead-serious expression on his face. Several of the vets in the back of the group shrugged and started to turn away, suddenly bored with a repetition of jokes that had made more rounds in Mimi's Bar than the booze. But before the rooks present could be distracted, Flak sprung up against the wall, feet spread and hands out to his sides, in the street search position, and said, "Because when God was spray-paintin' 'em black, they was all up against da wall!"

Mild laughter and a loud fart from the rear of the bar. Even Davis managed a chuckle, though he had heard the joke a dozen times before from Fort Gordon to Frankfurt. The tiger bent forward and licked the black MP's arm with its sandpaper tongue, winked at Davis, and the man laughed again.

"He likes you." Flak wrapped an arm around Davis. "At least he likes the way you *taste*!" More muffled laughter, then the shuffling of feet as the men returned to their tables.

"A round of drinks for every MP here!" The canh-sat Tri toasted Davis and the legendary Jack Flak with his raised glass. Flak still had his arm around Craig, and soon Cob Carmosino had returned to the bar and was hugging both men from behind. A stranger to Mimi's, walking in for the first time, might have thought the joint a homosexual bathhouse.

The cute waitress with the shake-and-bake bottom reappeared, making her way through the dense cigarette smoke with a platter full of glasses balanced precariously atop her palm. She went out of her way to avoid the patron in the baggy shorts with the tiger cub on his lap, and Flak and Davis, in turn, ignored her for the most part: They were immersed in shop talk, about what had gone down on the street last night. It was no secret they were the closest of friends. "Craig here's gonna be my kid's godfather," Jack Flak often professed loudly to the men of the 716th. The racial jokes that pursued the duo everywhere they went were just part of the necessary entourage. After all, it *was* Saigon, land of intrigue and suspense: Polish jokes did not seem to go over well in the 'Nam.

Jack Flak pulled his wallet out for the hundredth time that week and showed the attentive bartender a photo of his Cholon-born wife. Clad in a form-hugging *ao dai*, she stood before a vine-covered wall in Hue, the orange of dusk behind her.

"Very nice." The bartender, a bent-over, middle-aged, mouselike character sounded sincere. "But why you marry Vietnamee girl?" He left the Z sound off at the end.

"Hey, this is my home!" Jack Flak looked dumbfounded the bartender could ask such a question. "I was born here, chump. I lived all my past lives here. I plan on being buried here."

The bartender frowned. You did not speak of funerals or future misfortune. The mere voicing of such events, the Vietnamese believed, could cause them to happen. In the Orient, words held incalculable power.

"You wouldn't travel to Texas, now would you papa-san, unless you planned on marrying one of them round-eyed southern-drawlin' Cowboy cheerleaders?"

Perplexed, the bartender smiled agreeably and poured another drink for his most dependable customers. "You'd like my old lady, pops," Flak continued. "And she's got a sister I bet you'd like even better," he said jokingly.

The bartender raised an eyebrow slightly at that remark, but kept pouring until one of the glasses began to overflow.

Ten feet away, at the nearest table, Captain Tri and his subordinate sat drinking with a couple of the men from the Decoy Squad. "Do you think this Specialist Fox will recover?" The canh-sat's younger driver posed the question with narrow eyes. He had not smiled once since entering the bar.

"Oh, no doubt about it." A weary Michael Broox finished his beer with one last, desperate drawn-out swallow. He wiped his mouth with his bare wrist and locked eyes with the captain across the table from him. "It'd take more than a couple lousy land mines to waste old Parlin the third."

Tri nodded slowly, smiling slightly. Thoughtful as he tried to place the wounded MP's face from the flash cards of his memory.

"Do you think he really saw anything besides smoke and somersaulting V-100s?" The canh-sat private persisted. "Do you think he will be able to identify his platoon's attackers?"

"Oh no doubt about it." Anthony Thomas reached across the table and patted the Vietnamese policeman's arm gently. "No doubt about it whatsoever, my friend. And when we figure out which VC leader or renegade bandit or who the fuck ever is behind the ambush, you can bet your balls we're gonna track 'em down and cook their eyelids in our c-ration cans after we paste their testicles to the trees with M-Sixty tracers!"

The canh-sat private recoiled slightly in his seat, but both he and Captain Tri beside him produced convincing smiles as they nodded along with the revenge-happy Americans.

Several feet away, at the farthest table in the corner, obscured by clouds of dense cigarette smoke, Sgt. Mark Stryker sat alone, staring back across the deserted dance floor at Captain Trinh Tri. But Stryker could not hear the conversation that was going on at the canh-sats' table, and he really wasn't seeing the Vietnamese police officer at all.

Stryker was thinking about the woman caller who had invited him to the Caravelle. She had never shown up, and now he felt haunted by the telephone conversation, wondering if, perhaps, it had ever taken place at all.

Rain clouds rolled in from the north as the military policemen filed out of Mimi's Bar an hour later, dragging their rotten moods, sour dispositions, and ragged carcasses back to the MP quarters at the International. As the dreary overcast quickly descended over the city, a warm drizzle fell suddenly across Saigon. It was a fitting prelude to the memorial the chaplain's squad was even then preparing at the cramped review stand in the rear courtyard of the hotel compound. The army-issue caskets were all in place, lined up in four neat rows before the makeshift altar. Thirty-five M-16 rifles, with fixed bayonetes, had been thrust barrel-down into the bright green grass beneath the caskets. MP helmets rested atop the black stocks of each weapon. Behind the raised platform where the commander's staff would review the ceremony, three flags flapped in the slight breeze: the American, with its striking collage of red, white, and blue, the South Vietnamese, with its three horizontal red lines across a gold field, and a smaller rain forest green flag, with gold crossed-pistols, symbol of the Military Police Corps, and the MP motto beneath them: Of The Troops And For The Troops.

Standing on the second floor balcony of the orderly room. Stryker smiled down at the military flag's elusive motto. So many of his young troopers considered themselves anything *but* soldiers. Supercops, yes. Master' sleuths, of course. But actual GIs? The boys with .45s on their hips would never hear of it. After all, this was Saigon, toughest beat in the world. Big city policework. *You say there's a war going on here too? Tell someone who cares: I've gotta go out and make my thousandth felony bust so I can top Jack Flak's arrest record.* Stryker blinked with inner pain as he focused in on the words across the green flag. When he realized he was beaming with pride, he wiped the smiled off with his fist, taking the tear away with it.

The men began arriving soon afterwards. He watched the boys from the Decoy Squad, in uniform for the first time in months, file respectfully, silently into the first row of metal folding chairs. He watched men from all five companies of the battalion, slowly followed by Broox, Thomas, and the rest into the courtyard. It quickly became standing room only. Outside the sand-filled barrels ringing the compound and the lines of sagging concertina, Assault tanks were pulling up to the wire. They would watch the ceremony from atop their V-100s. The Alert teams would remain alert.

Some of the men wore rain ponchos to protect them from the slight drizzle, but most chose to attend the memorial in uncovered khakis, chest ribbons exposed to the elements. Stryker often judged an MP, perhaps unjustly, by how much smog discolored the gold and red Vietnam service ribbon, the green and white campaign ribbon, the red and yellow National Defense ribbons, and all the others lined up above them. The more discolored, the more time the man had spent on the street, in his eyes. Now they could finish their Tour 365 someday and take their chest ribbons home with them, and, in ten or twenty years perhaps, pull them out of a dusty souvenir trunk and remember the mist that had soaked them the day they honored their fallen dead in Saigon.

Stryker watched Jack Flak arrive with his wife in tow. She took her role as police spouse very seriously. Stryker thought he spotted genuine grief in her eyes. After all, it could have been Jack's Reactionary Force that heard Mr. Death's punch line instead of these thirty-five valiant warriors lined up before her now. She wore a mint-white *ao dai* gown over white silk pantaloons. Stryker nodded silently at her choice of colors. They were most appropriate. In Vietnam, white was the color of mourning. He watched her long black hair, now soaked from the fine mist, cling to her shoulders and high, distinguished cheekbones. She had refused an umbrella from the ushers.

After the provost marshal and battalion commander found their positions on the review platform above and behind the rows of caskets and opposite the assemblage of enlisted men and NCOs, the chaplain stepped up to a large teakwood podium. A giant crucifix, crafted in mother-of-pearl, sparkled in the rain across the front of the podium. "This is indeed a sad day in Saigon," he began, raising his palms to the dark clouds overhead.

Stryker expected thunder to boom back at him from above, but the skies remained silent. The chaplain, a full-bird colonel, wore summer greens, with no chest decorations other than the small silver crosses on his collar. His eyes remained locked on the storm rolling past above the silent men all around him, and as best friends of the dead filed in front of the caskets with large photos of the slain MPs, draped in black diagonal ribbon in their hands, the chaplain talked about the war, the role of the military police in Vietnam, the reasons he believed they sacrificed their lives, what should be gained by all this, and the utter senselessness of the whole tragedy. The sermon, lacking of any true mass because of the large number of denominations among the dead, lasted fifteen minutes, and with an affirmative nod from the 716th commander, the chaplain signaled his honor guard to step forward for the traditional twenty-one gun salute—traditional because these were policemen, and they were not used to sacrificing so many brothers in a single pitched battle. Traditional because, in Saigon, the ranking top cop decided, on the spot, what was appropriate. Twenty-one muzzle flashes cracking against the falling drizzle was certainly appropriate in this case.

In haunting half notes that echoed back and forth beneath the storm and reminded many of the men of the peculiar tonal quality of Vietnamese music, Lieutenant Slipka and Sergeant Farthing stood side by side with their bugles, playing a somber string of taps.

The honor guard, rifles at port arms, slowly took up their positions in front of the formation of caskets, and as the last notes from the buglers rang across the courtyard and some of Saigon, uncaring as she might be but listening nonetheless, the soldiers raised their rifles, aiming at God.

The first discharge exploding through the silence seemed a bit premature.

When the AK-47 bullet slammed into the flat patch of skin between the chaplain's eyes, splitting his skull open partially in front and knocking him back off the podium, arms fluttering in midair, helplessly trying to retain a balance the brain no longer cared about, the courtyard began filling with screams from the women in the crowd.

Stryker went down on one knee, scanning the distant rooflines for the sniper, but smoke from the idling Assault tanks made detection difficult. Five more shots rang out even before the mass of men could scatter for cover, and he watched Craig Davis's head jump off his shoulders in a crimson splash and bounce off the wall behind his slowly tumbling torso. Stryker watched the black face, still frowning but startled tense, roll back out of sight between two caskets. In the bat of an eye, four more MPs were catapulted off their feet and somersaulted across the courtyard lawn by the impacting slugs.

"My God—" Stryker heard himself mutter as he hopped over the railing and landed thirty feet below, on his feet, pistol drawn. But where to start? The Assault tanks were kicking their engines over now, rumbling back and forth, also unsure who they were seeking. Sirens filled the air at the same time the whistle of the first descending mortars did.

Stryker went down in a crouch as the unseen enemy began "walking" the projectiles from one side of the courtyard to the other. Caskets exploded, sending splinters of wood and bone across the people running for cover.

"My God—" The words escaped the big buck sergeant who only went to church when it was a cop's funeral. He thought of Kim screaming at him only the night before about her temple curse, and he found himself praying he was not somehow responsible for this unholy desecration. "My God—" His heart sank to the pit of his stomach as he floated into phase-red watching the dead on all sides being insulted one last time as they were blasted from their coffins by indiscriminate waves of hot, smoking shrapnel.

Stryker knew he'd be wasting his time rushing out the compound in search of the sniper or mortar team. The V-100s were already crisscrossing the tenements, led by more than capable NCOs as professional as he. Better to remain in the thick of the kill zone, saving those he could. Stryker was a leader. As men scattered through the swirling groundsmoke, blinded by blood and confusion, he sought out the seriously wounded—he would start there. This barrage of endless explosions could not go on forever!

Stryker watched a string of glowing red tracers from a rooftop high above the courtyard kick up clods of grass around the feet of the legendary Jack Flak. The MP's wife was down on one knee, her *ao dai* soiled, holding onto his waist as Flak returned fire with his .45 pistol. Blood trickled across her forehead from a minor scalp wound, and though her features were laced with terror, Stryker saw in the woman's calm eyes a faith and trust in her man no God would ever replace.

Damnit Flak! Stryker thought as he raced toward the couple. *Fuck the hero's limelight for once and get your woman under cover!*

But Jack Flak kept blasting away at the rooftop, and when his eight rounds were expended, he popped in the clip release and pulled a fresh magazine from his web belt as the empty container clattered off his jungle boots.

And his wife remained by Jack Flak's side. Faithfully. Without protest. Until the AK round caught the cover boy in the clavicle and spun him out of her arms. The impact knocked the hero of *Time* magazine flat on his back, and his wife screamed forth her fears as she saw the fountain of blood erupt from the gaping hole in his shoulder.

She rose to her feet to run to him, and Stryker, only fifty feet away himself now, sprinted toward her from behind, intent on covering them both with his massive frame until the attack died down.

Only a mortar round could interrupt Sgt. Mark Stryker's headlong path. When the jarring explosion consumed Jack Flak's wife in a puff of smoke, Stryker stopped dead in his tracks, ignoring the shrapnel flying by on all sides as his eyes rested on the gossamer-thin pieces of *ao dai* gown, now streaked with crimson, floating on the warm courtyard breeze.

7. Death On The Wind

Sgt. Cob Carmosino was torn between two impulses: sprint to the useless aid of Davis (how could the easy-going black MP they had all been razzing just that morning possibly survive the separation of his startled head from his shoulders?) or rush over to assist and comfort the legendary Jack Flak. Could the saucy package of dynamite that had been his wife only a moment ago now really be just so much ash floating on the sticky breeze swirling through downtown Saigon?

Another barrage of mortars made the decision for Carmosino. The blast caught him below the beltline, knocking his legs out from under him. One jagged sliver of shrapnel slammed into his flak jacket, between the shoulder blades, on his way down, and though the sergeant from Danang had sustained no serious injuries on his jaunt through the whirlwind of smoking steel, the sudden pressure from behind pounded the breath from him: He would lie there unable to move for the duration of the attack.

Mark Stryker felt the same blast slap past him as he upended caskets to reach Jack Flak, but the force had dissipated somewhat as it rolled out across the courtyard after felling Carmosino. Jamming small wads of cotton in his ears—Stryker kept a supply readily available in the top of his FA pouch for those tenement sniper shoot-outs that always roused his migraines; the rooftop phantoms usually faded with the night, and the ex-Green Beret had decided long ago they weren't worth the headache of urban firefights in close quarters—he was beside Jack Flak even before the man realized what he had just survived.

On his knees now, and hands held out in front of him, covered with blood, Flak was staring more at his crimson-coated fingers than the mangled slab of meat sprawled across the grass before him.

"She told me we were going to the Miramar tomorrow for a special dinner." Flak stared at the space between his frozen hands, as if he were seeing the wife he had only known through three monsoons.

"Come on, brother." Stryker wrapped a massive arm around the younger MP protectively, fully aware flying lead and hot metal didn't give a shit how many push-ups you did every morning. "One of them rounds are gonna take our heads off—time to beat feet—make a hasty—"

"She said it was going to be her treat." Flak spoke as if he were not aware another man had invaded his space. "She was going to tell me she was pregnant. She didn't know I already knew."

"Come *on*, brother!" Stryker made a move to lift the dazed MP off his knees, but Flak seemed frozen to the spot, refusing to budge. He would not be rushed. "Them damn mortars are *way* too close for comfort!" The terrorists were walking the projectiles back toward the military policemen huddled among the dead, after destroying the reviewing stand and two jeeps beside the orderly room steps.

"I remember when I first met her—" Another blast sent shrapnel screaming past both men. Smoking bits of metal sizzled by as if in slow motion. Stryker caught them out of the corner of his eye. "When she was just a cherry-girl who wouldn't even look me in the eye—"

Stryker slapped Jack Flak against the temple, but even that stinging shock failed to bring the man back from never-never land. "Let's go, Flak!" He rammed his wrists under the grieving MP's arms and started to drag him away from the body at his knees when another explosion caught both Americans from behind and flung them forward.

Flak stumbled across the twisted torso of his wife, and Stryker himself, trying to keep his balance, plunged one hand down through what once had been the woman's back. She was now so badly riddled by shrapnel that his palm came to rest in the matted grass beneath her.

Rolling to the side, Stryker grabbed a handful of Flak's uniform and pulled him away. There was blood in his eyes now—he wasn't sure whose. "Corpsman up!" He heard the words crystal clear, though he was unaware they were coming from his own lips.

Stryker knew every man in that courtyard was certified in advanced first aid, but there were no medics at the ceremony. Nevertheless, two MPs were hustling up through the drifting smoke and rolling concussions. Were lifting Jack Flak off the grass while still on the run. More men were grabbing him from behind. He felt his ankles being dragged through the unkempt lawn as if he were not even wearing boots. "No. No. I'm okay! I'm okay!" he heard himself saying now, though he wanted them to drag him through the grass some more. The sensation was so carefree—like he was a punk kid back on the block, ditching school to laze down by the riverbanks. "I'm fine—take care of the others!" *Drag me a little bit more! Just a little bit more! But watch out for snakes! Lotsa Red Racers down by the Arkansas! Watch your ass in the grass!*

The weightless sensation Stryker was feeling just then, the mixture of fear, anger, bewilderment, but above all physical helplessness, told the ex-paratrooper he was most probably wounded. "Okay, sarge!" The men were dropping him back down now, and he waited for the pit to swallow him up, but darkness never came and the impact against the lawn was painful, jarring him from the surge of adrenaline.

The whole episode, from mortar blast until being abandoned by the two privates seeking medals, lasted only a few seconds at most.

"Over here!" somebody was yelling on his right, the words shooting out at him like rifle discharges now. Ear shattering, probing, painful—*electric*. He felt a finger pushing the cotton in deeper. In the past, it had served to muffle the crack of harmful blasts without affecting normal conversation, but today *nothing* was working.

Stryker glanced over his right shoulder.

One of the rooks fresh in from a Camp Alpha processing bus was down on one knee, trying to prop up the decapitated Craig Davis. "I need some assistance over here!" Bright red blood was streaming down into his eyes from a scalp wound—probably not serious but messy.

Scalp wounds. Real bleeders. He remembered that now from the medical course he had taken back at Special Forces camp. And from all the scalps his Strikers up in Pleiku had taken when he sometimes lost control of the boys.

Stryker ran his fingers through his scalp as another dual explosion dug holes in the lawn on either side of him. His thumb snagged the flap of skin hanging down above his eyebrow, and the bolt of pain brought him back to reality. Once again he could feel the earth beneath his buttocks. The walls of sagging concertina were no longer spinning around him.

Damn! Stryker gritted his teeth and planted his hands firmly on the ground. *Thirty seconds had been lost by now—at least thirty seconds!* Men were now rushing past all around him, tending the wounded, rushing for the Assault tanks beyond the wire, freaking at the sight of so much blood and carnage—so much insanity. It did not matter to Stryker that he was obviously wounded—stunned at the least. But that was no excuse. Men he had trained were racing about, making him proud. He'd best get his act together and charge in. *Supervise!* Not let them down. Set an example. *Never abandon your partners!*

And still the mortars rained down on them.

"Let's go!" Stryker heard himself yelling as though a stranger off in the distance was screaming the words. He was on his feet now, racing alongside other MPs caked with blood. They were all rushing past the newbie, vaulting the coiled strands of barbed wire where mortars had torn down the fence line.

"Leave him!" Stryker reached down and grabbed the

rook by the collar, jerking him to his feet. "The man's dead!" And they ran.

Dozens of them, rifles or pistols in their hands. Past frightened and panicky Vietnamese clustered on the other side of the compound wall.

"You! That one!" Stryker pointed to a buck sergeant, then one of the leaning tenements off to the left. "You! That one, and you! That one!" He had them splitting up into three groups now, heading for the most likely buildings that jutted up behind the International's rear courtyard.

"Floor to floor?" a man was demanding on the run as he chambered his M-16.

"Negative!" Stryker yelled against the roar of gunships swooping in from Tan Son Nhut Airport. *Thank God for Air-Cav!* "Post men front and back, but kick ass up to the roof, ASAP! We'll sweep it from the top down after we secure those tubes!"

Risky, Stryker knew. Damned dangerous, in fact. To protect your men, you went slowly up, one flight at a time, until the target building was completely cleared, but time was tight. He felt more MPs would die—in fact, all of headquarters could be decimated, if he did not take out that mortar team.

On both sides, V-100s, held five feet off the ground by their immense balloon-like tractor tires, rumbled by, circling the tenements, prowling the alleys, restraining the trigger fingers on the 50-cals.

Overhead, two Hueys hovered motionless on either side of the housing project, nose cannons pointed in toward the three apartment buildings rising seven stories high. Two more choppers glided around the kill-zone and the stationary craft in a counter-clockwise pattern, buzzing the rooftops without unleashing any of their deadly hardware. You couldn't just pounce in and zap occupied dwellings, especially in the heart of Saigon-town. The ambassador would shit a brick.

Stryker made eye contact with the nearest helicopter pilot, gave him a hand signal for directions, but the Huey merely wagged its slender tail slightly from side to side, and the warrant officer behind the cyclic shrugged his shoulders in resignation.

Great. Stryker sighed as he led the charge up the wooden stairwell of the building in the middle. If the choppers couldn't spot even an abandoned tube, perhaps the Cong were long gone.

The storm of mortars had tapered off rapidly then ceased altogether with the first sound of approaching aircraft.

With every new set of stairs, Stryker envisioned a brilliant, tracer-laced confrontation with the descending terrorists, but as his men climbed each successive floor of the building, all they encountered were terrified women, sobbing in panic as they dragged their children down through the American MPs, praying aloud in Vietnamese they would not be cut down in the middle of a crossfire before they could get safely to the ground.

The men charging up the stairs ahead of him had slowed considerably. At first irritated, Stryker quickly realized they were playing the game by the rules. Only a few MPs had wide eyes glued to the steps overhead. The vets alternated between glancing above and inspecting the women rushing past in the opposite direction. Too many of the cops had experienced, firsthand, the abilities of a Vietnamese woman to shoot just as straight as her male counterpart.

"Niner to the ground!" Stryker jerked his radio pak-set off its web belt clamp and sent the PR transmitting. "Detain every subject—male or female—leaving the ground floor of all three buildings, over!"

"Roger-wilco, sarge." He recognized Broox's excited voice. Sirens were converging on him from all directions in the background. "Got ya covered on this end."

All three rooftops were deserted.

There was not even the stench of cordite or the licorice taste of gunsmoke to greet them when they rolled forth through the top floor fire hatches, one at a time.

Stryker halted in his tracks momentarily as one of the Hueys, looking ten times bigger now up close, suddenly rose above the edge of the roofline, hovering like some massive curious dragonfly fifty feet away, staring directly at him, black bug-eyes and all. As the flapping of the rotors filled his ears and the downblast scattered particles of dust and debris across the rooftop, Stryker stared past the heat waves floating between his men and the huge craft, and tried to make out the pilot inside, but his helmet was blending too well with the tinted glass. He found himself, along with the MPs on either side, swallowing in temporary awe at the intimidating sight of the nose cannon pointing directly at them. A scene showing the gunship pursuing a VC across a rice paddy flashed through his mind, then vanished, and he wondered how many Cong that cannon had killed.

Wasting time! His instincts screamed at him from within. *You're wasting time!*

"Where the fuck are they?" Stryker's lips formed the words without any sound really leaving his mouth. The roar of the rotors would have made speech useless anyway.

Again, the pilot—the sun behind him now as part of the overcast broke, and the chopper slowly shifted along from one side of the building to the other—merely shrugged his shoulders, also bewildered.

One of the helicopters off to the right suddenly broke pitch and descended swiftly down through the towering tenements, disappearing beyond the concrete jungle as it went to investigate something on its own.

"Christ, sarge!" One of the privates from Delta Company was close beside him now. "If the flyboys can't even come up with ol' Charlie, this thing's gonna turn into a real bitch!"

"Take two men and run a quick grid search of this rooftop." Stryker ignored the first MP and directed a second private farther away. "I want evidence a sniper or Mike-squad was up here. And I mean *run*! Shell casings, blast residue, anything! Now beat feet!" The private, four campaign stars on his gold and red 'Nam service ribbon, nodded but did not run. He motioned for the closest men to join him, then they began walking off the rooftop in a careful crime-scene pattern, breaking it off into smaller squares as they searched for anything out of the ordinary.

"I'm tellin' you, sarge," the nineteen-year-old beside him said as he holstered his pistol, well aware they had happened upon a cold stretch of contested territory, "this whole damned thing is takin' on orgasmic proportions. Just this morning my cunt downtown begged me to call in sick. She said something terrible-bad was gonna go down on the job today!"

"Oh yah?" Stryker frowned, thinking about Kim and

her temple curse and how the government didn't pay him enough to endure all-knowing buck privates and chase phantoms across rooftops at the same time. He switched the channel selector on his portable radio.

"Yah, sarge! She showed me her damn astro—astro—"

"Astrology," Stryker said as another chopper banked sharply to the left from a stationary position and disappeared beyond the buildings.

"Her damn astrology charts. None of our stars are in the right orbits, sarge! I'm tellin' ya—everything's all out of whack!"

Stryker raised his radio to his lips as if to speak, but the private didn't take the hint, or didn't want to. He kept on. "She even read my palm, sarge! I'll bet even *your* palm don't jive with the planets this month, Sergeant Stryker!" His jaw dropped, leaving his mouth open.

"Stars don't orbit." The MP in charge of the middle rooftop pressed the transmit lever on the side of his radio. "Niner to Mike-Papa Broox," he said, as another Huey floated past overhead, its downblast hitting them like the brief breeze from a giant oscillating fan.

"Niner, this is Broox, over," came the scratchy reply. *Damned concrete always getting in the way.* Stryker moved over to the edge of the rooftop.

"Any possibles on the Victor-Novembers detained exiting target buildings? Over."

"Negative on your last, sarge," came the reply. "Just a lotta old mama-sans—"

"And a buncha—" another MP started to say over Broox's shoulder before the senior man ended the transmission. Stryker could imagine what he had been about to say. Probably something about the little bloodsuckers swarming over the few MPs left on the ground, begging for bubblegum. Stryker could see dozens of the street orphans converging on the bobbing black helmets far below.

"Do you need any assistance? Over," Stryker asked. He squinted down at the squad of white hats exiting the ground floor entrance of the building across the alleyway, where Broox was positioned.

"I believe we got it under control, Niner. Bookoo canh-sats just emerged from one of the target buildings. They musta gone in from the back. They're dispersing the juveniles now."

Stryker watched the kids scatter.

"Did they have any luck clearing the building?" Stryker asked.

After a short pause, Broox returned to the air with, "That's negative, sarge. They had a dry run too. Over."

"Roger—out." Stryker snapped his pak-set back on his belt and started for the stairs, but he halted in midstride and turned back to face the edge of the rooftop, ten feet away.

A gut feeling tried to nudge Stryker back over to the edge—tried to make him look down at the street one last time. Something did not *feel* right. Either something Broox had just said, or something about the Vietnamese policemen appearing on the scene so quickly. But the radio was alive with frantic voices calling for ambulances down in the courtyard of the International Hotel, and Stryker dismissed the notion.

"Follow me!" He motioned for the men conducting the search to abandon the fruitless maneuver and return with him down to the street.

* * *

"Take a hike!" Lieutenant Slipka stepped in front of him as Stryker and his men returned on foot through the downed fence line, into the pulverized courtyard.

"What?" Stryker almost shoved past the lieutenant, but there were enlisted men watching, and it just wasn't worth it.

"Straight to the dispensary," Slipka continued, placing his hand on Stryker's forehead to move back locks of hair. "Christ, you should see yourself in a mirror. Looks like somebody came after you with a hacksaw, Mark." Behind the officer, both on and off-duty MPs were rushing about, tending to the wounded, covering the dead. Digging through the rubble.

"Gotta search for my men, Lou."

"Just a scalp wound, you lucky sonofabitch." Slipka jerked his hand back as early as possible. He wasn't really listening to Stryker, though he never missed what was going on around him. "I don't know why they don't just ship your leatherhide ass back to The World! This must be your tenth Heart."

"Million dollar wound!" Sergeant Richards sauntered up to the group, himself covered with blood—that of other military policemen. "Another million dollar wound, but the Stryk won't leave the 'Nam, Lou." Richards sounded bitter. All would have agreed this was not the place for raw humor—even Richard's brand. "He'll never leave. It's all he's got left. Besides—"

"You know they don't give MPs Purple Hearts." Broox had reappeared in the courtyard, too. His remark was also intended to come across matter-of-factly. It sounded even drier than that—totally emotionless.

Stryker had had enough of all of them. The seconds had shifted into minutes: Time was ticking away. He finally brushed past Lieutenant Slipka. "Any of you got a count yet?" He headed for the closest set of stripes: Schultz.

Raunchy Raul never looked so exhausted. His normally rosy cheeks had gone dull, lifeless. His uniform was in shreds; every inch of exposed skin either caked in blood or mud. When he looked up at Stryker—he was down on one knee, helping two corpsmen lift Carmosino onto a backboard—his eyes seemed bottomless. And empty. Uncaring, after all this, yet driven on by some motivation they all shared—some dedication. *Of The Troops And For The Troops.*

He focused on the white letters of Stryker's black nametag. "Nine KIA," he finally said, reaching into his shirt for a pocket notebook. "Twenty-two wounded. The names are all down there. I believe."

"You believe?" One of the captains had walked up from the Commo van. "What the hell does that mean?"

Without saying anything, Schultz just waved a hand, palm up, at the collapsed reviewing stand. Two squads of men were frantically digging through the twisted boards and sandbagged foundation. "Oh yes—yes, of course." The captain returned a salute that hadn't been given, and rushed off to supervise the sergeants supervising the hastily assembled rescue team.

"Where are the COs that count?" Stryker turned back to Schultz, ignoring Slipka's reaction. He knew the lieutenant was still an NCO at heart, having risen through the ranks, and wasn't offended by the ex-Green Beret's manner.

"The caps are all out crisscrossing the boonies with

the Alert Teams, running down dry leads on possibles called in by the gunships." Schultz seemed suddenly pleased that he could remember anything after all that happened. But the slight pleasure radiated from his eyes. He did not smile. "Both majors are downtown: one on an MP-involved shooting at a liquor store hold-up; the other checking on the street patrols and briefing the line lieutenants on Intelligence just received from the VNP. The PM and CO are upstairs," he said, pointing to a helicopter slowly circling the International Hotel compound, "coordinating the whole thing from Eye In The Sky."

"And I bet you thought *you* were in charge of this whole cluster-fuck, didn't you Stryker?" Slipka gave the big sergeant a compassionate grin. "Now you see, Mark Stryker doesn't catch all the flak when hell busts loose in the glorious capital of South Vietnam. Keeping a lid on Sin City is not a responsibility that falls squarely on your back alone, my friend."

Flak.

Granting the lieutenant an appreciative nod, Stryker moved off toward the collapsed reviewing stand. He could feel several of the privates following him through the courtyard grass. And as he neared the spot where Jack Flak's wife had died, he could feel something more powerful. More personal. Something devastating yet serene.

Sergeant Stryker could feel *her*.

He felt he could see her spirit floating above the lawn where the walking mortars had so cruelly torn the life from her, flinging her soul to the wind. He thought of Kim and the temple curse, and how she stared *into* him during the little speech and the threats and the love-hate farewell. Stryker saw all the disembowled pregnant villagers the VC had tortured outside Duc Co, and he saw the arms from the little innoculated hamlet children the same bastards had piled up in the center square of the terrified community. He saw every display of insanity that he had ever witnessed flash before his eyes, and then he saw the spot where Jack Flak's wife had been kidnapped from him by bad bad Mr. Death and the rain forest goblins from never-never land.

The body was gone.

"Where is the woman?" He turned and locked eyes with Slipka.

Broox answered. "They shoveled her into a body bag, Stryker. Dragged what was left of her over to Third Field Morgue, I guess. She was a dependent, I suppose." His tone told the men gathered around that he didn't really care either.

"She was an American citizen," Stryker said. "That's all that matters—all that should matter to any of you." He turned and let Mike see the coals glowing in his eyes, beyond the jungle green. "Go and find her, Broox." He said it like she was alive. "Find where they took her, so I can tell Jack when he asks."

"Okay, sarge." Broox slid his hands into his pockets and shifted his boots slightly, then stared down at the ground.

"Now." Stryker's tone was firm, almost threatening.

"Right." Without looking up, Broox turned and walked back toward the charred and smoldering rear doors of the International.

"One of you beat feet over to that E Five medic over there and find out where they took the coverboy," Stryker said, running a finger under his eyelids. From a distance, it might have looked like he was wiping away a tear, but Stryker was scraping the dried blood from the hollows of his eye sockets. His entire face felt like it was an inch beneath a cosmetic mud cake. He could imagine why the Vietnamese he had passed between the tenement across the street and this courtyard had stared at him, wide-eyed, like they had confronted a ghoul. One woman had even shielded her child from him with her shawl and darted down an alley corridor rather than cross his path.

Stryker went down on one knee beside a dusty private digging with an entrenching tool. He reached out and grabbed the shovel. "Take a break, brother."

Surprised, the off-duty MP grabbed a hand offered by Sergeant Richards and let the Decoy Squad NCO pull him up out of the pit being dug beneath the reviewing stand. "Smoke 'em if you got 'em," Richards muttered grimly, staring at the bleak hole and the men who were digging it deeper.

"It's hopeless, sarge." The private brushed off his fatigues and sat on a pile of torn and leaking sandbags. "You're talking tons of weight under just the boards alone. Nobody could have survi—"

Frantic cursing and a sudden frenzy of activity down in the hole signaled a discovery of some sort had been made.

"What is it?" Richards yelled past Stryker, as both sergeants jumped down into the outer lip of the excavation.

Three more MPs were crowded into the five-foot-tall and yard-wide tunnel that extended about ten meters underground. "Who the fuck wants to know?" an irritated voice replied as the blades from three shovels began rapidly tearing at the moist earth. Roots and dirt clods sailed back toward the two NCOs, and a flashlight beam flickered about in the dark. "Oh shit, I'm sorry, sarge." A grimy face surfaced. "I was just gonna call for supervision. I thought—"

"Cut the chatter," Richards snapped. "You got a survivor down there, or what?"

"Moans, sarge. Yah, moans. Somebody down there—*right*!" He squatted down in front of the two sergeants, waiting for them to make the next move, say the next word. Take over. Assume control of a nightmare come true.

"Rest your arms," Stryker directed calmly, brushing past the enlisted man in the cramped space. Richards joined him, taking a shovel from one of the other men. "You get some air, too," he told the third MP. "We need more room to work."

And go to work they did.

Striking the wall of earth with alternate picklike blows, both men put their shoulders into each swing, using their body weight like martial arts fighters seeking the best leverage when cornered in a narrow, dead-end alley. Dirt flew, sweat poured, the earth overhead trembled as more men rushed to the pit, offering their help. Slipka finally ordered them back away from the excavation lest more ground collapse onto the sergeants beneath their feet.

"Wait!" Stryker raised a hand a few minutes later, after both men were breathing hard and drenched in sweat. He placed his ear up against the wall, as Richards tore off his shirt, leaving his trousers and web belt on.

"Can you hear him? Can you hear him?"

Stryker listened intently, but there was nothing. "Yah. Yah," he said, excitement in his own voice, renewed strength flooding his muscles. "I hear the poor guy. He's alive, Gary!" He was beginning to believe his words. "Keep digging, man, keep digging, but not so hard. I don't wanna knock off the guy's head with a shovel when we finally break through."

"They found something!" voices above ground called out in unison, drifting down to the men in the pit.

"Then dig!" Richards yelled, hacking away again at the earthen bank, mentally calculating how long the victims had been buried, and how much longer a human could survive without oxygen before suffering brain damage. He knew the odds were in favor of Mr. Death and the Deep Sleep. But neither of them could stop. *You never abandon your partner. You never abandon your partner. You never abandon. . . .*

"You never abandon your partner." Richards forced the words out slowly under his breath just as the wall trembled and a small section collapsed inward. Cool air seemed to suck past both men, into the small, dark cavity, then surge back, putrid and oppressive.

"Your light! Gimme your light!" Stryker yelled back at one of the privates. Richards reached up the tunnel slope, and a steel, four-battery cylinder was handed to him automatically.

With his hands now, Stryker was enlarging the hole. Richards flipped on the flashlight and shined it over his partner's shoulder.

Two white letters glowed back faintly against a black background: MP.

A few seconds later, Stryker, ignoring the threat of

their ceiling collapsing around them, widened the hole until he could squeeze through.

"How many?" Richards's voice seemed to crack with emotion when he spoke the words.

"Two," Stryker muttered softly, working to get into a better position.

"Alive?" Richards sensed the hope in his own tone. For the first time since the mortar attack itself, they were confronting something they could deal with: not singing shrapnel, which wasn't in the mood to negotiate, but the chance to rekindle the spark of life. A body no one had pronounced dead yet. A brother cop Mr. Death had missed on his reckless rampage through Mark Stryker's favorite neighborhood "Alive?" Richards repeated his question after receiving no immediate response.

"One of 'em." Stryker was pushing his forefinger in against the man's throat. "Yah—yah, I'm getting a weak pulse on this one. . . ."

"Which one—who is he?" Richards shifted around to play the flashlight beam across the face of the man lying on his back in the hole, but his face was coated with dirt and unrecognizable.

"Fox."

"Fox?" Richards's mind raced back to the opening of the memorial, when two nurses arrived, pushing Spec4 Parlin Fox the third toward the reviewing stand in a wheelchair. The lone survivor of the ambush outside Bien Hoa had come to bid his brothers farewell.

"The wheelchair saved his ass." Stryker was cursing it now as he struggled to move it out of the way. "Landed on him upside down, but created an air pocket of sorts above his head." He finally got the large wheels out of the way so he could slide a hand under Fox's neck and tilt his head back, opening the man's airway.

"You sure the other one's not alive, too?" Richards could see what Stryker was doing and wanted to squeeze into the hole beside him and perform some life-saving maneuvers also. "Are you really sure, Stryker?"

"He's dead, Gary."

"But how can you be sure? You haven't even—"

After rapidly clearing dirt and vomit from Fox's mouth, Stryker reached across the specialist's chest and tore something from the collar of the other man in the hole. He tossed it out the opening toward Richards and stated, "Take my word for it: He's dead." Then he placed his mouth over Fox's and forced air into the unconscious MP's lungs.

When Gary Richards shined the flashlight down at the piece of metal that had landed at his feet, a small cross sparkled back up at him. It was the collar brass of the chaplain who had been shot between the eyes.

8. Mindgames and Catspaw

Like grey ghosts gliding beneath a dull moon, thick layers of thundercloud moved in to replace the fine mist that had been cooling Saigon all morning. The sun's disc vanished behind the silver blanket, and a vast shadow fell across the city as heavy rain again began to fall in thick, stinging sheets.

"Waco—Waco, this is Car Twenty-two-Echo." A tense but low-volumed voice broke through the static on the dozen radio receivers turned on in the patrol jeeps parked in the rear of the International Hotel compound. A bolt of lightning spiderwebbed across the northern edge of the city, lingered, then sizzled away, wiping all transmissions off the net temporarily. Then, " . . . is Car Twenty-two . . ." and another wave of static, followed by a dual thunderclap overhead.

"Unit calling, this is Waco . . ." A more powerful transmission broke through the interference as the base station dispatcher came on the air with his usual unemotional drone. "Ten-thirteen your last, over. . ."

"Waco, this is Twenty-two-Echo." The MP's siren and straining engine came across loud and clear above the squealing of tires this time. "Requesting backup with a chase, Ten-thirty-two . . . now proceeding south along Bach Dang from Ham Nghi. Also requesting Code One at this time."

A triple-toned scrambler yelped like a burglar alarm across all four channels of the MP radio net for a couple of seconds, demanding silence, then the dispatcher came back on the air. "All units—Code-One—Car Twenty-two-Echo is Ten-One hundred, Ten-Two at this time, last proceeding southbound on Bach Dang from Han Nghi—that would put him on the west bank of the Saigon River, just below the USEM annex at Nguyen Hue." The dispatcher rapidly gave additional aids to help those rooks who were still mystified by the Saigon street system; but everyone knew where Nguyen Hue and the American embassy annex was. "Units in Precinct One and Sector Seven intercept—Okay, Twenty-two-Echo, gimme your present location—talk it up."

"Now southwest-bound on Chuong Duong, approaching the Nguyen Thai Hoc Bridge, Waco. Suggest all responding patrols exercise Code-Zero." The private's voice could barely be heard above the screaming dual hood sirens. "We've got shots fired."

Nearly a minute of silence on Channel One followed as units on Channel Two acknowledged the chase and radioed in their locations and the points at which they'd attempt to intercept the pursuit.

It was a long sixty seconds for the dispatcher. Finally, he pressed down the lever that broke squelch. "Talk it up, Twenty-two-Echo—gimme a location."

He quickly jerked his fingers back, praying he had not just covered someone's transmission from the street.

"They're taking a left turn onto the bridge, Waco." The private in Car 22-Echo was beginning to sound worried: Chases across bridges often meant nothing but trouble for the MPs of the 716th.

"Give us a vehicle description, Nick." A husky voice broke static for a single second as the words were crammed together to save valuable airtime. Sgt. Ron Brickmann's confident tone added that extra charm to the chase.

The private pursuing the green jeep across the Nguyen Thai Hoc Bridge sounded a bit more relieved, knowing the best cops in Asia were backing him up, when he replied, "Appears to be one of those old canh-sat jeeps, Sierra-Four—no top—five Novembers inside—civilian clothes." The transmission ended when the kid had to use both hands to steer through the cluster of motorcycle traffic on the east side of the canal.

"Damn!" Brickmann slammed his fist against his jeep's steering wheel as he roared down Ton Dan Boulevard, forcing cyclos and bluebird taxis onto the shoulder of the roadway. "Wish they'd quit putting these hotdogs out on solo patrols just 'cause the sun's up!"

"License plate!" another anonymous voice requested additional information.

"Unreadable, Car Thirty-five—they've got tape across the plate."

"What's your p.c., Twenty-Two-Echo?" One of the line lieutenants from MACV came over the air unexpectedly. "Besides the gunplay—what's your original p.c.?"

"Lima-Three, this is Twenty-two-Echo—this Mike-Papa first observed subjects fleeing the vicinity of the mortar attack on headquarters at high speed—believe they also ran down a Saigon traffic cop at intersection of Ham Nghi and Tran Hung Dao, over—"

"That's confirmed, Lima-Three—" the dispatcher cut in. "One Delta-Oscar-Alpha at that location."

"This Mike-Papa first initiated pursuit on Tran Hung Dao north of HQ, Lou. They led me in and out of traffic all the way to the railyards, then east to Bach Dang before Waco could read me through all the interference."

Another blast of thunder rolled down across the city in reply, as if the storm were listening in and laughing at them all—their little inconsequential games.

"Shee-it!" Brickmann slammed his fist against the steering wheel again as he coasted up to Trinh Minh The Street, only to find the intersection flooded with rainwater. "Well, fuck me anyway!" He gritted his teeth helplessly as the siren slowly died down and a score of alley kids wearing nothing but baggy GI shorts waded out into the hubcap-deep murky current to beg for candy and gum. "Wish they'd knock off all the chatter," he said, ignoring the boys splashing up to the jeep as he turned to face his partner, referring to the radio transmissions, "so we can get down to some real police work."

A chorus of multi-pitched sirens was quickly growing in the distance. Brickmann casually pulled a rare packet of *Dentyne* from his shirt pocket and slowly distributed the small pieces of gum to the boys as the sound mingled with rain pelting the tin roofs all around. He never looked at any of the kids but kept his eyes on the street up ahead, hoping against the odds the honorable bad-guys-of-the-day would stumble down his block on a random turn of the steering wheel. With his free hand, he slipped the cover strap off the butt of his automatic.

His partner had a shotgun balanced across his thigh, the barrel out. One of the Vietnamese boys was rubbing his stomach against the choke, massaging himself, to the entertained laughter of all his friends. "Maybe you like adopt gutter boy, Joe?" The kid ran his fingers through the hair on the private's thick forearms. "I cut lawn, shine shoes, clean house, feed dog—everything *American* boy-san do for fatha."

"Maybe you like adopt?" Another one appeared at the private's elbow, pushing the first aside, then they all began chanting, "Maybe you like adopt?" totally oblivious to all the sirens converging on their neighborhood.

"Maybe you'd like to eat some double-aught buckshot, ya little rug rat!" The MP lifted the butt of the shotgun suddenly like he was going to bash in some baby-san teeth, and the kids scattered through the deepening sewer water backing up in the gutters.

"You numba-ten cheap Charlie!" came the inevitable cry of an insulted shoeshine boy.

"Numba-fucking-ten!" a second kid amended his friend's assessment of the American.

"One, two, three . . ." Everyone within earshot began the usual chant.

"Motherfuckin' *di di*!" The private cut in, ending the challenge with a rhyme of his own. *Di di* was Vietnamese for scat! (to say the least).

"A poet, and he don' even know it," muttered Brickmann, his eyes scanning the maze of side streets up ahead. *Where were they?*

"In my opinion, we oughta gas these little sonofabitchin' bastards with some CS, sarge. That'd scatter 'em *rikky-tik*!"

But The Brick reached back over the seat and turned the radio up louder, ignoring the suggestion. Though it was an idea, he thought to himself, tear gas in this rain would sting like a bee! Add a little Huey rotor overhead to whip up the brew, and we could throw a hell of a party! He thought about it for a moment, grinning, and wondered if Egor from the Fifty-seventh Med Dust-Offs would accommodate him in just such a little escapade. Naw. They probably got Johnson busy runnin' slicks back and forth from the International to Seventeenth Field Hospital.

"Talk it up, Twenty-two-Echo." The dispatcher's voice fought to be heard through the increasing waves of static. "Talk it up."

"Now proceeding south along—"

Another lightshow of brilliant spiderwebs crackled directly over the area just then, and the MP's transmission was lost in the sudden wall of static.

A loud *pop* came across the receivers in the back seat, and both Brickmann and his partner turned to stare at the radio. The static abruptly ended—all sound, in fact, ceased emitting from the unit's built-in speakers, and for a moment the men in Sierra-4 feared Waco had been knocked off the air by the powerful bolt of heat lightning.

After they cringed at the numbing thunderclap that followed, both men again turned to inspect the radio. Slowly, power seemed to surge back into the system, but there were no transmissions.

Brickmann wondered if all the fuses in the 716th motorpool might have been blown out just then, but his partner reached up and grabbed the mike clipped to the dashboard. He squeezed the transmitter lever in for a fraction of a second then released it. The red Transmit light glowed for a moment then faded, and both men sighed in relief.

"Look!" The private, rain draining off the edge of his helmet like a small waterfall, pointed straight ahead, up the block.

A green jeep, followed by four MP jeeps, raced through an intersection, eight or nine blocks away, heading east to west. Brickmann almost missed it.

He jammed the stickshift into reverse, revved the overheating engine once, then let the clutch fly. Rear tires sprayed water out from the undercarriage like a vandalized fire hydrant, and the jeep roared back up out of the flooded intersection.

Motor straining against the liquid obstruction, Brickmann executed a U-turn and deposited a respectable amount of tire rubber along the wet pavement as he guided his vehicle down a narrow side street running parallel to the pursuit. His partner automatically reached forward, activated the siren toggles again, and motioned the pedestrians ahead out of the way with his arms. So many of them just stared blankly at the speeding jeeps, oblivious to all the commotion as they walked their water buffalos along the sidewalk or persuaded chickens to market with a stick.

"Waco, this is Sierra-Four." The private grabbed the microphone again, unsure if his transmission would even clear squelch. "Chase now proceeding toward Nguyen Than Hien. This unit to intercept at Trinh Minh The. Suggest additional patrols head toward the Loop just in case."

"All units copy?" A faint voice came across the net. Waco was rapidly fading with the storm, it seemed.

"If your suspects make it across the canal, you can kiss this one good-bye. Over. . . ." An anonymous voice announced what everyone refused to think about: Once outside of Precinct One, the suspects had a greater chance of escaping into the rubber plantations along the southeast edge of the city.

"Ten niner-one." The line lieutenant from MACV came across the air again, his tone unmasked irritation. "Repeat: Ten niner-one." Several transmitter clicks over the air signalled anonymous protest: a Code-Ninety-one meant cease all unnecessary radio traffic. "Cut the chatter, boys. So we can fini this dinky-dauness and live to chase another day."

"Fourteen hundred hours." The dispatcher noted the time dryly. For the record, of course.

Water was swirling down around Stryker's knees now as he and Sergeant Richards struggled to move Fox out of the pit before runoff from the storm drowned them all. Walls of earth on both sides were rapidly crumbling away as the stream rushed past, disappearing somewhere underground.

"We're piling sandbags as quick as possible, Mark!" a worried voice called down to them from above the surface of the earth. "But we're unable to keep the water out!"

"Hurry!" Another MP slid down into the hole beneath the reviewing stand foundation when Stryker and Richards were spotted climbing out. Everyone wanted to help.

Richards was doing most of the backwork. Stryker was still forcing life into the unconscious soldier's lungs. Rain that had drenched the men topside like a warm shower felt cool as tea to Stryker and the other sergeant after their ordeal below.

"To the Mike-Whiskey!" Another NCO was directing the entourage as they climbed up out of the muck. "Get them over to the Mike-Whiskey!"

Stryker glanced up at the E8 with irritation creasing skin between the waterlines on his mud-caked face. He hated it when they referred to the ambulances as Mike-Whiskeys, or meat wagons. Especially when the man in his arms was not technically dead.

Yet.

"Christ!" A man ran backwards several steps as the ground began to tremble. With a muffled sucking sound, the earth around the already leaning reviewing stand collapsed, and the structure began to sink into the hole amidst a loud gurgling noise.

The edge of the foundation that had been hanging precariously along the edge of the crevice rose almost vertically into the air as the heavier side, with all the chairs and podiums atop it, disappeared from view.

A patrol jeep that had been parked ten feet away began to lean forward suddenly, but before its driver could move it to safety, the front wheels sank into the muck, the ground pulled away halfway under the chassis, and the engine compartment fell from sight, leaving the rear tires sticking up in the air.

"Damned French sewer system," somebody muttered as the sinkhole stopped gurgling and the shifting ground became silent.

"Nothin' but a maze of catacombs down there, brother," another MP commented as Fox was hustled into the back of the four-wheel drive army ambulance. "Jon Toi took me down there one time chasing a fucking AWOL—never wanna pay the place another visit. Rats the size of tomcats down there, friend. *Ching-ching!*"

"Aw, hey—"

"I shit you not, pard. I still dream about it when the power goes out at night and I run out of candles."

The MP made a creep-show whistle and said, "How much would *you* accept to spend a night in the haunted Saigon underworld?" With a Vincent Price accent.

"Laugh all you want." Their conversation mingled with the rainfall and thunder, fading away as Stryker climbed into the ambulance. "Did I ever tell you about the time Reilly and the Uke followed a pimp down there and—"

Stryker watched the medics place a facemask over Fox's nose and mouth and turn on the oxygen tank. His ears began picking up metallic-sounding voices, and instinctively he moved back toward the rear doors. His ears practically perked up as he strained to pick up the radio conversation out of the numbing sounds of the storm.

"Okay, okay," said an excited voice across the airwaves, "they stacked it up at coordinates—" Heavy static wiped the numbers off the air, as far as the field units were concerned, but the Waco dispatcher might have picked them up at headquarters.

"Whatta they got goin' down out on the street?" Stryker wiped the rainwater out of his eyes and stared hard into those of a buck private fresh over from The School.

"They have a hot pursuit, sergeant," he replied instantly, eagerly. "A Code Zero with a Ten-Thirty-two, Ten Ninety-seven, Signal-Three hundred and last I heard—"

"Whoa—wait a minute, bud." Stryker held up a hand. The movement felt like it required every ounce of energy left in his system. "Fuck the radio jargon—and I don't wanna hear no phonetic alphabet either. Just tell me what's going down out there!"

"Sergeant Brick and some of the guys are chasing suspects that might be involved in this enemy attack." He swallowed hard, wondering how he should word the rest of it, but Stryker was off the bench and on his feet. From a bent-over crouch, he grabbed onto the private's shoulder and vaulted back out into the rain, commandeering the nearest patrol jeep.

As he threw the vehicle into gear, slid around in a half circle aiming for the hole in the fence line, and also threw a wave of mud out uncomfortably close to a group of reporters with his spinning tires, Stryker reached back with one hand and flipped on the power booster of the radio welded to the rear wall. The volume was already cranked high as it would go. Activating the siren with his knee, he slid onto Tran Hung Dao on two wheels. Civilians and soldiers alike scattered frantically from his path as he barreled down the hill, heading for the main artery that would take him quickly up out of downtown, to where the action was.

Ten minutes later and a pound of rubber lighter, Stryker's jeep rumbled up to the crash scene, engine knocking, undercarriage steaming. One tire hissing.

A sea of lazily twirling red lights greeted him. Beyond the two dozen MP jeeps, abandoned haphazardly everywhere, blocking the street was the light green jeep, lying on its top across the sidewalk, half into a demolished jewelry store. Two bloodied legs hung out from beneath the warped jeep's frame.

Stryker chuckled out loud as he stepped from his own unit. Just like the Wicked Witch of the West!

But the big ex-Green Beret from San Marcos was mistaken. No character from the *Wizard of Oz* would be able to match the anger of the woman rushing up behind him just then.

"Who will pay for this?" A short, slender Vietnamese woman was suddenly beating against the small of his back with her tiny fists.

Stryker whirled around, but his own temperament immediately softened when he saw the size of the lady in the western business suit. "I don't believe *we've* had the pleasure." He gave her a half-grin, then resumed scanning the treeline on the other side of the road. There was no sign which way the chase had proceeded on foot, but there was little doubt in his mind which way the hunted would flee: into the jungle.

"I want to know *who* is going to pay for all this damage?" she screamed up at him, waving her fragile arm back at the totally destroyed shop, shards of plate glass still crashing to the ground every now and then.

"I can assure you, madame," Stryker said, his .45 sliding out of its holster as he started for the jungle, "the parties responsible for this—"

But the sight that usually shut people up on the spot—the drawing of his automatic—didn't phase the little dragon lady a bit. In fact, she reached out and latched onto Stryker's web belt from behind, pulling the canteen pouch off as she dragged him to a stop. "I want your name, *sir*!" She stabbed his chest with a rigid forefinger. "And I want the badge numbers of every—"

Stryker's patience ran out with the talk of badge numbers. "Do you see a badge on this chest, honey?" He picked her up off her feet and flung her over his shoulder roughly, thinking about some of his men that *did* wear gold and silver shields above the service ribbons. But they were customized jobs, bought downtown with one's personal funds, and the PM got a case of the ass every time he spotted them. Never mind. The MPs in Korea had been wearing them for years, and it was of the highest priority on an air force flyboy's uniform roster, next to the .38 and blue beret.

As Stryker carried the woman over toward her shop, two more MP units rolled up to the scene of the crash, sirens wailing. "What's the latest?" he yelled over to them impatiently, gently depositing the female storeowner on the steps of her establishment. He cupped her chin in his right hand so that their eyes met, then he whispered in a no-nonesense tone, "Stay right here, *miss*." Though her narrow, angry eyes still seemed like orbs filled with hot coals, she did not budge, choosing to remain on her haunches, frozen.

"They're proceeding through that stretch of mangroves!" one of the privates replied, helmet liner bobbing atop his head as he raced to keep up with his partner, one hand grasping his rifle, the other holding a portable radio to his ear. He had the squelch off: Static danced out at them loudly with each footfall.

Stryker palmed the bottom of his automatic to make sure the clip was seated firmly, then he double checked the safety with his thumb and fell in behind the four enlisted men sprinting through the reeds at the edge of the highway. A hot load was already locked into the chamber of the pistol.

Behind him: ramshackle ground-floor buildings that housed a variety of failing businesses. And behind them, charred and blackened tenements that slowly rose up in the distance, becoming the outskirts of Saigon. Ahead of him: rolling stretches of green harboring all manner of flora: elephant grass, reeds sharp as razors, wait-a-minute vines, and thorny shrubs, and sparse tamarind trees that eventually gave way to leaning palms on the left and a dark rubber plantation on the right. Acres away, adding still another contrast to the multiple shades of green: the edge of the rain forest.

With the reeds slashing at his khakis, Stryker

poured steam into his leg muscles, struggling to catch up with the younger cops ahead. As the four privates approached the nearly invisible strands of barbed wire marking the edge of the rubber plantation, they slowed, catching the momentary gleam of wire despite the overcast skies and intermittent sheets of rain blowing in on the wind.

One could barely see the recent trail left by the military policemen who had preceded them: the trampled and pushed-aside reeds were slowly springing back, one or two at a time.

The first two men to reach the wire opened up the two strands by stepping down on the lower one with their boots and holding the top one above their heads so that the other two, and Stryker, could run through. The nearest fence posts were twenty feet away. The wire sagged considerably but could be deadly if sprinted into. (The barbs were the battle-ax razor blades that had been outlawed in the United States decades earlier.)

As he approached the two men holding the wire open for him, Stryker's eyes gazed beyond the fence line, searching the trail for anything out of the ordinary—something he always did out of habit when in phase red. Especially since none of them had actually seen the first units on scene run through here on foot. It wouldn't take that long to leave a boobytrap or two behind.

Though the trail zigzagged through the first ten or twenty rows of rubber trees—the straight rows and buckets hanging from lower trunks the only sign of man in an otherwise primitive setting—it quickly veered off to the left, straight into the mangroves, and failed to continue down into the heart of the rubber plantation itself.

Passing from the orderly rows of branchless trees to the tangle of vegetation they were suddenly entering gave the once eager rookies a reason to slow down and ponder the situation. The terrain up ahead looked more than hostile: It smelled of a trap. It stank so bad, in fact, that even these men with mosquito wings for rank paused to stare back at Stryker for guidance.

The big MP sergeant, sweat glistening on his forehead, scratched at the bullet hole scar over his left earlobe as he violated the cardinal rule of not bunching up, and he glided into the midst of his privates. "I'm getting a bad feeling here, brothers." He motioned with palms out for all of them to fall into a squat, so he could just observe for a while. Listen to the jungle ahead, feel out the vibes they were all getting. Come to terms with the ominous *thickness* in the air reaching out to envelop them.

Some would argue it was merely a shifting in the humidity, or the clouds, racing past above, pressing the mist down against the earth—and the men racing across it. All Stryker saw just then was Kim's face back in that doorway of the Miramar, telling him he was now cursed. Telling him nothing would ever go well for him again.

He turned the volume on his pak-set down low and tested the squelch. It was working, but there was absolutely no traffic on the band. The absence of transmissions gave him an eerie feeling in the pit of his gut, but it just meant they would be off the air temporarily, prowling the mangroves and whatever else lay up ahead of the treeline, patrolling in silence, the way they had been taught back at The School. And the way Stryker had honed and polished them after their arrival in the 'Nam.

Stryker glanced at the nametags of each man as he listened to the jungle. Three of them he didn't even recognize. He wished it was like back in the old days, when they'd filter into the battalion one or two at a time, so he could take them out on patrol individually, to get to know the man, learn his reactions. Show him *how* to react. Properly. The Saigon style. Stryker glanced at the men's faces. He saw fear in their expressions. Courage, and even cockiness perhaps, in the tense muscles around the lips, but fear in their eyes, where emotions could rarely be masked. And certainly not by rooks who had yet to experience what the streets of Saigon had in store for them during their Tour 365. He checked their eyes closer: All four men had green eyes. Jungle green, like his own. The odds seemed astronomical. The possibilities made him smile, and one of the privates cocked his head slightly in response, curious. Maybe they just might survive whatever lay ahead of them this rain-soaked afternoon. Maybe Stryker's temple curse wouldn't get them all blown into Buddha smoke after all. But Stryker perked his ears and listened for the birds. This was lush, teeming jungle, even though it lay right at the edge of Sin City. But there were no birds. At least no birds singing. And that was a powerful-bad omen. It reminded him of the white parrots outside Pleiku. They had sat silently perched above the banks of the Dak Ba, in branches hanging over the murky river, and watched in anticipation (or so it seemed) as Stryker and his A Team ambushed a sampan filled with Cong cadre. Not until after the hail of lead tore the communists apart and sunk their boat did the parrots lash out at the Americans with noisy squawking.

Stryker raised his right hand slowly, the two first fingers and thumb extended. He made eye contact with the man nearest the treeline, then motioned for him to set out for the unknown. The others would cover him. After he reached the nearest point of cover, he'd signal the next man to follow, and they would move in that manner the rest of the way, until they either met up with the other MPs, or engaged the enemy. Stryker voiced none of this. What they would do now had been drilled into them so many times by the sergeants back at The School that it was now second nature.

But before the man could even rise from his crouch and start off down the trail, there came a long, drawn-out exchange of automatic weapons fire, in the distance, several hundred meters into the trees to their left. The private sank back down into a reed-hidden squat, and the shooting peaked to a dull crescendo, then slowly tapered off.

A few minutes later, Stryker again motioned for the private to start his move, but when he raised his hand like before, there came a loud chattering overhead that sent all five men prone, hugging the earth. One of the privates rolled onto his back and sent off a half magazine of rounds into the branches. Flapping wings responded, and with shrills of alarm, a pillow load of bright feathers fluttered down across their position, and several dead birds dropped into the bushes around them.

"The parrots have spoken," Stryker muttered, "so it must be safe to move." Though sporadic rifle discharges were still sounding in the distance, Stryker motioned his men to advance into the trees.

Just then, as the MPs began to move off from his left, there came a fluttering noise over Stryker's right shoulder, and a short, sleek projectile ascended from the center of the rubber plantation, a silver smoke plume trailing it as it climbed through the sheets of rain, heading for the heart of the city.

Again, all five soldiers with badges went into a cautious crouch.

"A fucking one-twenty-two." The private nearest Stryker followed the rocket with intense eyes, his mouth open in awe. *This was what the 'Nam was all about!*

Stryker's own eyes narrowed. "A one-oh-seven," he said in disagreement. "Chinese made, not Soviet." His words were a hushed whisper as he motioned the others to continue heading in the opposite direction from where the projectile had been launched. "One-twenty-twos are about twice as long and twirl the other way because of the slant in the fins."

The youngest MP in the group stared back at Stryker incredulously. What the hell do I care about diameters and dimensions at a time like this he thought. His boot snagged a wait-a-minute vine, and he concentrated on the trail ahead again.

Overhead, thunder crashed among the looming storm clouds, and in the distance, a loud, piercing explosion from the vicinity where they had seen the rocket first appear above the backdrop of rubber trees.

Stryker, without the others noticing, pulled a small, folding field compass from his web belt, plotted the area where the rocket exhaust vapors were still lingering, then continued after his men before ten seconds had passed.

Moments later, a dull, muffled tearing blast erupted miles off, back in the city—a world away. Stryker envisioned the nose piercing the tin rooftop of a dilapidated tenement and burrowing down several floors before exploding, knocking a ten foot crater out one side of the building, and probably leaving several families homeless. Or dead.

Stryker cocked an ear toward the rubber plantation as they moved further away from it, into the tamarinds, but he heard no further launches.

"There." One of the rooks leading the five of them slid to a stop, raising one hand to signal their halt while the other pointed ahead. A dozen black helmets were lined up along a dike, barely visible from where Stryker's men had stopped. Now and then an M-16 cracked. The group had their backs to Stryker's people.

"Niner to Three-five," he whispered into his pakset after four quick clicks. "A Ten-Two of four coming up on your romeo, over."

Several of the black helmets turned as the transmission apparently got through, and a hand waved them up. "Awright, move out!" Stryker instructed the privates crouched in front of him. "And take off the damn helmets." He still couldn't believe most of the MPs within a hundred feet of him had left their steel pots back at their units, preferring the lighter helmet liners. "Leave 'em here in the bush, or snap 'em onto your web belts, letters to the rear."

"The white letters *do* make quite a target," one of the rooks said nodding to the man beside him as all four clipped their liners to their belts and started off toward the dike at a brisk trot.

Stryker's boots made bamboo crunch lightly as he found cover beside Sgt. Raul Schultz, ranking military policeman on scene—if one could call this stretch of jungle the scene. Schultz was the only man present wearing his steel pot. The thick strap dug into his chin, making his cheeks appear rosier than usual as his whole face seemed to get forced up closer to his thick brows. "What's the situation, Schultzy?" Stryker did not look at the other sergeant but gazed out over the dike instead. Schultz stared back at him suspiciously, even though one of his men was popping off some rounds again at a distant hedgerow. Schultz pursed his lips silently and made his thick eyebrows do a little dance. Stryker had not addressed him as Raunchy Raul. He had not called him the roly-poly policeman, either. True, enlisted men were all around, but that had never stopped Stryker before.

"Well?"

Dirt kicked up on the other side of the dike as a tracer ricocheted inches above their helmets and climbed up through the mist, rapidly burning out as it zinged toward the clouds.

"Bad guys there, there, and *there*!" A spec4 with his rank patch failing to completely cover the phantom mark of old sergeant chevrons flew up above the dike top, sprayed the last position with a half magazine of rifle rounds, then plopped back down, breathing hard. Stryker didn't recognize the man.

Every man near him expected a hundred rounds to answer his challenge, but instead, a painful scream pierced the sound of rainfall across the jungle floor, even as the discharges were bouncing back at them off the distant treeline.

"Payback is a royal *motherfucker*!" The MP who had just fired fifteen rounds yelled above the fury of the storm as he resumed his seat, back against the dike, rifle between his legs, giggling. Then, his expression turning suddenly serious, he stared up at Schultz and, with sad eyes, said, "That leaves three, sarge."

Stryker stared back at the man, wondering how much was an act, how much was the insanity of the moment, and how much was normal. Schultz himself chose not to answer with words but merely nodded. "I've got three men circling around," he turned back and told Stryker, "to form a modified L ambush, and—"

"Then we'll bring smoke down on their asses," the man who had just sprayed the treeline interrupted, still staring off in the opposite direction from which he had just fired, like he'd done his part. The rest was up to the others.

Stryker frowned. He hated unearned cockiness. The scream they had all just heard was no different from phony death cries he had heard countless times in steaming battlefields outside Pleiku: when the cong got bored with gunplay and tired at watching the Americans waste their ammo in twenty-round blind bursts; when each spray of harmless tracers was met with an exaggerated scream, the same way profane insults were sometimes exchanged on fruitless Lurp missions in the middle of the night.

"Did you get a make on them?" Stryker asked the men all around Schultz. "Any of them?"

"Civvies, sarge." A private with calm fingers wrapped around his M-16 but horror in his unblinking eyes spoke soft and quickly. "They were all wearing civvies!"

"But did you *recognize* any of—" The question, had Stryker been allowed to complete it, would not have come across as unusual. Not in Saigon, where the MPs dealt more with well-known terrorist cell leaders than anonymous NVA faces on strangers in the bush. But Schultz cut him off.

"I got a pretty good eyeball of them after they stacked it up back there," he said. He paused to emphasize his point, and looked calmly into Stryker's eyes as a lull developed in the shooting. "And none of those faces out there," he said motioning toward the top of the dike without letting his rifle muzzle actually clear it, "are in my files back at the International, Mark."

Stryker, his weapon's sling across his left shoulder while the rifle itself rested against his right hip, horizontal to the ground, slowly rose his eyes to the top of the dike, careful to keep the top of his head below the tangle of glasses matted along its edge. He immediately spotted activity in two places. Neither movements were made by MPs.

Ignoring his M-16, he drew his pistol, flipped off the safety with his thumb, then drew down on one of the guerillas. Careful to keep the front sight about five feet off the ground, he took in a deep breath, held it, and gently squeezed in the trigger.

As the discharge bucked the pistol up an inch or two and sent the slide back to chamber another round, Stryker was already pulling the trigger again.

The second hollow point caught the Vietnamese in the forehead, even before the first had completely doubled him over, and like a rag doll punched in the belly then slapped in the chops, he was catapulted off his feet, backwards, his brains monkey food; a haven for the marsh leeches, memories spread across the rotting floor of the moving jungle, sliced apart by the razor-sharp reeds shimmering like a restless green ocean between the rising trunks of massive tamarind trees. All these thoughts, all these visions raced through Stryker's mind, seemingly swept into an emotional frenzy yet dismissed as his gunhand shifted to the right and he, firing four rounds this time, took out another Vietnamese, sending his blood splashing along on the wind. "And that leaves one." Stryker looked down at the spec4 with the faded sergeant chevrons. Now he could vaguely remember the man from somewhere, and as they locked eyes, both men grinned. A Death's Head grin.

Though they were not smiling about the same thing.

Imagining the three MPs a hundred yards away even then sneaking up behind the lone survivor on the other side of the dike, Stryker said to Schultz, "I think you gentlemen can handle it from here on out." He flipped the safety back on his .45, popped out the magazine with one round remaining in it, and inserted a fresh clip. Holstering the weapon then, he sprung to his feet, whirling away from the dike.

"Where the hell you going, Stryk?" Raunchy Raul asked, startled, and almost rose to his feet, but caught himself before his head cleared the top of the dike.

Where Stryker had disappeared through the elephant grass, only a swirl of mist remained.

Mark Stryker checked the compass again while still on the run through the tall reeds, altered his course slightly, then increased his speed. But even though he was almost at a sprint, his boots made little noise, and he chose his path through the vegetation so smoothly that he failed to encounter any obstructions.

Less than a minute after leaving Schultz and the others, he ran past the spot where he and the three rooks had spotted the Chicom rocket roaring past overhead like a small locomotive. Stryker had no idea what he'd find as he raced for the spot where the projectile had surely been launched from: the same area from which a sudden explosion had mingled with the applause of thunder.

He felt no apprehension, no fear. He was back in the jungle. On foot, running across the forest floor, his boots a mere extension of his soles, the feeling of the earth beneath him vibrating through every fiber of his being. Stryker was back in his domain: the wild. Where he had felt at home since his youth, long before they had put him through the special forces training, trying to break him, along with the others: The ninety-seven fabled to fail. But how could you master a jungle expert? How could you conquer the spirit of a forest phantom, totally at home in the night mist, comfortable in the cold—or his healthiest in the heat?

As he zigzagged through the mangroves, pitting his wilderness skills against the surprises of the unknown, Stryker's mind took in everything he approached, yet along the sides of that mind's eye he saw a bar scene where his buddies from the A Team in Pleiku, snockered on *ba-muoi-ba*, sat around a table stacked high with Death-From-Above playing cards, discussing a soldier's coveted right to choose the time, place, and manner of his death. And they had all agreed a jungle firefight was the place to give one's all in total flame-out, passing into that warrior's never-never land in style, tracers flying ahead of your ghost, announcing your spectacular departure and, at the same time, grand entrance on another plane—another combat zone.

Grinning with job satisfaction, Stryker held his left hand out as thorn bushes slapped at his face, leaving small scratches that bled, streaked his whiskers, then burned from the mixture of rainwater and salty sweat. His right hand held out the .45, an extension of his arm. He did not even think about the rifle swinging against his side, for Stryker's aim was as legendary as Jack Flak's. He could knock down a seven-inch-square wood block at fifty meters with all eight rounds of a fully loaded pistol, using a weapon for which the maximum effective range was rated as twenty-five meters.

Here in the jungle, Stryker was an animal, not an MP. His senses adapted like a wild creature's, and he used them all: testing the air, feeling the ground, trusting his instincts more than his training, though in tight spots he always fell back on that training to survive.

An acrid aroma assaulted Stryker's nostrils suddenly. The heat of the afternoon, mingling with the rain, produced thick mist that rose nearly to his shoulders in spots, and the greenery all around gave it a turquoise tint that shifted about on all sides, as if in a surrealistic haze. The smoke drifting along on the mist was barely noticeable.

And then he smelled death.

The odor that accompanies much bloodletting. The smell that is flesh charred black, curling up, growing tough and tight, despite the sheets of rain that kept the ground soggy, growing, alive, and wild.

As if he had been here before—as though he knew every inch of this dark stretch of jungled plantation, Stryker found himself suddenly slowing, pausing at a wall of dense foliage that sprang up between one row of rubber trees. His hands cautiously drew back the vines, revealing a blackened circle of ground where no trees grew. Where a guerilla rocket team had set up their launch planks, only to have their second projectile, perhaps damaged by the intense downpour, explode upon ignition.

Six Vietnamese lay dead, scattered around the smoldering bamboo pad, horribly twisted and mutilated by the exploding rocket. Stryker doubted these people were in any way connected with the men his MPs had chased down into this plantation from the vicinity of the International. But such a stroke of luck: an actual communist rocket team, permanently detained on the spot. It was like searching for trilobites in an ancient, dry seabed, only to discover a perfectly preserved allosaur, revealed by a mudslide.

Stryker's eyes surveyed the clearing like the paleontologist, who would carefully plot out his excavation of dinosaur bones, except that the big MP sergeant was schooled in survival and not science: He did not poke and prod about the outcropping of rocks. He remained silent and unmoving behind the wall of greenery, scanning each individual body until he was confident no survivors awaited him out in the clearing.

His ears listened for any hostile warning noises, but the only sound was shouts in the forest he had just left: The last fugitive from the overturned jeep was being coaxed into surrender.

Finally satisfied he could safely proceed with a closer inspection of the carnage, Stryker slowly advanced into the clearing, allowing several seconds for each boot to move along on the rotting vegetation underfoot. Then, moments after he left the cover of the treeline, his nostrils picked up the offensive odor of wild power, restrained yet tensing to attack, mere feet away, intruding on his territory—and Stryker on its.

Suddenly the hand of one of the corpses flew up ten yards away, and Stryker shot out in reply to the almost comical waving gesture from the dead. Three rapidly fired rounds tore the hand off at the wrist and flung it back into the trees gnarled at the edge of the clearing.

An angry roar sliced at the air like a dull knife tearing through wrapping paper, and the tiger that had been trying to rip the dead soldier's arm off at the shoulder leaped out from behind the cover of patchy reeds and bounded towards Stryker.

In the small amount of time he was allowed to react, the MP sergeant brought the front pistol sights to bear down on the running tiger, but the snarling animal was too quick. Four carefully placed slugs only kicked up dirt and rotten leaves, and in the fraction of a second the beast was hurtling through the air and upon him.

Its huge paws slammed into his chest, and as the tiger tried to lock its jaws across his throat, they both tumbled to the ground and rolled away in opposite directions. His pistol knocked from his hands, Stryker instinctively reached for the rifle against his side—*but the weapon was also gone*!

His eyes swept over the ground frantically and finally came to rest on the flash of silver metal—the M-16, ironically, had come to rest between the paws of the huge cat. The animal now stood unmoving, except for its heaving chest, sucking in the hot, sticky air of the jungle. Jaws apart slightly, saliva drooled from between the gleaming lower teeth as it locked eyes with Stryker, hesitating, playing his game, allowing him the first move. His last try at escape. Like a dog that had chased him repeatedly across some backyard yet refused to bite, this animal's sparkling eyes were laughing at him, daring him to see if he could get away.

Stryker used the slight recess between rounds to size up his opponent. Though the tiger was not yet an adult and seemed more like an overgrown, playful cub, he knew he was no match for it, one-on-one. He flashed back to those evenings outside Pleiku, atop his lonely hilltop, scanning the fields with his sniper scope, searching for Cong, yet often spending hours tracking the tigers through the night bush with the starlight scope—a device that enabled one to virtually see in the dark by amplifying all available starlight and transposing it across a small green screen in front of the hunter's eye. Back then, *those* tigers had prowled about playfully, too, seemingly smiling as they glanced at each other while on the prowl for game. Yet let some unsuspecting deer or water buffalo venture in front of them, and those smiles became cold grins as flashing teeth sliced into jugulars, freeing yet another life from the Asian jungle.

The seconds quickly merged into a score of heartbeats, then Stryker made his move. Rubbing the tiger claw necklace around his neck for luck he felt was running more alongside the cat across from him, he bolted for the nearest tree, letting loose a savage war cry.

Momentarily startled by the barking scream, the tiger ducked to one side out of instinct, as if dodging the hostile sound, then bounded in pursuit of the big human, roaring itself now.

Stryker calculated the rapidly dwindling distance between himself and the nearest rubber tree, then fell into an awkward long jumper's rhythm and threw himself airborne while still fifteen feet away from the slender trunk. His judgment was accurate, though, and his right boot landed across the top of the sap bucket pegged to the bark, a couple feet above the ground. Pumping his leg muscles like giant springs, he skimmed skyward, feeling the bark tear at his hands and uniform. The rainfall seemed to increase, striking his face like the silver hands of angry jungle spirits, pushing him back down.

The tiger roared again as it, too, leaped up into the tree, swiping at his buttocks with the extended claws from one front paw.

The swinging act took the animal's hindquarters out from under it, and she tumbled back to the ground, landing not like a cat on her feet but painfully across her back.

Rolling to her feet and angry now, the tiger leaned up against the tree, jaws open as she stared up at him, hind legs still on the ground lazily but front paws reaching up to him again.

Stryker skimmed up another dozen feet, well aware his rump had sustained five deep gashes that were now dripping blood down onto the tiger's golden face. The animal licked her chops and continued to stare up at him, growing impatient as it slowly moved around the slick trunk, awkward on only its hind legs. Stryker reached for the pak-set on his belt, started to lose his balance on the rain-slick trunk, and lost the radio as he struggled to regain his hold on the smooth bark. The PR fell directly onto the tiger's snout, bounced off and split in half on the ground between its paws. The big cat growled up at him again, its anger fueled further. A vibrant roar filled the wet, humid air.

Stryker knew he was now out of communication with his men. They would eventually come searching for him, but he was not sure how long he could maintain hold of the slippery bark. Fire ants were already stinging the moist wedges between his fingers. A terrible thought struck him just then: Might he bleed to death from the buttocks wounds? He would turn in his grave if they wrote on his tombstone anything about these embarrassing circumstances of his death: The Notorious Mark Stryker, Ex-Green Beret, Killed By A Cub Tigress That Dealt A Fatal Blow To His Behind! Gary Richards would love that. And it would make Raunchy Raul, the roly-poly policeman's day! He stared down into the tiger's eyes. Blood no longer trickled onto her coat of fur. Perhaps the wound was not that serious after all. Never mind that his buttocks and thighs were starting to tingle—like they were falling asleep from loss of blood. He smiled, knowing that was not how death from bleeding felt when it set in.

The tiger seemed to smile back up at Stryker, and in its savage expression, he saw Kim's face, screaming at him about temple curses and jungle justice. But he would not die this way! Perhaps in a firefight, with bullets flying, tracers glowing, discharges singing their mournful song, but not at the paws of a displaced rubber plantation cat!

"Go home!" he yelled down at her, almost comically. The tiger yawned back up at him, then slowly pawed at the steaming air between them. "Go home, woman! *Di di mau*! This is Saigon, damnit! You're out of your territory." Then, under his breath: "Not supposed to be any fuckin' felines even *this* close to the outskirts of town."

They stared at each other for the next five minutes, man and beast. Silent, both playing their own individual mind games. The tiger had probably stared countless smaller animals straight into heart attacks before. No doubt she felt she could accomplish that trick here again today. Stryker played his Fearless Frank game, trying to delve deep into the animal's mind through its eyes, jerking suddenly at the strings of fear that lurked inside every creature, regardless of the legend behind it—even the king of the jungle. Hell, it had always worked on barking dog calls in the past. But the tigress only yawned again.

Eventually, it cautiously lowered itself into the prone position, content to sleepily gaze up at its prey, waiting. Patiently waiting.

Stryker checked his watch again. Thirty minutes had slowly passed. Where were his men? His ears twitched slightly, catching a distant sound: a jeep motor turning over, then the vehicle being driven away. He hoped it was only some shoeshine boy, stealing the unit.

The tiger was now resting its chops across its front legs, body unmoving but eyes tilted upward, following Stryker's every move. Now and then, one paw would swat the disabled portable radio back and forth out of boredom, intrigued perhaps by the weak bursts of static.

Stryker knew he had to make his move soon, before he was too weak from clinging to the trunk to fight once back on the ground. He could only hold on another ten minutes anyway, tops—the downpour was just too intense. It was seemingly batting him down. Trying to keep the element of surprise on his side, he slowly ran one hand down to his calf, increasing the pressure of his other arm around the tree trunk. He allowed himself a full minute to unsnap the velcro sheath and slide free the long, black commando knife. Tarzan would have been proud, he decided, preparing to make his move. This was the only way out. He thought about chunks of his meat floating about in the bowels of the animal an hour from now. Maybe I *will* win this one! He grinned inwardly. I'll kill the bitch with indigestion!

Stryker slowly drew the blade back, preparing to drop down onto the tiger's back. This is a barfight. I'm getting the biggest, baddest drunk into a headlock from behind. He mapped strategy in his mind. Then I'm leaping into ambush. He drew the knife back farther, tensing his bicep. I'll plunge the blade down through her throat until it pierces the heart. It's my only chance—

"*Dung lai*!" a feminine voice screamed up at him from within the treeline. "Put back, or you die sooner than you thought, GI Joe!"

Stryker's eyes narrowed as he ignored the tiger now and searched for the owner of the businesslike voice. The cat itself casually twisted its enormous head around over its back, apparently familiar with the voice, then gazed back up at Stryker, smiling with its gleaming fangs again as it panted against the smothering heat of the storm. "I'm dead serious, *mista*!" the voice ordered. He swallowed hard, bewildered. One thing was certain: He was not growing delirious from loss of blood.

"Show yourself!" he challenged.

A soft laugh filtered out through the forest and drifted up to him. Then there came a slight ruffling of leaves, and a young Vietnamese woman cautiously appeared inside the edge of the treeline. The tiger glanced back over its shoulder at her, wagged its thick tail in apparent recognition for a few seconds, then let its massive head return to face the tree harboring the helpless MP. It dropped its heavy snout to inspect the radio again, swatted the gray plastic with a lazy paw, then resumed staring up at Stryker.

"Climb down," the woman in the black calico trousers and khaki blouse ordered. A new, smoothly polished AK-47 Assault rifle was cradled in her arms like a favorite son, the barrel pointed up at the American. Stryker did not immediately respond. His eyes slowly inspected her from head to foot, then glanced beyond her to the treeline, but she appeared to be alone. Except for her tiger friend. "Climb down," she repeated. "Go for weapon, and today you meet Buddha."

He guessed her age to be mid-twenties at first. Her eyes had a mature sparkle, or lack of sparkle in them—a sophistication—but as he started down the tree and grew closer to her, he found she was much younger. Perhaps seventeen, eighteen at most. Her hair, normally long, jet-black and shiny as strands of fine silk, was now tied neatly back in braided pigtails. He could tell from the way she held her rifle, and her confident stance, that her figure was firmer than most women he had encountered in Asia. The words *dedicated swimmer's body*, came to mind, but he didn't know why. Perhaps it had something to do with Lai. She loved to picnic down by the Dak Ba, later swimming in the river at night, bathed by moonlight, protected by his watchful glance from the flowered banks.

"She will not harm you." The woman motioned toward her tiger with the rifle barrel, producing a disarming smile as Stryker lightly dropped his boots back onto earth. "Unless I command her to."

The tiger produced a loud, satisfied roar, as if to confirm the remark.

"What is it you—" Stryker started to ask, but the woman waved his question aside with a violent jerk of her AK, silencing him.

"*I* will ask the questions!" she informed him, losing her smile as she stepped away from the treeline and slowly approached him. "What are you doing on our land?"

"*Your* land?" Stryker produced his best puzzled look. "You are French, miss? I was under the impression this plantation—all these plantations south of Saigon clear to Long Thanh belong to the French. I believe this one in particular is owned by my old friend Servonnat, who lives up in—"

"Silence!" she snapped, halting about thirty feet away from him. The tiger, now midway between them, was concentrating on Stryker's boots. They had maintained their spitshine throughout the whole ordeal thus far. It cocked its head from side to side each time the MP sergeant moved, and the gleam shifted about on the smooth toes.

"I was just trying to answer your—"

"This is Vietnam, GI Joe." Her smile returned, but now it was a sardonic grin. "Not France. Not United States." Her deep accent excited him—*aroused him*, even at the point of a gun. "You Americans have a lot to learn about my country."

Stryker searched her casual uniform for any sign of allegiance, but he could find none. "You are a communist?" he finally asked, suddenly feeling a presence growing nearer them in the jungle.

The emotion mirrored in her eyes sent a shiver up Stryker's spine as she hesitated, then slowly said, "I—am—a—"

"Yes?" He carefully stepped around the tiger at the base of the tree trunk.

"A—nationalist. Not that it is any of your business." She shifted her feet about so that only her side was presented to him should he try a surprise offensive move amidst all the talk.

"You are going to kill me?" Stryker asked matter-of-factly.

"But of course," she replied just as coldly, raising the AK-47 to her shoulder.

At the same instant, several M-16 charging handles sounded behind her in the treeline as bolts slammed forward onto live rounds. "*Dau hang*!" A rough voice exploded from the greenery, above the sound of rain falling on the canopy of leaves overhead. "Drop the weapon, honey, or you'll never see sixteen candles!"

A mixed look of both disappointment and terror shot across the woman's expression as indecision wracked her mind against the instincts of survival. Finally, she lowered the weapon, and three MPs emerged from the treeline and jerked it from her hands. She locked eyes with Stryker, smiled in resignation, and gave him a well-I-tried downcast look. The tiger sluggishly rose to its feet, but she launched a torrent of angry Vietnamese at it. The animal ceased looking hungrily from man to man and eventually lay back down on the wet ground and resumed pushing the pak-set around with a padded paw.

Four more military policemen appeared just inside the treeline, and two of them automatically split apart and moved to either side of the uncaring tiger, careful to keep their rifle barrels aimed at the big cat's head. "What is your name?" Stryker asked the woman as he walked a few paces closer to her and bent over, retrieving his pistol from the tall grass at her sandaled feet. He slid an o.d. green handkerchief from a thigh pocket and pressed it against his wound—the claw cuts had stopped bleeding and weren't so serious after all.

She stared at him in silence for a few seconds, searching his eyes for hidden intentions, then shrugged her shoulders and placed her hands on sturdy hips. "*Low-ann*." She stretched the single word out until it came across more like a love potion than just a simple name. Stryker stepped back as he checked his pistol for mud or obstructions. And he smiled across the reeds at her, impressed with her cleverness, but he would not fall under the spell of another Vietnamese woman, even this woman-child. He already had enough temple curses to worry about.

"Just one name is all you have?" A challenge danced in the depth of his eyes.

The woman remained silent for a moment, then said, "And now it is *you* that must kill *me*."

Stryker let his gaze fall slowly from the woman's almond eyes to her sensuous figure, its wildness enhanced by the web belt draped across her hips. He took his time preparing his reply. This jungle bunny deserved special words.

"Ah—" Cob Carmosino appeared at the treeline,

trailing behind another squad of MPs emerging from the rain forest. "What have we got here—another Dragon Lady?"

"What'd she try and do, Stryker?" Raunchy Raul staggered out of the bush behind his fellow buck sergeant. "Waste you with the AK over there?"

"Actually," Stryker started to say and scratched the slight stubble on his chin as he stared into her eyes again, contemplating something private between them, something they had shared in that short amount of time. He found her so beautiful, so appealing. *So much emotion exchanged through our eyes, yet we have never even touched*. "Actually, I guess she saved my life, in a manner of speaking." He laughed and gestured over to the tiger a few feet away. "Fang there had me treed a few minutes ago. Was sharpening its claws on the bark right there." Several heads turned to stare at the claw marks six feet above the ground. "But this Mekong Miss appeared out of nowhere to come to my rescue." He smiled at her again, and she smiled back, but then he remembered her saying she must save him only to kill him, and he turned to one of the privates. "Uke!" he growled. "Pat her down! Get me some ID."

Private first class Uhernik latched onto the woman's wrist as he slung his M-16 over a shoulder. A sheet of rain swept in over them, seemingly in protest, and as the wind howled, she slipped free. But instead of trying to flee, she merely folded her arms across her ample chest defiantly. The Pfc smiled over at Stryker. "It'll be my pleasure, sarge." He wrapped his arm around her waist and dragged her from the clearing toward the nearest rubber tree.

The tiger whirled its head around upon hearing her angry breathing, but she did not resist, and the animal let loose with an ear-splitting roar but did not get up. The two men with their rifles trained on the beast looked nervous as they shifted their boots around in the mud. "That thing's a *pet*?" Carmosino asked Stryker, resting his hand on his holstered automatic.

"Apparently so." Stryker frowned, no longer amused.

Uhernik now had the woman leaning against one of the trees as he searched her, beginning under the long, silky hair over her shoulders and working down.

"She's clean," he announced two minutes later, handing a national ID card over to Stryker.

He stared at the laminated identification for several seconds, shifting his eyes back and forth between the lifeless picture on the card and the woman standing a few feet away. "Nguyen Thuy Loan," he finally read her name aloud, suspiciously. He scratched his fingernail along the card again, comparing the likeness beneath the plastic with the dark complected girl in the khaki blouse. Her face was flawless. Stryker just knew she was a descendent of royal heritage. "You are from the Imperial City." He did not ask her—he told her.

"I am from Hue," she admitted. "But, for now, the jungle is my home." She glanced down at the tiger between them, then let her eyes take in the treetops all around. "The forest . . ." She waved a hand out slowly to encompass the trees. "or the city. It does not really matter. It is all Vietnam. It is all my country."

He waited for her to say *and not yours*, but she did not. "It is too bad you did not shoot me out of that tree while you had the chance." His face remained expressionless. He tried to picture himself in bed on top of her, but the vision would not come.

"Now I pay the price for my hesitation: Your men take me go to the monkey house." One of the MPs had already produced his handcuffs.

"Now you pay the price," he said but his words came out sad.

"But I spared you, Mr. Stryker." She focused on his nametag. "Because there is something special about you, my friend. You were not born to die on this spot this day."

"I'm flattered." He shifted about nervously, expecting the men behind him to chuckle or even applaud, but they remained strangely silent, mesmerized perhaps by her beauty also. "But you must be more careful in the future, my dear. Unlike that big cat of yours there, you only live twice."

"Or so it seems." She smiled, losing the fear in her eyes.

"Once for yourself—and one time for your dreams." They locked eyes again, and Stryker felt aroused like never before in his life.

"Take her away," Carmosino motioned to Uhernik to put the handcuffs on, but the woman pulled her hands free, standing her ground. She was not finished talking to Mark.

"I believe the earth is round," she told him softly, a lone tear sliding down her cheek as one of the MPs slapped a handcuff across her wrist. She ignored the sudden pain. "We'll see each other again if we're destined to." She pulled her eyes away from him, turning to face the opposite direction, submitting to the policemen on either side of her.

"Wait." Stryker wanted to tell them to forget the cuffs for once, but his voice was covered by a sudden thunderclap directly overhead. The heat blast knocked every man there to his knees as a brilliant spiderweb of light blinded them at the same time. The wind swirled wildly all around without warning, and there came a terrible crashing and splitting sound as several trees were struck by the bolt of lightning.

When he regained consciousness, moments later, Stryker was lying on his back between two fallen trees, the fierce sheets of rain still slapping his face. The air was thick with smoke, and the odor of electrical flames was everywhere. Beneath the branches of one of the trees, two sets of boots protruded: Schultz's and Uhernik's.

Stryker glanced around quickly, ignoring the migraine that set to drilling at his temples with the sudden movement, but Nguyen Thuy Loan and her pet tiger were gone, memories on the mist.

9. Some Men Welcome Their Nightmares

Breathing hard, sweat rolling down his face and chest, Mark Stryker sat bolt upright in his bed, suddenly terrified of the darkness in the hotel room. Yet almost magically, the clouds smothering the city broke apart outside his balcony window, and moonlight filtered in through the bamboo curtain, drenching the teakwood floor, the Buddha statue, and all the joss sticks hanging from the wall altar, in liquid silver. When he realized he was safely on the third floor of the Miramar Hotel on Tu Do Street and not along the banks of the Dak Bo, outside Pleiku, his heart slowed, and he sighed deeply, letting himself lean back against the plush pillows Kim had left behind.

He couldn't understand his dreams lately, since she had gone. Since all his women had slowly, methodically disappeared from his life.

He used to anticipate the nightmares. Sometimes it was the weather: wind rustling through the balcony beads at dusk, or a storm brewing on the horizon—a sudden change in the normally constant humidity. Other times it was the food they dined on at the

Caravelle. Clams often brought them on, or so he believed. And mix one platter of fishheads with a six-pack of "thirty-three" beer, you were guaranteed eight hours of grief. After that much booze, the *tom kho* and *ca thu* began looking like eyesockets of the decapitated Cong his A Team had ambushed outside Duc Co so long ago.

But he welcomed those nightmares—the ones where he felt so helpless. Where his sidearm never worked, where his M-16 always malfunctioned. Where he couldn't run worth a damn, and when he punched out the enemy they only laughed—his fist always turned to jelly—there was never any strength, or force, behind the blow. And damned Charlie Cong always grinned back at him, unscathed, preparing to leap out at him in retaliation. He welcomed all that grief on the dinky-dau level of never-never land, because, in the end, when things looked real bad and he just knew he was about to kiss Mr. Death on the lips, she appeared to save him. Lai. Love that sustained. Her eyes alone, or the memory of them, was a spiritual force that kept him from claiming that privilege afforded all warriors—that right to choose the place and the time and the circumstances of their death.

Lai always saved him in those nightmares. Sometimes she was naked, sometimes clothed only in heavenly white silk that hugged her curves, arousing him even more. When she appeared, Mr. Death vanished. With the mere wave of her slender hands, everything threatening disappeared. The black of night melted into pre-dawn pink, and he always fell into her arms, secure in a soldier's heaven. Even back when they shared that hut-on-stilts in Pleiku, before he had left the Green Berets and moved to Saigon, he had languished in the aftermath of the nightmares, knowing that when he woke, she would be draped across his chest, trying to meet him in her own dreams, but she would not be the same Lai he had left behind in his mind. Stryker realized the woman who appeared to save him was a combination of every Asian woman he had ever loved. And that, too, scared him.

He had heard the stories in Mimi's Bar, from the Third Field Hospital medics. The night-class shrinks. Bozos who swore they knew men on the psycho wards who had died in their dreams because reality offered them nothing and never-never land promised everything. The corpsmen, at least some of them, were convinced a soldier recovering from battlefield wounds (or love in a war zone) treaded on thin ice when he escaped the real world with pain killers the Vietnamese nurses were so freely cooperative about dispensing. Why return to the combat patrols when you could permanently escape the pain and the horror and the uncertainty of it all by simply jumping off that mental cliff into the depths of blackness, only to surprise all the bastards by suddenly taking flight, ascending up through the silver heavens to where only warriors and their women existed—no angels allowed.

But lately his nightmares had changed. Now he could easily escape his enemies. And, if he chose, skillfully circle back and destroy them all—*powerfully*. With his bare hands. That made them nightmares no longer.

Except that Lai, or whoever she was, had abandoned him. There were mornings, when he awoke, that he could not even remember her face. Or Kim's.

Soaked in sweat, he watched the moonbeams shift about on the balcony outside, playing with the clouds, and he tried to think of the woman's face.

The woman who had saved him from the tiger in the jungle. The woman who had locked eyes with him, delved into his soul, sifted through all his secrets, exchanged a million emotions with him—all without even touching.

Loan.

A muffled explosion sounded in the distance, miles away. He knew it was a VC rocket, launched randomly into the heart of the city. A lone, solitary missile. None would follow. Not this night. It was a terrorist act conceived by a clever group of nationalists. Keep the Saigonese waiting and wondering. Tense. Nervous. At least until three or four in the morning. Then shoot one at 'em. Just one. Knock down a tenement here or a hotel there. Then fade into the darkness. Until tomorrow night.

Stryker wondered how many people had just died—their spirits at that very moment escaping on the warm evening breeze. Would they glide in this direction? He hoped they headed north. Toward Hanoi.

He wondered how many young couples—how many *lovers* had just perished. Yet even in such a blinding, searing explosion, how could they dread such a fate? If one had to die, why not in the arms of your woman, beneath a slowly twirling Casablanca fan, flares sizzling past outside your window, illuminating the edge of the most intense city in the world, soft music drifting along on the warm, wet air from the all-night rooftop cafe across the alley, while the two of you meet in your dreams to make love all over again?

The sweat rolling down off his brow began to sting his eyes, and Stryker wiped them with the back of his hand and forced his legs over the edge of the bed. He walked over to the balcony and stepped outside. A light drizzle still fell across Saigon, but nothing like earlier that evening, or in the afternoon. Several dozen blocks away, flames danced along the skyline as a housing project in Cholon burned to the ground. Police and fire sirens were beginning their slow, mournful midnight cry.

In the street below, two MPs from Bravo Company walked past on their beat, .45s holstered but nightsticks in their hand. They had seen him first, had recognized him from way off, and were staring up at him now even as they walked along. Both privates were grinning. They probably thought he was out for some fresh air after getting his rocks off for the fourth time tonight, he decided. Stryker returned their wave, then left the balcony and sat back down on the bed. If only the two cocky bucks down there really knew how alone he actually was right now. He'd give practically anything to have a woman beside him just then. *Any woman.* Stryker reached for the phone, intending to give Chay downstairs a call. The trusty porter would come up with someone. Some cherry-girl who didn't speak English and would therefore listen attentively to his sad, sob story while she massaged his pain away and walked on his back till he fell asleep again. But he released the receiver without picking it up, changing his mind.

He concentrated on the woman's face. The girl who had escaped them in the jungle only that afternoon. The girl with the tiger. Ann. Or Nguyen Thuy Loan, or whoever she was. It didn't really matter. *I believe the earth is round. We'll see each other again if we're destined to.*

He tried to remember the flawless, amber complexion, the disarming smile, the long, black, shining hair, cut straight across the bottom. But all he could see was the tiger, fangs gleaming as it smiled up at him, separating them.

Stryker rose from the bed again and walked over to the dresser. He lit a candle and stared at his reflection in the mirror, but all he saw was a ghost. Death mist, wavering in the glass and dim light like midday heat over blacktop. *Le Thai Mai*. Rodgers's woman.

The lady in the tiger.

He thought about them—whether they had actually met again in never-never land. He doubted fate could be so kind. Even Rodgers had questioned that, should she wait for him, how someone so innocent could still love and embrace the monster he had become.

Stryker turned away from the mirror. The image would not fade away this time when he blinked his eyes, the way it always had in the past.

He lay down on the bed and stared up at the map tacked to the ceiling. It had been folded and reopened so many times that the creases were splitting apart. The different precincts of Saigon were now held together by butterfly bandages and wisps of Kim's thread. Blue stars marked spots where he had been forced to kill men. Gold stars indicated scenes of felony arrests he had survived.

Some mornings he'd wake up to find another star had separated itself from his beloved map and fluttered down onto the bedsheets. It always seemed to be a blue star. Perhaps the map was trying to tell him something. Maybe his time in the Orient was up, his days in Asia numbered.

He concentrated on the red stars, which outnumbered the others combined. He had told Kim they indicated homicide scenes, but they really marked bungalows where he had made love to other women while on duty, away from her side.

Other women, Vietnamese, were his weakness.

His eyes fell to the far wall again and focused on the black-and-white poster beside the bureau, where Lai's portrait had hung before Kim destroyed it. The poster showed a woman in the traditional *ao dai*, wearing a straw conical hat and highheels, strolling down a boulevard, alone. The picture always inspired Stryker. It was all that symbolized Saigon for him, and had been taken by a buddy of his with the Thirty-fifth Combat Engineers up in Binh Dinh Province, Bill Tobin. He tried to imagine where the woman in the photograph was now—in whose arms. He found himself hoping she had just been killed by the rocket that fell in Cholon.

Suddenly angry with himself, Stryker picked up one of the Buffy elephant statues beside the bed and tossed it at the dresser. Amid crashing plaster, the candle disappeared, snatching the dim flickering light away with it. But his ghosts remained to taunt him.

He closed his eyes tightly, grasping the tiger claw necklace around his neck, and saw the jungle clearing earlier that day, when a bolt of lightning had saved Ann from a jail cell and buried Schultz and Uhernik beneath a rubber tree.

Appropriate. He shifted into an attitude adjustment. *Nasty Nick and Raunchy Raul.* A smile crept across his lips. *Floored by a fucking rubber tree.*

Both MPs, private and sergeant, had survived with only painful scratches and bruised egos. Nearly every man at the scene had been knocked out by the thunderclap directly overhead. He couldn't understand how the woman had escaped when she was standing in the midst of them all, but he was intent on dwelling on the mystery as little as possible: Stryker had given up trying to understand what transpired in the heart of the jungle long ago. Man was not made to understand the rain forest. He could travel through it, survive in it, fight and die under its triple canopy. But only the animals *understood* the jungle.

At least they had her ID card. He had a couple canhsats checking up on it now.

The latest report from the hospital was the Spec4 Parlin Fox the third would survive the additional injuries he had sustained in the surprise mortar attack on the memorial ceremony. Stryker stopped breathing when he thought about the kid. How much more was one soldier expected to endure during his Tour 365?

Jack Flak was still on the active duty roster. He had taken his dead wife's body back to Dinh Tuong Province, down in the Delta, stating he would return in time for tomorrow's guardmount. Flak had refused emergency leave-of-absence. Stryker knew he was having other personal problems: His parents had died in a car accident two months earlier, and the bank was after their house.

Investigators at the scene of the rocket launchpad explosion had already concluded the dead guerillas were in no way connected with the attack on Military Police Headquarters. Their missile had landed between Gia Dinh and Tan Son Nhut, miles from the International Hotel. Stryker's boys had just gotten lucky when they stumbled across the rubber plantation clearing. Nobody told the CID agents about the woman and her tiger. It was too embarrassing. And they probably wouldn't have believed any of it anyway. Lightning bopping Raunchy Raul up side the head with a rubber tree was incredible enough as it was.

The terrorist Carmosino's squad had captured after Stryker took out two of the Vietnamese sprinting away from the overturned jeep refused to talk, but a check with the VNP revealed he was a former canh-sat, fired from the police force in Saigon ten weeks earlier for participating in an extortion racket. At this point, none of the dead men appeared to be white mice, however. Jon Toi, Stryker's buddy at VNP Headquarters downtown, suspected they were mercenaries wanted for highway robberies up north, in Bien Hoa, but he was awaiting fingerprint checks. The green jeep was indeed a former police jeep, recently liberated from the VNP motorpool by a thief within the department.

Stryker felt it was all coming together, somehow, yet at the same time he realized the case was so complex the investigation could go on for months. He had the time, he decided. If Lady-Saigon would only grant him a reprieve. He stared out the window again, at the temple rising in the hot mist. *You're all I've got, baby*.

A small brown lizard, clinging upside down to a corner of the ceiling, seemed to answer his thoughts when it began the chirping mating call that literally sounded more like the words, *fuck you*! than anything else. Two other lizards scampered, also upside down, across the ceiling overhead to join the first. They were the source of countless jokes from the men.

Outside, the rain began to increase again, until the sheets pounding the fiberglass covering over the balcony began sounding like an angry child's drumrolls.

Was this storm ever going to move on? The choppers were still grounded. Even the Phantoms remained on the ground. (Now *that* was a change: lying awake at four in the morning, and no jets racing their engines at Tan Son Nhut.) In two hours he'd be giving a guard-mount to brief fifty men chosen to run another payroll convoy north to Bien Hoa. This time they had to make it. The soldiers there were getting restless. And understandably so: Next to mail, that monthly paycheck, tiny as it might be, was a big morale booster. Without scrip, there was little motivation to lace up one's jungle boots, let alone engage the Cong in hand-to-hand.

Stryker thought about his little walk through the rain that evening, after reviewing the piles of reports Schultz's men had left on his desk. (Schultz himself had gone home early. Stryker couldn't blame him. A rubber tree across the cranium would do that to you.) He had strolled past the apartment complex on Phan Dinh Phung, where Johnny Powers had been killed a few months earlier. Powers's Vietnamese wife and little daughter had also been gunned down by two communist agents when the family stumbled into the middle of a foot chase involving Stryker and two of his rooks. Tiny Ling had died instantly on the spot, but they had rushed Johnny's wife, Wann, to Third Field, and she had survived.

Stryker still took flowers to her now and then, though the visits were like spending an hour with a zombie. Wann just stared out the window, nodding now and then, but never smiling. He wondered what she was seeing in the street outside—if the ghosts of her family remained on earth to keep her company until she withered away to join them. The men had chipped

in to rent her a small apartment on Bui Vien. It wa
only a few blocks from MP Headquarters on Tra
Hung Dao, and as the weeks progressed, he wondere
if perhaps that had been a bad idea. All those patro
jeeps screaming by at all hours of the day and night.

On the other side of Precinct One another wa
widow lived. Though she had never really been mar
ried to Dave Schramm, Thuy had been his woman
and that was enough, as far as the men of the 716t
were concerned. Schramm had been killed by the V
while infiltrating an infantry unit up in the boonies:
cavalry platoon where several of the men were sus
pected of trying to frag their captain, a flamboyant offi
cer known notoriously as "Moast The Ghost.
Schramm had even put Thuy on his GI life insuranc
policy before his death, and though she had bee
known by the beat cops of Tu Do as a "girl of question
able virtue," Thuy now played the role of grieving wif
without protest, refusing to touch any of the money th
provost marshal had tried to present her with. She jus
sat by her window on Mac Dinh Chi, clasping the gol
coin David had left her, waiting for her man to retur
from the jungle.

Broox told Stryker she was pregnant with Schramm'
child, probably about four months along now. Th
men were informed at one of the briefings, and a collec
tion was taken up again. It was added to the twent
thousand the PM had set aside in a trust fund. For th
boy. Thuy would need help raising what all the me
knew would just have to be a son.

Stryker rubbed the bullet hole scar on his left earlob
as his thoughts shifted again, and he began thinkin
about Sindy. For the thousandth time he watched he

car, peppered with his own bullets, spin out of control and crash through the cemetery fence. When the trunk sprang up and he saw the little baggies of dope spilling their white gold onto the filthy street again, he was jerked from his memories by the phone ringing.

Stryker glanced at his watch, then let it ring five more times before reaching over to pick the receiver up—there were too many wrong numbers dialed across Saigon in the middle of the night.

"Yes?"

"Mark Stryker." It was the woman who had arranged to meet him at the Caravelle but had never shown up.

"Yes, this is Stryker." He felt the chill go down his spine again.

"Where were you the other morning?" she asked, irritation making her voice sharp as a jagged can top, being slowly opened with a rusty P-38.

"You know I was there." He was in no mood for games but also could not sleep. He might as well play along—he would see the sun rise faster.

"My crotch grows moist just listening to your voice, Mr. MP." Her tone changed slightly, though it still sounded threatening.

"Really." The word was soaked in sarcasm.

"My lips quiver at the thought of engulfing you—of making you feel like you've never felt befo—"

"How did you get this number?" He interrupted her, but she in turn cut him off.

"*Listen to me*!" she screamed. "If you want to know who is behind the ambush of your men in Bien Hoa, meet me in two hours on the terrace of the Continental."

Stryker did not immediately reply. His lips curled

back involuntarily: He hated the Continental. All those fucking foreign correspondents covering the war from a Saigon rooftop with a glass of bourbon in each hand.

"Did you hear what I just said?" She sounded impatient, suddenly worried.

Stryker tried to place her voice. She was definitely Vietnamese. Someone from his past, or at least someone he had met somewhere in one of his Saigon escapades. She was not any of the women he had been thinking about during the last few hours. And she was definitely not the woman who had saved him from the tiger earlier. He thought about coming right out and asking her, but somehow he knew she'd just hang up.

"Well?" she persisted. He waited for her to slam the receiver down on the other end of the line.

"I have to attend a guardmount in two hours," he finally revealed. "I have to give a briefing."

"Then you will not meet with me?" she sounded intensely disappointed.

"I would be wasting my time. I do not feel you would show up."

"I was unavoidably detained last time." She sounded apologetic now. He was impressed with her fluency. That alone should place her face for him, but he still couldn't do it. "This morning I will be there."

"I have a briefing to give," he repeated.

"Then you will not come?" Her voice went cold, sinister.

"No."

"Then it is your loss, *fool*!"

"I cannot make it."

"Very well." Her attitude changed again and she laughed before breaking the connection.

* * *

"Make a note of that, Stryker," Lt. Tony Slipka muttered as the two of them slowly walked behind the formation of young military policemen standing at the position of attention in front of their patrol jeeps behind the International. "I'm tired of seeing all the graffiti on the back of these helmets." The lieutenant raised his voice: "Did you hear that gentlemen? Dispense with the profanity, okay? Knock off the 'FTA' and other crap. You've got one week to clean up your acts, then—" He hesitated as he walked up behind Nilmes, his attention caught by something dangling from the private's web belt. "And what the hell is *that*, sergeant?" He reached over and grabbed an odd-looking contraption from Carl's nightstick holder, examined it for an unimpressed second, then handed it to the NCO standing beside him.

Stryker immediately recognized the *tonfa* hardwood fighting stick. Shaped somewhat like a billy club, a handle protruded out a fourth of the way down from the top of the shaft, enabling the martial artist to increase the thrust with which he swung the weapon at an opponent. In policework, it would come in especially handy when subduing violent resisters. "Aw, that's just one of them Japanese nightsticks, Lou. Lots of the guys are starting to—"

"None of my *guys* are going to start carrying them, *sergeant*. It's not—military issue, for Christ's sake."

Carl Nilmes, still sporting purple crescents under both lids from black eyes he had sustained in a record-breaking bar fight the week before, glanced back at Lieutenant Slipka. "The *tonfa* is much more practical than your regular nightstick, sir," he said confidently,

prepared to launch into a condensed critique of th
weapon.

"Eyes *front*, private!" Slipka snapped, leaning for
ward. "You're at the position of attention." Then, turn
ing to Stryker: "My ass is grass, Mark, if he ever bop
some old papa-san with this friggin' thing and we ge
our butts sued by the Viets."

"I understand, Lou." Stryker produced his most com
passionate expression as he stared at the brown stick
avoiding the lieutenant's eyes for fear of laughing ou
loud.

"It's just not—*uniform*."

"Right."

"Mark my words," Nilmes whispered over to the ma
beside him after the lieutenant confiscated the *tonfa* an
moved on. "Someday every fuckin' department back i
The World's gonna be issuing them honies as manda
tory equipment. Just wait and see, bro. When yo
snooze—you lose—"

"Submit a report on the matter," the man behind hi
muttered sarcastically, confident it would just be shit
canned like all the rest.

"I think I will." Nilmes grinned. "I just think I fuck
ing will, as a matter of fact. Wait and see, schmucks
Someday you're *all* gonna be carrying Ma*nilm*knock
right next to your .45 there!"

"We'll bank on it, Carl baby—we'll bank on it, fer
sures."

Lieutenant Slipka skidded to a halt in front of Pri
vate Steve Writter, his eyes glued to the stocky MP'
customized belt buckle. Made of pure gold, it sparkle
back up at the incensed officer. "Do you see that?" h
demanded of the sergeant beside him. "Do you se

what this clown's got inscribed in half-inch letters across that damn thing?" A couple men closeby snickered but quickly fell silent.

"Well, no, Lou." Stryker bent over slightly to get a better look at the huge buckle holding Writter's web belt in place. "I never really noticed."

"You know perfectly well what it says, Stryker! I told this clown to get a new buckle last week!" Slipka executed a sharp turn on his heels and moved on to the next man. "Make a note of it on your clipboard, Stryker. One more time and he gets written up!" Then, under his breath: "To think the man's out there representing the Seven-Sixteenth while he's wearing that abomination."

Stryker glanced over and winked at Writter and the private just nodded back with a *no-sweat* grin. One of the men in the rank behind him reached over and slapped Steve on the back, proud of him.

After Slipka and Stryker had advanced up to another row of cops, Writter's line fell into parade-rest, and the private with the thick black glasses reached down and polished the sparkling buckle that read: Gimme Head Til I'm Dead

"Get a haircut," came the repeated directive as row upon row was inspected.

"Assemble inside." Stryker finally announced the conclusion of the rare uniform inspection, to the relief of the men. "For the briefing."

Fifteen minutes later, he had completed the checklist that informed each man present which Assault tank he'd be riding north. "Any questions?"

"How much in greenbacks we transportin' up there to Bien Hoa, sarge?" a youthful voice asked.

"That's classified," Stryker muttered. "You all know what type of questions I was calling for."

"Bookoo bucks," an anonymous voice replied from the rear of the room.

Just then the doors to the briefing chamber swung open, and Sgt. Cob Carmosino, self-proclaimed, most handsome Italian in the battalion, sauntered in, cocky smile beaming across the dimly lit room.

"You're late." Stryker checked his wristwatch dramatically.

"Whatta ya mean I'm late?" Carmosino checked his own watch in reply, juicing up the Italian accent to the eager approval of the men. "I'm early, Stryker—I'm *always* early." Stryker frowned, folding his arms across his chest. "By the way, mellow-Mark speaking of being tardy, do you know the definition—*excuse me*—the *Italian* definition of copulate?"

Several snickers rose from every corner of the room in reply, but Stryker just cocked his head to the side, perplexed and prepared for the worst.

"It's when the police sergeant in Rome saunters in fifteen minutes late for a briefing, and the chief says, 'Cop-uh, you late!' "

The room fell dead silent with the punch line, and a paper airplane shot across from the cluster of Spec4's beside the burping watercooler, striking Carmosino on the bridge of the nose.

Still silent, the sergeant with the thick black mustache waded through the collage of chairs encircling the podium and found a seat. "I don't see that goofy Gary Richards or any of his Decoy douche-bags here," he said in a hurt tone.

Stryker did not explain that he had assigned

Richards's squad to stake out the Continental that morning. Just in case his mystery phone caller happened to show up. He instructed Gary to card every gorgeous raven-haired beauty that entered the premises alone. Somehow he just knew that was what the caller looked like.

As soon as Stryker saw that Carmosino was comfórtable in his seat, he dismissed the briefing, telling the men, "Hit the street, gentlemen. I'll see you in Bien Hoa."

After pounding his fist down onto the tabletop to reinforce his point, Saigon police captain Trinh Tri directed unwavering eyes at the man standing in front of him. "You fool!" he yelled. "We are on the verge of both capturing another payroll and slipping up an ambush that would mean death or life behind bars, and you have the gall to demand more money for this scrap of information?"

His cheek quivering now with tension, the slender man in front of Tri fought to keep his skinny arms from shaking. "It is not inconsequential," he replied in Vietnamese, "if it supplies you with the time and the date and the route of the next American payroll convoy."

Tri bit his lip and twisted his knuckles as he considered this. He was well aware this weasel of a snitch got his information from a corrupt American major at MACV. The army officer was, in turn, granted a free reign on blackmarket activities downtown, backed by under-the-table canh-sat protection. He knew he could easily trap the major himself and get the goods on him, thus eliminating the sniveling middle man who now stood before him. But no—it was better to have an intermediary in place, in the event his operation began to fall apart. That would increase Tri's chances of survival. Nobody wanted to lose their pension and retire to the bamboo cages of lizard island.

"You have the nerve to approach me about more money *after* I already have the required information to complete my mission?" Tri laughed. "You are a fool!"

"Unless you pay me the required sum, I will be forced to go to the authorities." The man forced the words out. "The *real* authorities, Captain Trinh."

Trinh had had enough. His eyes darted over to the two armed sentries guarding the entrance to his tiny thatched hut on the outskirts of Bien Hoa. "Take this bastard out and shoot him!" he directed.

Without hesitation, the mercenaries moved forward, but at that very same time the air was filled with the terrible noise of metal grating upon metal and steel clanking upon the earth. The ground beneath the hut began to shake, and the bamboo walls started vibrating. Clouds of dust rolled in through the opening behind the two stocky bodyguards.

And just as suddenly, the earthquakelike disturbance ceased, though a powerful rumbling sound remained directly outside the doorway.

As the dust cleared, Trinh Tri glanced about the floor. The man he had just ordered executed had slipped out in all the confusion.

Tri rushed toward the exit, but the gaping hole was suddenly filled with form of a giant Arvin, clad in flak jacket, camouflaged helmet, and bristling sidearms. "Ah—Colonel Ng." Trinh Tri staggered back a few steps, retreating from the tank commander's space.

"And what brings you to my neck of the woods?"

The huge Ng roared with laughter as he drew his pistol and pointed it directly at Tri's face. Five smaller soldiers had appeared behind him in the doorway, sporting M-60 machineguns. The giant weapons all but dwarfed the tiny Vietnamese. "What brings *me* to *your* neck of the woods?" He stomped forward and jammed the barrel of the .45 between Tri's wide eyes. "I am the tank commander for this military region!" he told Trinh. "This is a combat zone, my friend. You are far from Saigon. Regardless of what you and your ragtag team of carpetbaggers are up to, you must first answer to me." Ng pulled an empty sandbag from his web belt and dropped it in front of Tri. "To be allowed to even set foot in this area, you must first deposit an escrow account with the Bank of Ng." He chuckled, increasing pressure on the weapon against Tri's forehead. "To insure your honesty."

"But of course."

"Now!"

Feeling ridiculous, Trinh Tri searched his pockets, ignoring the bulging wallet totally. "But we have nothing yet." He feigned helplessness. "The sting has not yet gone down." His eyes pleaded with Ng for more time. In his gut, Trinh felt sick. He couldn't remember the last time he had been humbled in front of another crook.

Ng seemed to consider the situation. He smiled again, this time sincerely, it seemed, and holstered his pistol. "Very well, very well." He patted Tri on the back like a long-lost brother.

"Yes? Yes?" Tri also smiled, though he directed icy glares at his two bodyguards for failing to act. After all, they were only outnumbered three to one!

"I will give you forty-eight hours, runt. Forty-eight hours to fill that sandbag with silver, or your ass is grass."

Colonel Ng turned and rushed out of the hut. More slowly and cautiously, his men followed him back to their tanks. Then, in a swirl of dust and deafening noise, the metal monsters clanked and clattered off down the road.

Capt. Trinh Tri, hands on his hips in awe, stared at the half dozen tanks as they lumbered away, oblivious to the rain that had already washed out sections of the highway. He stared at the thunderheads gathering dark and ominous on the horizon, and wondered how many more tanks waited over the hill.

"Well fuck me," Trinh Tri muttered Mike Broox's favorite expression. The Saigon police captain had obviously paid off the wrong Armour officer. You just couldn't stay ahead of the mob, he decided. This lousy country was just overflowing with con men.

10. Burn Down the Night

Jack Flak hadn't smiled in days. Not since the surprise mortar attack on MP Headquarters. He hadn't slept much, either. Jack Flak had vowed he would not rest until the terrorists, be they hardcore NVA, elusive VC, or just rooftop sympathizers responsible for his wife's murder, were brought to justice.

He ran up, grabbed onto one of the handholds above the enormous tractor tires, and pulled himself up onto the rumbling V-100 Assault tank as it coasted out of the compound's main gate.

The endless sheets of rain made it hard to maintain his grip on the slippery hull of the cumbersome vehicle, but an MP manning the 50-cal latched onto an arm and pulled him up behind the dual Hog-60s straddling the turret windows.

"Gonna bag us some Cong today, brother!" Jack Flak said eagerly, still unsmiling. He turned a switch on the right side of the M-60 nearest him, raised the metal flapcover, then flipped down the thin feeder tray. The tray held the tracers steady so that the bolt could eat them up without misfiring. Flak gently slipped the first four bullets of a long belt beneath the cover, then slapped the Hog on the side proudly. "Yep, gonna bag us some Cong before the storm clears."

"No, no, no, no." Carl Nilmes shook his head from side to side in reply. "This is a simple payroll convoy, Mr. Showbusiness. Quick in and quick out. Drop off the MPC, pick up a couple signatures, then beat feet back to ole Saigontown. Eight and skate, my friend, eight and skate. No hostile contact on *this* GI's schedule!"

"We'll see." Flak stared out at the castlelike clouds massing black as night along the horizon. "We'll see."

A jeep ferrying Stryker, Brickmann, and Carmosino to the head of the eight tank convoy cruised up beside Flak's V-100 as it turned onto busy Tran Hung Dao. "I see you made it!" Stryker called out, pride in his smile. He had missed Flak at the guardmount but somehow knew the man would show up for the ride north.

"Let's get this show on the road!" Flak replied, still unsmiling, his features set grimly as he stared straight ahead.

Steve Writter was no dummy. He knew when a conversation had been abruptly terminated in so many words. Detached, grinning himself with the excitement of the mission, the private floored the accelerator, oblivious to the problems of the men around him, intent only on getting his super-sarges to the head of the convoy.

Stryker produced one of those melancholy smiles supervisors always fall victim to when they sadly start to worrying about the behavior of their men. But what was he to do? They were in the middle of a multi-million dollar convoy, using sophisticated equipment that probably cost twice as much! Flak's therapy would just have to wait.

Sergeant Carmosino felt his gut tingle as they fell in place ahead of the massive Assault tanks. Vietnamese atop motorscooters or crowded into three-wheeled cyclos swerved out of the way upon seeing all the flashing red lights. Even the V-100s had firetruck sirens mounted on their front bumpers, above the colorful Thor and Captain American murals, but thus far it had been a silent, Ten-40 run. Quiet, low-profile, except for the powerful motors propelling the monstrous, bobbing tanks down the narrow streets of downtown Saigon.

Carmosino locked eyes with the women on every street corner, the ladies of questionable virtue, girls who paused to watch the convoy roar past, straining to recognize the faces on board. Old boyfriends, perhaps—husbands they had split from. Men who had arrested them a dozen times, only to fall in love with them in the end. Carmosino wondered how many men aboard the tanks behind his jeep were weak enough to fall for their deceptive tricks. How many cherry-boys would fall under their spell. How many would fork over that precious ticket Stateside, only to lose them once again back in The World. And he wondered how many would resist, leaving Vietnam unscathed after their Tour 365 was up. How many, a decade later, or twenty years afterwards, would finally realize what the pain was really all about—why they had left their heart in Saigon.

He glanced over at Mark Stryker. The ex-Green Beret was also watching the women straddling the street corners. Searching for a face he recognized, perhaps? A monsoon memory from months long gone? *What the hell was the man always grinning about?*

Crazy Cob, all foolishness aside, could understand why Americans were held in awe by the sheer intensity of Saigon—the electricity in the air, the nonstop excitement underfoot—but he was puzzled by their enchantment with Vietnam's women. Carmosino found them cold, conniving. Evil. He wanted nothing to do with them, yet he realized that, secretly, he wanted to accompany Stryker and the boys downtown one night after day watch. Wanted them to show him Tu Do. Or Nguyen Hue, or Le Loi. Wanted them to fix him up with a woman who would walk across his back, casting her spell on him, bringing him, too, under Saigon's curse. He stared at two off-duty soldiers strolling off the main boulevard, down into a back alley, their women on their arms. One man glanced back at the MPs as the convoy rumbled past, and though he was not 95-Bravo, he gave Sergeant Cob the thumbs-up sign. Then he returned his attention to his woman, pecking her on the cheek, and the four of them disappeared between food stalls on the edge of a vast open-air cafe.

Why the thumbs-up? Carmosino wondered. Was it thanks for protecting the city while he and his woman enjoyed their short time together? Or was it guarded admiration of a job none of the other soldiers wanted? Carmosino wanted to jump out of the jeep and follow them—be a witness to the carefree evening they were obviously about to enjoy.

An underpowered motorcycle screamed past on the side of the jeep, carrying a white-shirted canh-sat. The policeman waved at the NCOs as he sputtered by, siren wailing. Then he accelerated ahead of the convoy, putting a half block between himself and the Americans.

"Well if it ain't good ole Toi," Stryker said, nodding over to Brickmann.

"Come to give us the royal escort." The Brick grinned, though his eyes narrowed, looking suspicious.

Jon Toi pulled up to the nearest intersection, hopped off his Honda-50, and halted all cross traffic, so that the convoy could pass through unhindered. (Not that any of the arrogant tank pilots would have yielded to a vehicle of Vietnamese persuasion.)

After the Assault tanks roared past, their eight-inch letters MILITARY POLICE emblazoned across the sides and red beacons twirling lazily atop the front fenders, Toi would race up to the next major intersection, repeating the practice, until Stryker and his men had reached the edge of the city.

"One hell of a decent copper," The Brick said after they made it through the northern sectors of Saigon without running over any pedestrians.

"Remind me to send a letter of appreciation to his honcho when we get back," Stryker replied. He could paste it between the gory glossies he had hanging throughout his spare room at the police family barracks, Stryker thought to himself.

At the intersection of Phan Thanh Gian and Highway 1, Toi waved good-bye to the men of the 716th, then waited for their dust to settle before returning to the heart of the city. Conflicting inner emotions made his face twitch slightly. He wanted to both accompany the Americans into the unknown and return to the arms of his living wife, back at the VNP housing project. Decisions. Decisions. He laughed at himself, concentrating on the whip antenna that jutted up from the last tank in the convoy as it rapidly disappeared over a line of rolling hills. Old Glory and a saffron RVN flag were tied to the top of the radio antenna. They seemed to be waving back at him. Then they faded over the horizon.

Toi wondered how many bullet holes they'd be sporting on the return trip back. He glanced down at the narrow wedding band on his finger and sighed.

Then he turned and started downhill, back into traffic. Halfway home he would stop and pick up some of the French bread rolls Nang loved so much, Toi decided. And he might even coast through Nguyen Hue and pick up an armful of flowers for his wife, Lan. It was about time tiny Diep got a new dress, too. Toi smiled as he merged in with heavy traffic and began thinking about his family.

It was times like this when he failed to notice the glaring looks of hostility from his countrymen all around him on the crowded street. And that made the time away from his woman go by much faster.

Stryker whirled the M-60, mounted on the bar in the middle of the jeep, around wildly, spraying the treeline with hot lead. Every fifth round was glowing green tracer that sizzled out through the drenching rainfall.

Writter, startled by seeing the Assault tank in front of him take a direct hit from an armor-piercing projectile, nevertheless managed to keep the jeep under control as he swerved around the smoldering debris. After the V-100 had been stopped dead in its tracks, all four tractor tires exploding after taking secondary blasts from two claymores, the metallic hull of the huge vehicle plopped down in the middle of the roadway as if the legs had been jerked out from under a wounded elephant.

The remaining seven tanks formed a protective laager around the first, and the three jeeps bringing up the convoy's rear joined Stryker's unit in saturating the jungle's edge with intense machinegun fire. A dry forest inferno would have done less damage in twice the time.

MPs from the closest V-100 rushed to the aid of the men in the disabled tank. The armor-piercing round had apparently burrowed into the engine compartment before detonating. Only one soldier had received slight shrapnel injuries, but there was much excited yelling as the survivors were dragged from the smoke-filled crews' quarters. The men riding on top had been thrown clear of the blast.

A rifleman clothed entirely in camouflaged strips began firing down on the convoy just as Stryker was confident the ambush team had retreated into the jungle.

"A suicide sapper," Brickmann muttered as he produced his M-16. "Left behind to make sure we stayed pinned down while the others escaped." The Brick took a bead on the silhouette halfway up a cluster of tamarinds. "Well, bye-bye, bozo!" He let loose with a half clip of lead. "You've done yourself honor! You've sacrificed your ass for your brave countrymen, your righteous cause, and your whore back home in Hanoi." The burst of rounds knocked several branches away, catapulting the guerilla backwards through the sky in a crimson spray. His arms and legs kicked about wildly in flight, but he was dead before he smashed into the ground.

"Check him out!" Stryker yelled at a jeepload of privates as lightning and thunder clashed about in the dark skies overhead. He reached for the mike clipped to the dashboard, then turned to one of the other units loaded down with rooks awaiting instructions. "You men canvass that treeline. I want answers! I wanna know who's behind this! Now move!"

Stryker immediately calmed himself as he kicked the piles of machinegun brass out of his way and moved into the back seat to be closer to the radio. "Waco, Waco—this is Charlie One-Alpha, over." He spoke into the microphone, slick with rainwater.

Waves of loud static answered him as thunder rolled down over the land around them. Leaves in the trees on either side of the roadway rustled as if terrified, trying to break free of their branches so they could flee on the breeze.

"Waco, Waco." He spoke the call sign of the base station back in Saigon like it was a cherished girlfriend's name, drawing out both syllables in a deep voice. "This is Charlie One-Alpha. How copy? We've a Signal-three hundred approximately niner klicks north of Saigon, over."

Lightning crackled over the radio net first, then flashed brilliantly all around the laagered convoy, knocking his transmission completely off the air. The red transmit light on the console popped and blew out. Taking cover below the jeep next to them, Raul Schultz pulled his steel pot down over his head as he pressed himself flat against the muddy blacktop. Another bolt of lightning spiderwebbed down from the sky, appearing like a brilliant silver umbrella opened directly above their position. "Oh no," he groaned softly to himself, "not again."

Stryker visually checked the man with the shrapnel injuries. He was no longer bleeding badly, but one leg was obviously suffering from a compound fracture, below the knee. Pink tissue surrounded the fragment of gleaming white bone jutting out through the man's pants. "Get him into unit eight!" Stryker pointed back to the last Assault tank in the convoy. "Sergeant Carmosino will escort you back to Saigon, code. None of this is worth losing a leg over! You can have one jeep taking up the rear, too!" He pointed at the vehicle carrying four rookies from Delta Company. Their eager expressions dissolved instantly, as if destroyed by the latest sheet of rainwater. "We've lost radio contact with Waco."

"We couldn't get a dust-off in here anyway," Brickmann said softly, so the enlisted men wouldn't hear. "Not with the way this storm is raising hell, Mark."

"Tell me something I don't already know, Brick."

"Nothing in the treeline, Sergeant Stryker!" Two MPs had returned from the position where the anti-tank weapon had been fired, their uniforms and faces caked with mud and twigs. "Just a lot of blood trails that end about fifty meters into the bush. There's a fucking canal in there. We lost 'em in the water."

"Which way is the current flowing?" Stryker glanced at the terrain, but the trees made it all look flat. He wanted these bastards bad.

One private glanced at another, and they all swallowed, unsure, but one finally ventured a guess. "Southwest!"

Behind them, the man with the fractured leg cried out as he was lifted up into another Assault tank.

"Awright!" Stryker's eyes chose the men off four V-

100s. "You MPs follow me! Now!" And he started for the treeline, on foot.

A dozen American boys scrambled off the slippery tanks as they raced to keep up with their convoy leader. Stryker had already disappeared into the sea of shimmering green elephant grass. Behind them, a powerful tank engine was revved up, and after one patrol jeep slid around in a half circle, aiming for the direction back to town, the V-100 spun its own balloonlike tires and fell in pursuit of the motor patrol. Waving halfheartedly, disappointment in their eyes, the rookies in the second jeep produced the thumbs-up as they fell in behind the rumbling Assault tank.

It couldn't be helped. Stryker wanted only experienced vets in on this one. He was tired of writing letters home to the parents of boys too young to drink real booze back in The World. Christ knew the officers left the dirty work to the chaplains. And it never got done that way: not when Charlie sent snipers out to terminate the army's priests right in the heart of Saigon!

Stryker made himself slow down and proceed with caution as soon as he came upon the waist-deep canal: It just wouldn't do to get careless and lose his head to a VC boobytrap when so many newbies were depending on him.

The canal was only about four feet wide. He went down prone at its bank, inspecting the murky water. Little snakes of blood floated along on the current. Stryker had raced down diagonally through the jungle after leaving the roadway. Upon reaching the canal, he was about two hundred yards downstream from the point at which the guerillas—or whoever they were—had ambushed the payroll convoy. His suspects were still somewhere *up*stream. The blood filling the canal was evidence of that.

His men quickly gathered around him, and Stryker, proud that they had arrived so silently, dispersed them into the most effective ambush positions.

He glanced about all around him—*perfect*. Now to position himself up in that treetop over there. Stryker would set off the rain of lead down into the killing zone.

"Drop your weapon, Sergeant Stryker!" A loud voice with a Vietnamese accent sliced through the din of rainfall, coming from somewhere downstream. He had been caught offguard by one of the oldest tricks in the book! Leave a casualty upstream, soiling the current, while a counter-ambush was set up below the stalkers. Stryker had read about lions doing the same thing in the African wild. His arms tensed. He wondered how many of them he could take out with a horizontal spray of lead from the hip before they'd cancel his own ticket with an overwhelming burst from a dozen different directions.

Even before he could react, Stryker was surrounded by two dozen heavily armed mercenaries who seemed to ooze from the tree trunks all around.

True to their training, several of his MPs unleashed a barrage of bullets downstream, concentrating on the area where the voice came from. They were answered by the deafening blast of a claymore anti-personnel mine that sheared branches above the hidden MPs and wounded many of the men. The air was soon filled with agonized screams as additional mines were brought into play, tearing the Americans' L-ambush to pieces.

A crescendo of discharges from both sides filled the jungle clearing, then the steaming battlefield fell ghostly silent. Stryker, surrounded by his captors, hugged the earth, gun barrels pressed into every section of his body.

"I suggest the rest of you brave warriors of the Seven-Sixteenth now lay down your arms and surrender." The voice drifted out through the trees again, more confident this time. "You will not be harmed, and I promise immediate medical aid to those of your comrades who have been wounded."

Stryker shifted his head about in the leaves and bark and debris of the decaying jungle floor. He knew that crafty voice from somewhere but, like the woman who had called him twice already in the middle of the night, couldn't place it.

His men remained silent, waiting. Confident he would give a command.

"If you do not cooperate," the voice continued, "I will be forced to execute your beloved Sgt. Mark Stryker."

As if on cue, the mercenaries jumped to their feet, pulling the big MP sergeant up off the ground with them. Ten rifles to his head, he was dragged out into the middle of the clearing, in full view of every military policeman still breathing.

"Surrender!" the voice again commanded.

Slowly, one by one, a half dozen MPs emerged from the bush, rifles held out over their heads. Some were smeared with blood.

"No!" Stryker yelled. "Get down! Blast these assholes into outer space!"

A rifle butt connected roughly with Stryker's jaw, knocking him off his feet and stunning him momentarily.

When he regained his senses, the six men who had

surrendered were standing a few feet away, hands bound behind their backs. Capt. Trinh Tri towered over Stryker, and as the sergeant's eyes came back into focus, he sighed deeply, finally remembering the voice now: The canh-sat Broox was always talking about—always treating to ice coffee at the side gate to MP Headquarters.

"And how is Mike?" Tri grinned ruefully down at Stryker, then shook his head slowly from side to side. Stryker surveyed the mercs around him. They appeared to be unworried about providing targets for any hidden eyes that might be sighting in on them right then. "Oh, don't concern yourself with the rest of your men," Tri said and laughed loudly. "They are either dead or—" He rolled his eyes up toward the branches growing together overhead, "How do you say? Missing in . . . hah: yes, *action*. MIA, Sergeant Stryker."

Stryker glanced over at the captive Americans. He knew none of them on a first-name basis, though he recognized them all instantly. Stryker felt a sudden, deep sadness in his chest. Brickmann, Schultz, Writter, Nilmes—they all appeared to be dead.

And for what? The so-called payroll convoy was empty of riches. The bowels of the Assault tanks were filled only with extra ammo. This had been a mission to flush out the bandits responsible for the earlier ambush. And Stryker had failed miserably.

The six privates wearing MP armbands—combined, they might have had a tenth the time Stryker had logged in the 'Nam—stared down at the man whose antics were required reading back at The School in Fort Gordon. Apology was heavy in all their eyes, but their expressions seemed to ask, "What was a rook to do?"

One of Tri's henchmen was already placing a blindfold over the eyes of the nearest American. Stryker envisioned their marching the privates all off to some secret jungle camp, in preparation for demanding ransoms from the U.S. government. Unfortunately, Tri had captured military policemen. This was all part of their job. Uncle Sammy would refuse to pay.

"On your feet, Stryker!" Tri ordered. The men not yet blindfolded retained a glow of hope. Perhaps this unpredictable ex-Green Beret would pull something out of his magical steel pot. Tri's expression went icy, unemotional. "Prepare to die like a man."

Stryker paused, then chuckled loudly as he forced himself up off the ground. "I have been prepared for that many years," he said with a laugh.

Tri smiled in response as he held his .45 out at arm's length. "Then perhaps Sergeant Stryker, in the other world, you will not take this personally. It is purely business. I'm sure you understand." He proceeded, without further hesitation, to fire four rapid rounds directly at the center of Mark Stryker's chest.

Thrown backwards off his feet by the blast, the MP sergeant landed on his back against the matted jungle floor. A snake, perhaps terrified, slithered out from under him and disappeared through a wall of high reeds. Blood dripping from the edge of his mouth, Stryker watched the python drop down into the canal, then he slowly closed his eyes, plunging backwards into the pit of darkness at the edge of never-never land.

11. Tanks for the Memories

"Bury him!"

The military police private with two weeks in-country looked up at the man beside him, then back down at Stryker. "I said *Bury him*!" Captain Trinh Tri bounced the barrel of his .45 off the MP's cheek. "And you too!" He motioned toward the man's partner. One of the mercenaries produced a folded entrenching tool and dropped it at the teenager's feet.

The ground was soft. Worms made up as much of it as roots because of the rotting nature of the jungle carpet. Snake holes appeared every few inches, allowing the moist earth to crumble and collapse quickly. They had a grave dug in less than ten minutes.

It was shallow, but it would suffice.

"Roll him over into it!" Tri directed impatiently. The MPs took Stryker gently by the arms and legs, and lowered him, face up, into the hole. "Quickly!" The police captain kicked one of the privates in the back, and, already dazed from the pistol whipping, the MP stumbled into the grave on top of Stryker.

Several of the mercenaries erupted into laughter, but

the second soldier rushed to pull his partner up out of the mud.

"Farewell, Mark Stryker," Tri muttered, somewhat relieved. "May this be your last battleground." He kicked a pile of dirt down onto the ex-Green Beret's face.

"Fill the hole!" Tri then ordered the two Americans. One youth picked up the small shovel and began placing piles of dirt on top of the big form, while his partner used his hands to cover Stryker's lifeless expression. A tear streamed down the private's face.

Thunder crashed overhead as the grave was finally entombed, and a strong wind swept down through the trees, nearly knocking Trinh off balance. He glanced around superstitiously and pulled his collar tightly around his throat.

"Over there now!" he told the grave diggers. "On your knees—with the others."

The privates both swallowed hard. Powerless to act, they knew what was coming. The four other men were all kneeling next to the canal, their faces against the cool earth.

Tri ejected the half-spent magazine from his pistol and inserted a fresh clip of seven rounds. "I should let you draw straws." He laughed softly. "The lucky man could stop *two* hollow points!"

A hundred feet away, Sgt. Ron Brickmann, lying facedown in the foul-smelling carpet of dead leaves, popped an eyelid open. At first, all he saw was a silver blur, but slowly the warm layer of air smothering the floor of the jungle swept the mist aside, and he spotted the group of men standing in the clearing.

Brickmann tried to move his arm, but it was horribly mutilated by shards of shrapnel, and the effort brought waves of pain down through him. He could tell that some of his men—the survivors—were lined up beside the canal and would soon be cold meat, floating back to Saigon. He tried again to react. He could see his rifle sparkling a few yards away, but his limbs would not respond.

Salty tears stinging his eyes, Brickmann stared out at the men he had laughed and joked with only that morning. He knew he was drifting back into unconciousness—a deep sleep he might never return from—and he struggled to keep his eyes open. For just a few moments longer.

He knew he was suffering from shock. That was why Sgt. Ron Brickmann wasn't startled when the ground between himself and police captain Trinh Tri exploded upward in a shower of roots, worms, and clods. If he could, Brickmann would have laughed. *What a funny thought: Stryker rising up from the dead! Imagine that.*

Captain Tri jerked the pistol from beneath the MP private's earlobe and whirled around at the sudden disturbance where he had witnessed Stryker's burial. When he saw the ex-Green Beret, larger than life, burst forth from the grave, back-up revolver blazing, the canh-sat nearly had a heart attack. All the childhood horror stories his mother had told him to make him behave were suddenly coming true! The thunder exploding above made it worse.

Tri's jaw dropped to his Adam's apple, and he froze in terror: *a leech was hanging out of the ashen-faced American's left nostril, swollen with blood!* Tri's incredulous expression was altered drastically when Stryker, never more alive, aimed at the gaping hole between the canh-sat's lips and fired off another hot round.

Capt. Trinh Tri's surprise chased half his brain out the new hole in the back of his skull.

"Into the canal!" Stryker screamed at his men, but the warning was unnecessary. Already, they were somersaulting forward into the swift current, ignoring their bonds and taking their captors by surprise.

Stryker fired off the two remaining slugs in the small .38 Special, then dove for an automatic rifle lying near Tri's body. The effort nearly knocked the breath from him. His chest was still one massive throbbing pain where the body armor beneath his fatigue shirt had stopped the four bullets earlier, but the MP sergeant managed to sweep up the AK and roll to the side in the opposite direction from which he had dived. Jerking in the trigger on full-auto, he unleashed a wild, unaimed spray of rounds that still dropped a half dozen of the mercenaries.

A few tracers zinged in around Stryker, but the freelancers were quickly melting into the forest without a fight. They felt no loyalty toward Tri. Their own skins came first, and though they outnumbered the American twenty to one, all it took was one slug to ruin their whole day.

Stryker glanced over his left shoulder: The men in the canal were rushing downstream, back on their boots now, the water only up to their chests. Another burst of tracers arced in through the trees, kicking up dirt at his feet, and he rolled into the reeds

Stryker crawled. He moved like a panther through the sharp elephant grass, ignoring the mercenaries because they were running full tilt in the opposite direction now. He headed for the location where he had left the rest of his men in the protective laager of the Assault tanks.

He could not understand why they had not come to his assistance when all the shooting started.

Five minutes later, after he had made it back up to the edge of the roadway, he understood the reason. Over a dozen South Vietnamese M-48 tanks, equipped with dual 40mm snubby cannons, had encircled the besieged laager. The MPs were heavily outgunned and outnumbered.

At first, Stryker couldn't figure out why the Arvins had encircled his men. Weren't they both on the same side in this crazy war? But then he spotted that insane Colonel Ng, and he sighed in resignation, careful to keep his head below the top of the reeds. Saigon policeman Jon Toi had briefed him often enough on Ng: The man was as corrupt as they came. Anything for the blackmarket profit. Stryker didn't know what the tank commander was up to. He was currently toe to toe with Lieutenant Slipka, unleashing a one-sided ultimatum. But he knew he had to get help.

So he turned and ran. He ran as hard as his legs would carry him. To hell with the pain in his chest! He ran in the direction of Thu Duc. It might take hours, but there'd be help available there. And Stryker knew right where to go.

Saigon policeman Jon Roi held the folded copy of the *Vietnam Guardian* over his head to protect him from the rain as he left the hospital compound.

Spec4 Parlin Fox the third was still not very talkative, but he sure knew how to nod his head. And when

Toi had shown him the ten small photos aligned on the eight-by-ten sheet of cardboard, his chin had bobbed rapidly up and down when the policeman pointed to VNP Capt. Trinh Tri.

So! As he had suspected, Tri *was* into graft. Toi must rush this information over to headquarters. Damn, but Stryker would be happy to hear the good news!

As he passed the emergency room entrance, Toi paused to watch several MPs pull one of their own from a giant tank that had rolled into the drive, both preceded and followed by jeeps. He spotted the fractured leg immediately and recognized Jack Flak's face, despite lines of intense pain crisscrossing it. He wondered what kind of trouble they had run into, and if these men were connected with Stryker's mystery convoy. He couldn't remember if this particular V-100 had been in the noisy procession up through the northern outskirts of town, or if the legendary Jack Flak had been aboard. Before he could ask, the MPs had hustled their brother off into the ward.

Toi did not have time to check into the matter anyway. He had important business to attend to at headquarters. But he felt intense friendship and sorrow for Flak. From the other MPs, mostly his buddies on the Decoy Squad, Toi learned that Jack Flak was going through sheer hell these last few months. Even before his wife had perished in the mortar attack on headquarters, the soldier had been suffering extreme anxiety over the deaths of his parents back in The World. A relative had written him about the traffic accident *after* the funeral.

He half expected as much would happen. His mother and father had slowly drifted away from him since he had volunteered for his second tour in Vietnam, and after he married the Vietnamese woman, they had stopped writing.

Now the bank was talking about foreclosing on the house. There was no way he could make the payments on an enlisted man's salary. But that was not what bothered Flak.

Someone had confiscated his souvenir trunks: the dusty old footlockers his parents had tolerated for so long. The metal boxes that held all his overseas memories, his war trophies. His Asian conquests that had been reduced to a score of faded photo albums. Now they were all missing. Missing in Action. And Toi understood how a man was nothing without his past.

He wiped the rainwater off the seat of his motorcycle, then drove off down to the white stucco police building on Vo Thanh.

The snitch was waiting there for him when he arrived.

"I'm telling you the truth!" Trinh Tri's excited informant exclaimed. The skinny man standing before Jon Toi now was the same Vietnamese whom the police captain was about to have shot up near Bien Hoa—before Colonel Ng and his tanks arrived with their clouds of dust, and the snitch escaped in all the confusion. "I'm telling you! At this very moment, Tri and his cutthroats are ambushing another payroll convoy!"

Ah—V-100s filled with greenbacks! Toi smiled to himself, finally enlightened. *So that's what all the secrecy was about!* "But why should I believe a weasel like yourself would have access to such Top Secret Intelligence?" Toi drilled a stare into the man's blinking eyes.

The skinny man swallowed hard. "I have a canh-sat

uniform at home," he revealed slowly. "And an ID card and a revolver." Toi folded his arms across his chest. "I noticed an American officer on the blackmarket several months ago. He is a Finance captain. I took pictures of him deeply involved in a currency scam. Then I put on my canh-sat uniform and approached him about the matter. I told him that for certain information my people in the Vietnamese National Police Force would not turn him over to the MPs. The ambush in Bien Hoa last week is the result: I in turn sold that information to Trinh Tri."

Jon Toi grabbed the weasel by the arm and dragged him over to a holding cell. He threw the skinny Vietnamese inside and slammed the door shut, then tossed the man a notebook and pencil. "Write down everything you have just told me," Toi said angrily, unlocking a gun cabinet on the wall. "Add names, places, and dates of every similar incident in which you have ever been involved. Otherwise, you can visit the White Room. And I'm sure you've heard the stories about what fieldphone wires can do to your testicles."

Toi grabbed an M-16 from the cabinet, several banana clips, and the keys to a police jeep. Then he got on the radio and began calling all the canh-sats he could trust.

Sgt. Don Brickmann glanced up at the skies. The clouds were starting to clear, it seemed. Night was falling, dusk retreating. He had no idea how long he had been out—how many hours, or how many days.

Darkness was quickly falling across the silent jungle. With considerable effort, he pulled himself up on his good elbow and glanced about, surveying the treeline around him. He could see the backs of several Americans, still unconscious. Most appeared to be breathing, though the breaths were shallow.

Brickmann knew he didn't have much time to save them. Where the hell was help? Had *all* of Stryker's boys been slaughtered? He tried to push himself up to his knees, but the wounded arm collapsed on him, and he fell face first into the leaves again. He closed his eyes tightly against the pain. When he opened them again, an ugly dragon lizard was staring straight into his eyes, flicking its long, purple tongue against his nose.

Brickmann rolled over onto his back, hoping the sudden movement would frighten the foot-long reptile off. Once again, an intense wave of pain racked his body, and the last thing The Brick saw before passing out was a weird, surrealistic maze of black patches against the emerging stars and moonlight.

Parachutes! I'm blacking out, and I'm going to dream about a goddamned airdrop! He groaned, rolling over again onto his side. Ron Brickmann hated memories of jump school and paratroopers and the silver wings he had earned but had never been allowed to wear. *Fucking parachutes!* As the dragon lizard climbed up on top of his chest in bored defiance, Brickmann started whistling a popular tune Barry Sadler was just then making famous. And then he passed out.

Stryker checked the two automatic rifles slung from his shoulders and dangling against opposite sides of his waist. He slowly pulled against one cord attached to the expanse of silk far above his head, guiding his descent better. The ground was rising up rapidly. He glanced over at the hundred-odd soldiers gliding down from the skies alongside him: troopers he had summoned from the little-known Special Forces Camp outside Thu Duc. One of them flipped the thumbs-up in return. Stryker smiled. He had to admit it, now that the wind was in his hair and he was flying: It felt good to be back among the Green Berets.

Far below, he saw the besieged laager of MP Assault tanks surrounded by units of Colonel Ng's forces. And up the road several miles, much to his delight, a full complement of American M-60 tanks rumbling to their rescue, across Highway 13 from the west.

A convoy of dim, yellow headlights to the south caught Stryker's attention suddenly, and he pulled folding binoculars from his flak jacket pocket and sighted in on them.

Canh-sats!

At least fifty jeeps, loaded down with Saigon policemen! Stryker's grin returned. Somehow he just knew Jon Toi was behind the two-pronged counterattack.

Though the plan called for them to land well outside the stretch of highway obstructed by the Arvin tanks, Stryker watched as several of the Green Berets dropped right in on top of the colonel and his men.

Before Stryker himself could roll through the reeds, the sky came alive with arching multicolored tracers and the shouts of men being shot.

Though he tried to land on his feet, upright, many months had passed since Stryker had made a night jump, and he crashed into a shroud of tree branches and fell head over heels into the sea of elephant grass at the edge of the highway.

Quickly separating himself from the parachute harness, Stryker instinctively rolled hard to his right, well aware experienced tankers would saturate the area he had just plummeted into. Seconds later, the stretch of elephant grass covered by his silk intruder was aglow with turret tracers from three separate M-48s. The air around him was one long, drawn-out discharge of large caliber bullets. Stryker ran. He sprinted for Ng's tank, crossing over the highway, now lit by crisscrossing beams from several of the vehicles blocking the road. White and red tracers bounced off the blacktop all around him. Stryker fanned four and five round bursts in return, knocking out several of the searchlights.

He slammed a fresh magazine into his rifle and rolled between the huge tractor tires of one of the MP fortresses. Col. Ng's tank was positioned directly against Slipka's V-100, but as Stryker grabbed a handhold and started to pull himself up onto the turret of the Arvin vehicle, he froze.

There was no activity aboard any of the Assault tanks. His Green Berets were racing about everywhere, and headlights were approaching from both directions down the highway, but the American military policemen were all missing!

A grating noise caught Stryker's attention too late. The turret of Ng's tank swung around without warning, and the long barrel slammed into his shoulder, throwing him back into the reeds, flat on his back.

Perhaps his moment of carelessness had been a blessing. Special Forces troopers were beneath nearly every tank now, planting thermite charges, and one of the tank commanders, out of desperation, fired a shell at a stretch of blacktop where a cluster of Green Berets had been an instant before.

The screaming projectile impacted against the V-100 fifteen yards away and lit up the night with a shower of sparks as metal dissolved and the tank's balloon tires exploded, throwing out a shock wave that flattened the elephant grass all around Stryker. He flinched as the ball of green-orange flame erupted from the hull of the MP vehicle, but there followed no screams. The V-100 was empty.

Stryker started to get up. The barrel of Ng's tank was moving slowly to line up with his position again when the hatch atop the colonel's vehicle sprang open and the ex-Green Beret was suddenly bathed with beams from two spotlights.

His hand still on it, Stryker left his rifle against the flattened reeds, in plain view. To move now would be suicide. But he had to bargain for time. "Surrender, Ng!" he yelled above the whine of the moving turret. *Ridiculous, but humor the bastard.* "Give it up! You don't have a chance!"

Colonel Ng's silhouette appeared atop the tank turret. He was laughing, though Stryker could barely hear him above the roar of motors all around and the discharges of sporadic weapons fire.

"Surrender?" Ng replied, incredulous. "You do not appear to be in a position to dictate terms, *sergeant*!"

"There are canh-sats galore racing this way right now!" Stryker advised him.

"I shall blow them off the face of the planet!" Ng countered. "I shall—"

"And there are a hornet's nest full of M-60 tanks rolling this way from the other direction!" Stryker said interrupting him. "You don't think I'd crash this party with just a handful of potbellied paratroopers, do you?" Stryker's smile was ear to ear, but his stomach was like a snake all knotted up, trapped in a corner. Aware its fangs were useless against the steel plate within the jungle boot's sole, unless it was swift enough to strike past the kick, injecting its poison in soft flesh.

"I am the tank commander of this region!" Ng remained confident. "I have done nothing wrong. These MP rustbuckets are not even carrying any loot, sergeant! I was just protecting my territory. This mission of your people was not cleared with my command! I was not informed!"

"You waste your time fabricating excuses, Ng!" Stryker slowly swung the barrel of his M-16 around, so slowly the movement was almost unnoticeable. "I think even a jury of Vietnamese would believe *me* before they would swallow your ration—"

"Then you must obviously not be allowed to testify against a patriot of my impeccable—"

A sudden explosion beneath Ng's tank knocked Stryker down flat on his back again and rocked the enormous vehicle back onto its top. Stryker, dazed and temporarily blinded by the blast, laughed loudly as he rolled away from the secondary explosions. He had not even noticed the American soldier planting the C-4—or whatever it was—beneath the colonel's tank. *Now that was truly a professional at work!* "Good-bye Ng," he muttered, rubbing the blur of sight back into his eyes. "Say hello to your fucking ancestors for me."

He rolled into an obstacle and stopped. His heart sank: South Vietnamese tiger cloth brushed against his skin. The blow came an instant later than he expected it. "*You* can say hello to my ancestors *for* me!" The colonel laughed louder after kicking Stryker in the mouth.

Somehow Ng had been thrown clear of the blast. Stryker had to give the Arvin credit: Miraculously he had landed without breaking any bones. Perhaps he wasn't such an old bastard after all.

"Enjoy yourself, colonel," he said softly. "I am the last American you will ever kill."

Ng just chuckled as he pressed the edge of his pistol barrel against Stryker's forehead. The cold steel against his skin produced an instant, intense headache, and the ex-Green Beret wondered if he had already been shot. He closed his eyes, and saw Kim's face, the Tu Do Street temple rising in the mist behind her. Kim was smiling, same as the colonel standing above him now. "You are also the *first*, sergeant," the tank commander said coldly. "Those foolish enough to cross my path in the past have always been South Vietnamese. Or, of course, Charlie."

"Of course," answered Stryker. He opened his eyes, tired of the talk. He had not anticipated such a delay in his death. It made accepting that one-way ticket to never-never land so much harder. When Stryker opened his eyes, he did not focus on the burly Vietnamese colonel.

The first thing he saw was the woman with the neatly braided pigtails and dedicated swimmer's body. Wearing the same black pantaloons and khaki blouse. Carrying the same AK-47 Assault rifle. Displaying that same disarming smile as she stood quietly behind Col. Ng.

"Farewell, sergeant." The tank commander laughed as he pulled the hammer back on his pistol.

"Good-bye, colonel," Stryker replied confidently.

"Say hello to your ancestors for me."

Ng's smile fell apart an instant before Nguyen Thuy Loan's Assault rifle barked a round of hot lead. The bullet struck the tank commander at the base of his skull. The force of the impact threw him forward, off his feet, directly onto the American.

Stryker pushed the heavy corpse away, its arms still twitching spasmodically, and glanced around, relieved. But the woman who had saved him from the tiger in the rubber plantation clearing less than forty-eight hours ago was gone.

He was not sure why, but he had felt all along the girl would shoot Ng instead of himself. The relief swelling up inside Stryker's gut did little to relieve the dizziness swirling about in his head again.

He stared down the hill to his left: His Green Beret buddies were escorting the rescued MPs back to their tanks. Ng's men had probably gathered them up to relocate the Americans while his own men searched the V-100s for the nonexistent payroll. The money was, at that very moment, being rushed to Bien Hoa by rail, protected by a complement of Alpha Company MPs.

Off to his right, a long line of canh-sats were emerging from the jungle, a cluster of prisoners, hands raised, in front of them. Jon Toi himself was leading the contingent of Saigon policemen who had scoured the trees, rounding up Trinh Tri's retreating mercenaries. Additional canh-sats were carrying stretchers that held his wounded men: Brickmann, Schultz, and the others.

Stryker's ears rang, but he knew the battle was over. American tanks had rolled up beside the Arvin M-48s. The Vietnamese tank commanders were all atop their turrets, hands also raised, surrendering without additional resistance. To fight a fleet of superior Armor would have been insane.

He tried to get up, to walk back to the Green Berets who were casually securing each tank and slapping each other on the backs, but his legs were jelly and they collapsed under him. Several MPs rushed up to help him, but Stryker could not seem to keep his eyes open.

The last thing he heard before blacking out was the roar of a tiger, then a woman laughing, somewhere far beyond the treeline, deep in the jungle.

12. Beyond Bien Hoa

"Car Thirty-six-Alpha, see the woman—number Twenty-three Lam Son Square—at the Caravelle—report of a domestic at that location."

Garbled static.

"Car Niner-Alpha, respond to the La Pagode on Tu Do—report of a fight in progress—Cars Ten-Bravo and fifty-zulu covering from Headquarters."

More static. A siren in the background.

"Code-Zero," the dispatcher added. "You have a man with a gun at that Ten-Fourteen."

Silence, another garbled transmission, then more static.

"Car Twenty-two-Echo, this is Waco—respond to the alley behind number Sixty-seven Pasteur—the Calypso—meet the canh-sats with a sexual assault victim at that fourteen—over."

An acknowledgement broke squelch, then static reclaimed the radio net.

"Suspects one U.S. salt-and-pepper team, Twenty-two-Echo, last seen on foot, northbound—unknown on weapons."

The military police radio transmissions drifted into Stryker's mightmare of tigers and temples, and he forced his eyelids open. A mosquito net above came into view. Beyond it, sterile white squares that were a hospital ceiling.

"Yah, wake up, you sorry-assed bastard." Gary Richards leaned into Stryker's field of vision, obscuring the ceiling and mosquito net. The Decoy Squad sergeant was holding a single finger up in front of his face—the middle one. "How many fingers do you see?" he asked seriously.

"Fuck you," Stryker muttered, trying to pull a pillow over his face.

"Yah, he's okay," Tim Bryant agreed. "The crazy fuck'll be outta here in no time."

"We brought you a pak-set," Anthony Thomas added cheerfully. "So you can listen to the radio calls. Wouldn't want you to miss nothing, sarge."

"That stakeout at the Continental fizzled out," Mike Broox said, disappointment in his tone. "Not a single *Co dep* entered the joint, Mark. Sorry."

Stryker opened his eyes again and looked at each man in turn, then smiled. Damn, but it *was* good to see their god-awful faces. Alive and uninjured.

Richards plopped a heavy gold bar down on Stryker's chest. "Toi wanted us to souvenir you this," he said. "Seems he and his boys raided that Trinh Tri's den out near Bien Hoa and found a footlocker full of the stuff. We were transferring the Finance captain's own private stock on our V-One hundreds without even knowing it!"

"And the captain from Payroll?" Stryker's head throbbed with each word.

"Behind bars, of course." Bryant grinned proudly. "On his way to the LBJ Monkey House."

"Nabbed him ourselves," added Thomas, "while you and the boys were out imitating heroes in the boonies."

"That's a federal offense, you know," chimed in Broox, his face dead serious, but his eyes were laughing along. Stryker wasn't sure if he was talking about imitating heroes or stealing gold from Uncle Sammy.

"Speaking of the boys," said Stryker, his voice cracking slightly as the last words trailed into a whisper. "How many casualties did we take?"

The room fell silent, then Richards sat down on the bed beside him. "It was bad, Mark. Real bad. We lost nine more men."

"Brickmann? Schultz? Gimme some names, Gary!"

"None of the sergeants got their tickets cancelled," revealed Bryant cautiously. "But they're all sharing this ward with you. Brickmann mighta caught a million-dollar wound—got his arm tore up pretty bad. He's on his way to Tokyo already. Nobody's sure if he'll be back or not."

"He'll be back," Stryker said confidently. "If I know The Brick, he'll be back—you can't crush *that* man with mere lead."

"The KIAs were all privates from Delta," Richards said. "I don't think you knew them."

Stryker's lower lip trembled, and he feared he might break down just then. It didn't matter whether he knew their names or not—they were—had been cops on the same team. Had been through the same police academy. Not that it all mattered now. Where they had been. What they had experienced. How they had lived. He wondered if their women downtown were waiting, even now, for them. Lighting candles in the window. Listening to the radio with baited breath. Preparing the bed, aware they loved men who might any night forsake them for the street, choosing that bullet in the chest—that instant of glory, over boredom. Over apathy and wasted life. Stryker hoped each man had left someone behind to remember him. Even if she was just a whore.

"Hey, check it out!" Broox reached over and snatched up the radio, increasing the volume.

"Now proceeding northbound on Le Van Duyet—about sixty klicks per hour, Waco—requesting units at Bac Hai to intercept, over."

"Roger, Twenty-two-Echo." The dispatcher set off the channel scrambler that got the attention of every MP within fifty feet of his radio. "All units—the vicinity of sector seven." The man's voice was an unemotional drone, "Code-One at this time—Twenty-two-Echo has a chase northbound Le Van Duyet—approaching Bac Hai—patrols to intercept, switch to Channel Two—the net's yours, Twenty-two-Echo—talk it up—vehicle description, p.c. and locations."

"That's Uhernik!" Bryant said, moving closer to the tiny portable radio.

Stryker nodded his head slowly from side to side after the private in 22-Echo aired the vehicle description. *The kid's going after Lt. Fuzznuts again.*

"Waco, this is Twenty-two-Echo—suspect has just stacked it up two blocks south of Bac Hai—*man,* I've *never* seen a fireball like that before, sarge—slid off the road and ran it right up a utility pole guide wire—better send a Ten-Five, Waco," he said, asking for an ambulance. "But I'd say the guy is a definite

Foxtrot—score another Delta Oscar Alpha—*this one's for Stryker!"*

Richards frowned at the improper radio language.

"Well *awright!"* cheered Broox and Bryant.

Richards got up off the edge of the bed and stretched his arms. "I think it's time we left super-sarge here to his beauty sleep," he said. "Besides, I gotta get over to HQ and give the nightwatch briefing. Slipka's up to his butter bar in paperwork."

"Be seeing ya, Mark." Thomas whipped a salute on Stryker as the Decoy Squad filed out of the room.

"Yah—okay, you guys." He struggled to keep his voice from cracking again. "Take care on the streets now, you hear?"

But they were gone, whistling out of tune as they sauntered down the hallway.

Stryker reached over and turned off the pak-set they had left him. It was alive with shrieking sirens, and he didn't need the noise. Saigon could wait. He still had eight months left on his latest extension. This concussion would only keep him in bed another day, at most.

He began to feel a strange presence behind the divider that separated his bed from the next cubicle over. Probably one of his fellow NCOs. "What you in for?" Stryker forced a weak laugh. "The clap?"

Nobody answered, and he started to grab hold of the curtain to swing it aside, but his attention was diverted by an army nurse down the hallway, wheeling a cart toward him with a long line attached to it.

"You've got a phone call, Sergeant Stryker." She grinned disapprovingly as she pushed the portable telephone into his stall.

"Me?" He feigned total innocence.

"She sounds very—" The nurse avoided using the word sexy. "Exotic."

Stryker saw Kim in his mind. He saw her begging forgiveness. Swearing she'd lifted the temple curse that had landed him in the hospital but had not been powerful enough to kill him.

He saw Lai. Swimming naked in the Dak Ba, flowers in her hair. But Lai hated Saigon, and all things Saigonish—like telephones. He doubted that she had ever used one in her life. He wondered where she was now. If she was even alive. If he would ever find her.

And he saw the woman with the tiger. The female guerilla with the disarming smile and dead aim who called herself Ann but carried an ID card that said Nguyen Thuy Loan. Somehow he felt he had not seen the last of her.

"Hello?" He glanced over his shoulder, slipping into phase yellow: *Something* behind that curtain was making the hairs along the back of his neck stand up.

"Mark?"

The voice belonged to none of the three women he had just been thinking about.

"Yes, this is Stryker." He immediately recognized her: It was his private little obscene phone caller.

"I missed you at the Continental earlier." Her voice was soft and seductive.

"I became involved with other matters." He hesitated. "I told you I'd be unable to come."

"But you sent four of your gestapo quick enough!" she snapped. "Does your goon platoon always do your dirty work?" Her voice was a snake's hiss.

Goon platoon. Stryker smiled. He liked the sound of that. "One must be extra careful if one expects to survive his Vietnam tour, my dear." He made his voice sound deep, inviting.

"Don't *'dear'* me, you sonofabitch!" she screamed into the phone. "That was a rotten trick you pulled. But it didn't work, did it?"

Stryker remained silent, waiting. Wondering why he didn't just hang up.

"I love you, Mark Stryker." She switched personalities on him again, growing instantly soft and helpless. "I want to feel you on top of me, spreading me apart, forcing all of you into me. I want—"

Stryker's eyes rolled up toward the ceiling. He wished he had a tape recorder: The guys at guard-mount would love to hear this one!

"I have to be going now, honey," he finally interrupted her gutter fantasies.

"You need me!" she cried out. "I have the name of the man responsible for the ambush on your MPs up in—"

"Trinh Tri is dead," he cut in softly. The story had obviously not broken in the papers yet.

There was a lengthy silence, then a deep sigh. "I have connections in the underground," she finally said, desperation in her tone. "I could tell you where murderers and blackmarketeers and rapists and pushers and pimps—and deserters are hiding," she assured him.

Stryker resisted the urge to cultivate another informant. "Forget it," he said.

"I won't forget it!" she insisted. "I want to please you, Mark. I want to—"

Stryker softly hung up the phone and wiped the sweat from his brow. One of these days he would remember where he had heard her voice before.

Something told him he had not heard the last from this lady psycho.

Stryker thought about all the Americans raising hell in the bars up in Bien Hoa right then—if they realized what *his* men had sacrificed just so they could pick up their paychecks. He thought about the MPs who had died—for nothing really. Paper. Scrip. It was all such a waste. None of the firefights or mortar attacks or rocket barrages they had weathered the last two weeks served to protect the South Vietnamese people from the threat of Communism. It was all connected to greed and profit. There were no ideals involved.

He knew his dead MPs were far beyond Bien Hoa now, patrolling never-never land with a vengeance. He almost wished he were with them.

Stryker thought about the woman warrior, Ann. Perhaps she was the only good that had come out of all this. He doubted he would ever see her again. And he knew if he did, he would have to kill her.

Or die trying.

Stryker felt the shiver run up and down his spine again. He glanced over his shoulder at the curtain separating his stall from the patient next door. He was getting the damnedest sensation in his gut, too—almost like those times when he shifted into phase red, prepared to lunge out and kill man or beast.

"You should have heard the broad on the phone just now," he called out to his roommate. "Weirdest bitch I've had the pleasure of talking to in a long time. Wanted to suck on my cock—the whole nine yards! Well, I mean—"

Stryker meant to correct himself—tell the man his whanger wasn't really nine yards long. *Close, but no cigar.* He laughed to himself.

His good naturedness quickly turned to irritation though, when the man behind the curtain remained silent. The entire ward was quiet. Too quiet!

Stryker reached for the curtain and drew it back. The bells of the telephone beside his bed began clanging frantically again, but Stryker did not move to answer the obscene phone caller. He was frozen to the spot by what he saw waiting for him behind the curtain.

Hanging from the ceiling rafters by the neck, his face grotesquely twisted, his tormented soul finally free, was the legendary Jack Flak. His body several hours dead, the MP's spirit was far beyond Bien Hoa, following his wife and his friends and his dreams to never-never land.

Jonathan Cain was awarded the Bronze Star Medal for service in the Republic of Vietnam. While with Saigon's 716th Military Police Battalion, his unit was awarded the Presidential Unit Citation and the Vietnamese Cross of Gallantry.